"Curtis '50 Cent' Jackson's first foray into fiction is a tense, suspenseful event that will keep readers on the edge of their proverbial seats."
—S. A. Cosby, *New York Times* bestselling author of *All the Sinners Bleed*

"Written with the excellent crime fiction veteran Aaron Philip Clark, Jackson's first work of adult fiction is an assured, classically rendered effort. Though the twisty ending is wobbly, and the novel lacks the depth of Southern gothics by Attica Locke and S. A. Cosby, it has its own special qualities—including a soundtrack in which patriotic Vietnamese hymns get swapped on a karaoke machine for the author's 'P.I.M.P.'"
—*Kirkus Reviews*

"In rapper 50 Cent's dynamic fiction debut, Vietnam-vet-turned-thief Desmond Bell breaks into the oldest bank in Texas and steals $2 million in Spanish gold.... Hot on Desmond's heels is Nia Adams, the first Black woman sworn into the Texas Rangers.... Much of the taut narrative is dedicated to Nia and Katz's pursuit of Desmond, which remains gripping all the way to the bang-up finale.... Fans of *John Wick*–style action thrillers will not be disappointed."
—*Publishers Weekly*

"Music artist, actor, producer, and entrepreneur Jackson's multitudes of fans will follow him on his first foray into crime fiction."
—*Booklist*

"*USA TODAY* Bestseller!"
—*USA Today*

THE ACCOMPLICE

A NOVEL

CURTIS "50 CENT" JACKSON

AARON PHILIP CLARK

AMISTAD
An Imprint of HarperCollinsPublishers

Without limiting the exclusive rights of any author, contributor or the publisher of this publication, any unauthorized use of this publication to train generative artificial intelligence (AI) technologies is expressly prohibited. HarperCollins also exercise their rights under Article 4(3) of the Digital Single Market Directive 2019/790 and expressly reserve this publication from the text and data mining exception.

This is a work of fiction. Names, characters, places, and incidents are products of the author's imagination or are used fictitiously and are not to be construed as real. Any resemblance to actual events, locales, organizations, or persons, living or dead, is entirely coincidental.

THE ACCOMPLICE. Copyright © 2024 by Curtis J. Jackson, III. All rights reserved. Printed in the United States of America. No part of this book may be used or reproduced in any manner whatsoever without written permission except in the case of brief quotations embodied in critical articles and reviews. For information, address HarperCollins Publishers, 195 Broadway, New York, NY 10007. In Europe, HarperCollins Publishers, Macken House, 39/40 Mayor Street Upper, Dublin 1, D01 C9W8, Ireland.

HarperCollins books may be purchased for educational, business, or sales promotional use. For information, please email the Special Markets Department at SPsales@harpercollins.com.

harpercollins.com

FIRST AMISTAD PAPERBACK PUBLISHED IN 2025

Designed by Yvonne Chan

Library of Congress Cataloging-in-Publication Data is available upon request.

ISBN 978-0-06-331291-3

25 26 27 28 29 LBC 5 4 3 2 1

THE ACCOMPLICE

PRELUDE
NIA

Palestine, Texas
2023

Nia Adams doesn't have a green thumb but waters her garden diligently, cares for the soil, tends to the flowers, and tames the weeds. Her favorite perennial is the *Lupinus texensis*, the Texas bluebonnet. The bright blue petals are the showpiece of her front yard. The flowers thrive on full sunlight and damp soil and are resilient during dry spells. Like Nia, they're survivors.

The midday sun warms Nia's skin as she pulls the last dandelions. She's worked up a sweat and welcomes the cool breeze that sets in. It shakes the leaves of the Mexican white oaks that shade her front yard. The sound of the air lashing the leaves makes her feel at home—makes her feel safe. She's approaching seventy, an age when a misstep can mean catastrophe: broken hip, snapped ankle, injured spine . . . She thinks a dog might be a nice companion, though she dreads the responsibility of cleaning, bathing, and walking a dog. But dogs make good deterrents against hot prowlers who target single women, looking for easy scores.

Maybe one day, she thinks, a dog might aid her—once her hearing fades. But, for now, her senses remain sharp. She hears the chortle of the white four-door diesel pickup truck before seeing it barrel up the road toward her property. Visitors are rare, especially these days, but the vehicle moves at a deliberate pace.

She places the bundle of weeds into a small trash bag, removes her yard gloves, and steps out of the flower bed into the driveway. She sets off down her driveway with her .22-caliber Ruger in the right pocket of her soiled cargo pants. As the truck closes in, she pulls the weapon, brandishes it for the driver to see, and stands calmly. Cop habits die hard.

Nia likes to think she's still intimidating without the badge. She's lost half an inch in height since her days as a Texas Ranger. She was already petite, and then age set in. A chatty date suggested she'd look fifty if she dyed her graying hair. But age doesn't matter to Nia—it means she's lived a life. She's got scars and stories to go with them.

The truck comes to a stop. Nia stands firm. A white man in a cowboy hat is behind the wheel. He looks young, but she couldn't guess how old. A dusty windshield can soften features. She recognizes the woman in the passenger seat as Texas Ranger Brianna Castro.

Nia doesn't lower the gun.

Brianna gets out of the truck. She's older than the last time Nia saw her—heavier, slower. Still pageant-pretty, though.

"What's with the sidearm, Adams?" Brianna asks.

"You just happen to be in the neighborhood?"

"Well, howdy to you, too, ma'am," the man says. "We don't mean to intrude."

Nia can see him better outside of the truck. He's got a hardened face—pockmarked, as though he's spent years shaving with dull razors. Ex-military, Nia thinks.

"She isn't intruding. Castro's always welcome here," Nia says, dropping the weapon to her side. "But I don't know who the hell you are."

"William Ray Boyd. Texas Ranger."

Boyd has a Down South twang, but he isn't a native Texan, just desperate to look like one. His gaudy belt buckle gleams. He probably polishes it daily.

"Boyd's my partner, Adams," Brianna says.

"For how long?"

"Ten years now."

"Ten years," Nia says. "I guess it has been a while."

"Castro's told me a lot about you," he says.

"She tell you why it took so long for her to see me?"

"I told him the truth," Brianna says. "You taught me everything worth learning. Helped me see things clearer. I'm hoping you can help me again."

Brianna still looks as if she lifts sandbags for fun. A man's sports coat hangs over her broad shoulders. Her attire is typical of a Ranger: a white oxford, basic tie, tan Ranger hat with matching pants, medium starch, and a pair of cowboy boots—short heels, rubber soles—brown. Always brown.

"I suppose any visit is better than no visit." Nia smiles. "We're good, Castro."

"Good enough for you to put that gun away?"

Nia puts the pistol back in her pocket but keeps her hands near her waist. Cop habits and all, or life in Texas. She isn't sure which.

"You two staying for supper?"

"I'm afraid this isn't a social call. We're here about a case."

"Desmond Bell," Boyd says. "Suspected of a string of robberies back in the 1990s. His last score might've been in 2004."

Nia hasn't heard the name spoken aloud for decades. It exists in her head, rattling and working her nerves, sometimes all night.

"What can you tell us about him?" Boyd asks.

"Come on in. I'll put some coffee on."

Nia leads the Rangers into her home. It's modest and comfortable, and it feels like a bed-and-breakfast, even to her. There's floral wallpaper, hardwood floors, and exposed brick. She hasn't had people over in years, but she tries to keep things tidy, aside from the dusty piano. Dust doesn't bother her the way it used to. Besides, Castro knows her too well to be bothered by Nia's poor housekeeping; as she said, this isn't a social call.

Nia scoops coffee from a tin can into unbleached filter paper. She turns on the coffee maker and returns to the living room, where the Rangers wait on the sofa.

She sits in a burgundy leather recliner. Her hand trembles. Must be nerves, she thinks.

Boyd looks uncomfortable. Nia wonders how often he visits Black folk's homes. He eyes an Annie Lee painting that hangs over her fireplace. The colors span a brown palette: rich, bold, and earthy. Children jump double Dutch in front of brownstone stoops, just Black people existing. It's idyllic; reminds Nia of Queens, New York, where she grew up. She hopes heaven is as magnificent as the painting . . . if she gets there.

"It's titled *Juneteenth*," she says. "Black Americana, according to the art world."

"Yes," Boyd says. "It's nice—real nice. But most art I see is."

"It is," Nia says, affirming Boyd's humble assessment of the work. He doesn't know shit about art, and he owns his ignorance. Most people work hard to sound smart, which annoys Nia.

"Do you remember the robbery at Colonial Trust?" Brianna asks. "2004."

Nia nods. "Of course I do."

"It's happened again," she says. "Not the same MO, but something about it feels similar to the Bell job."

"What's that mean? No—never mind. Spare me the details." She rebuffs her question with the wave of her hand. "I don't want to know anything about it. I'm past all that now."

"Bell was never apprehended, was he?" Boyd asks.

"You know he wasn't," Nia says, failing to keep quiet. "But even if he were alive, which I doubt, he'd have to be over seventy. Y'all see many septuagenarians pulling off heists these days?"

"We're only asking for your insights," he says, opening his briefcase. "Maybe take a look at the case file . . ."

"Don't," Nia says sternly. "Don't you dare open that damn case. I said I'm not interested."

"You'd be helping us a great deal."

"You don't get it . . . Take my advice. Leave it be. Whatever it is, it's bigger than you think, and believe me, you don't want any part of it. It'll ruin you. Same as it did me."

"Please, Adams." Brianna brings her hands together. She looks as though she wants to beg. Nia hopes she doesn't.

The coffee maker *clicks*.

Nia sniffs the aroma. It smells like the Ranger's station and the Houston Police Department precinct before that. "Coffee's ready," she says. "All I got is sugar."

"Sure," Brianna says. "Sugar's fine."

There's a tingle in Nia's chest. Starts small but grows and pulses. She can't get up from the chair. She can't move her arms. Legs, either. She's not even sure she feels them.

It's a goddamn heart attack or stroke, she thinks.

"Adams?" Brianna asks. "You all right?"

Nia can't speak. Half her body feels numb.

She slumps and can't see straight. Desmond Bell—she never wanted to die with him on her mind . . .

That son of a bitch . . .

Wherever you are, I hope you're rotting.

CHAPTER ONE

NIA

Houston, Texas
2004

The radio cackles. *10–35. Robbery is in progress. Central Bank of Texas. 1100 Main Street.*

Nia hates these calls. They never go well. She's intercepted nine active robberies in her six-year career as a Texas Ranger, and she knows two things: suspects don't surrender willingly, and there will be casualties. Sometimes, hostages. Other times, law enforcement. Usually, suspects.

Five minutes away.

Nia can see the bank in the distance. A Houston PD helicopter is already hovering.

Sirens wail. Lights flash. She drives the Blazer eighty miles per hour down Main Street. Abandoned cars line the shoulder. Local police have cleared a path. There are no civilians in sight. A Suburban carrying members of the Special Response Team follows behind Nia's Blazer.

Some of them have been waiting for this, itching for it—it's the ticket to the show.

Downtown is the city's epicenter, its heartbeat: energy companies, law firms, airline headquarters, St. John's Downtown Church, Sam Houston Park, and banks—lots of banks. The city has approximately 150, with more than two thousand branches. As in most cities, the largest branches are downtown and usually hold the most money. Central Bank of Texas is no different.

The city has had twenty-two armed bank robberies in the past three months. Many suspects are serial offenders, hitting more than one branch in a day. Budget cuts have decimated the Houston PD. They're low on resources and officers. They use the FBI to augment investigations involving major crimes—armed robberies, hostage situations, and terrorism. The FBI uses the Special Response Team as first contact because the SRT officers mobilize more quickly, know the area better, and typically are native Texans.

Nia wasn't born in Texas but considers it her adopted home. She knows its culture and people—and wants to protect it. That's what she told background investigators during her vetting process, but it isn't the only reason she became a Ranger. There's never just one reason anyone does anything.

The Blazer stops hard behind a police barricade. Nia glances at the Suburban in the rearview. It comes in hot and squeals out of sight. Her squad leader, Ranger Josiah Powers, is driving. He knows how to make a show of it.

Houston PD has done what it can. Cleared out the civilians. A half dozen squad cars are lined up. Plenty of blue suits are in position with guns drawn.

Members of the SRT fan out of the Suburban. Tactical vests over oxfords and ties. Six men: three Army veterans turned Rangers, one highway patrolman, and two DPS Special Agents from the Department of Public Safety's Criminal Investigations Division.

Nia's the seventh member of the squad. When they're jelled and working like a machine, she swears they can read each other's thoughts; it feels biblical. She'd never say they were of one accord, like the Babylonians, but something close to it. She tells herself that police work is God's work. The tattoo on her right shoulder reads: *Blessed are the peacemakers*. But there's a price for peace; it's paid in blood. Nia knows this—the squad knows this.

"We'll need to get set up here," Powers says. "Who do you think is in charge?"

"Check your six," Nia says. "Tan coat."

"Copy." Powers chews bubble gum like cud. It annoys Nia, but it's his thing. Says it keeps him sharp. She watches as he canvasses the crowd of blue suits. He's a big man who knows how to throw his weight around. Other cops don't look him in the eye. He plucks a tall man from the crowd. He's white with shaggy gray hair, wearing a Perry Mason trench coat. A pair of binoculars around his neck.

Trench Coat and Powers briefly converse, then the man in the coat walks over to Nia.

"Adams," he says. "Always good to see you. Wish it was under better circumstances."

"Likewise, Sergeant Keeler."

"I hate that you had to come down here," he says. "I'm not sure who called you, but we've got it covered."

"You know who called us."

Keeler draws in his cheeks and gulps air like a fish. "You know it's bullshit, don't you?"

"You rather the feds were here?"

"She's got it out for our department. Thinks we can't handle it."

"The mayor just wants a peaceful end to this. We've been working these robberies north to south. We're keyed in."

"So who's behind them?"

"We think it's a gang. Fairly organized. Aside from robbing banks, they're running guns and drugs. Cocaine. Heroin. Got a pipeline into California, Chicago, Detroit, even Mexico."

"Cartel suppliers?"

"Balls aren't that big yet. They're working on it, though."

"Not if we end it today," Keeler says.

"That's the plan. You establish contact?"

"Tried to. They won't pick up."

"Any idea how many suspects are inside?"

"One of my guys thinks he saw three. Another says four. Can't be sure."

"Hostages?"

"Take a look," he says, handing her the binoculars. "Midday crowd. I estimate fifteen to twenty."

Nia brings the binoculars to her eyes and scans the bank. "Looks like they're corralled on the east wall."

She gives Keeler back the binoculars; he loses the stale face. "Still can't get used to it," he says.

"What's that?"

"The hat. The boots. The whole getup . . . You mean to tell me you don't miss HPD?"

"Of course I do," Nia says. "Needed a change, that's all."

"Yeah, but the Rangers? It's not the same. We had a place for you."

"Adams! We got movement on the second floor," Powers shouts from the line. "Look alive!"

A second-floor window shatters. Glass rains on the street. A long barrel appears.

"Gun!" Nia and Keeler take cover behind the Blazer.

Pop . . . Pop . . . Pop . . . Pop . . .

"You get a look at it?" Keeler's huffing; he's out of shape. "What's he packing?"

"Semiautomatic. Military-grade assault rifle." Nia peeks from around the taillight and looks up at the window. "Shit. Here we go!"

A fusillade of bullets sprays onto the police cars. The bullets cut into metal and glass. Officers shout, voices taut with panic. Keeler radios for backup. He's talking fast, still out of breath. It sounds like gibberish.

They're outgunned. Nia watches an officer go down. More casualties follow. They're dropping fast, Nia thinks. An officer's rear cranium pops. She'd swear the detonation came from inside his skull. Other officers limp to safety, along with two of her team members, Powers and Cooper.

"Dammit," Keeler says. "They've got us pinned down."

The suspects have the high ground. Assault weapons. Maybe body armor. Firepower seems endless. It's a disaster—a failure in command.

"Please tell me SWAT is en route," Nia says.

"Ten minutes."

The windows of the SRT's Suburban are blown out. Cars are riddled with bullets, gaping smoking holes. Nia smells gasoline. "We need to move," she says.

Some officers hunker behind an industrial work truck. Big tires. Lots of metal. Lots of open spaces, too. Not ideal cover, but there aren't many options.

"You think we can make it?" Keeler asks.

"What?"

"The CenterPoint Energy truck," he says. "It's our best chance."

"You go," Nia says. "I'll cover you."

Keeler nods. He comes off his knees. Fixes his body like a sprinter—head straight, right leg back, chest square. He eyes the work truck. "Say when."

There's a lull in gunfire. She looks up at the window. Suspects must be reloading.

"Go!" Nia aims her Colt M1911 and fires. Keeler makes his move: he stays low and runs at a slight diagonal. "Get there," Nia mumbles. "Get there."

Keeler is struck down less than a foot from the truck. The impact propels him forward. His body strikes the pavement, arms outstretched and motionless. Seconds later, blood pools from his pelvis and abdomen.

"Shit," she says. He'd once been her commanding officer during her time in Vice. He was a good man. Fair and honest. Never tried to grab her ass. Never called her out of her name. There will be time to mourn later. Right now, she needs to stay alive and put an end to the bank assault. Nia radios her team: "Status?"

"Cortez and Jimenez are down," Powers says. "Cooper's injured." He sounds winded; words come out as fragments. "Browning and Navarro . . ." He tries to gather himself. "I saw them get hit, Adams. Nothing I could do."

"Are you okay?"

"Grazed. Nothing critical."

"I'm going in," she says.

"No," Powers says. "We hold until SWAT arrives."

"We won't make it that long."

Everything that was once apt cover is splintered metal and crumbling cement. The suspects have turned the block into a war zone. Hundreds of bullets have pierced vehicles, store walls, and windows. The air is saturated with cordite.

The HPD helicopter circles and then hovers closer to the building. It retreats when it takes gunfire. There are no eyes on them. No one knows their location for certain. When SWAT arrives, they'll be overwhelmed by gunfire. They won't be ready. Their best approach will be gaining access from the bank's roof, a tactical nightmare. It'll take air support and coordination.

There isn't much time for that.

"I won't die here," she says. "I'm going in."

"Don't be stupid, Adams."

"You coming with me or not?"

Powers is silent, just heavy breathing over the radio.

"Powers?" Nia asks.

"Goddammit," he says. "What's the plan?"

"I'll use the Blazer to gain entry into the bank," she says. "We mobilize and take cover. Then make our way through."

The day Nia was sworn in as a police officer, she understood the job increased her likelihood of death. Not an ordinary death, but a violent one. She revered that part of the profession, but human nature demands self-preservation. There's a desire to live, to thrive. She can't think about that now, though. If she is to die, she'll at least put a few bullets into the people responsible for the carnage perpetrated on the city.

Nia moves around the Blazer, opens the driver-side rear door, and climbs across the back seat. Bits of glass press into her knees and shins. She takes hold of her tactical rifle, along with additional magazines. She tosses the gun into the passenger seat, then pitches her body forward until she can squeeze behind the wheel. She belts in and starts the Blazer. The engine grumbles. Nia shifts into drive and then mashes the pedal, sending the Blazer through the wooden barricade. It travels across a strip of green and banks into the street. Bullets enter through the roof, burning holes into the cloth seats. Pedal to the floor, the Blazer smashes through the bank's window and stops short of demolishing the teller's station.

Smoke pours from the engine bay and fills the cabin. Nia's hat is lost in the wreckage. She feels a gash along her forehead. Blood is smeared on her fingers. She's been cut, maybe by the jagged pieces of windshield that have collected on the dash and seats.

Powers appears at the vehicle's rear holding a shotgun; shells are strapped across his chest. "Come on, Adams. Move out!"

Nia's dazed. She looks to her right and sees hostages huddled near an open vault. Two lie dead—a security guard still holding his pistol and a woman in a pencil skirt and blouse. There are nine others. Some are rendering aid to the injured.

"Adams, you okay?" Powers asks.

Nia's chest feels sore from where she hit the steering wheel. She coughs hard. No blood. "I'm okay. Let's move." She snatches the rifle from the passenger seat, gets out of the Blazer, and falls in behind Powers, who takes point.

"Tight on me," he says, moving toward a staircase to the left of an elevator.

Powers goes upstairs, keeping snug to the wall. Nia listens for suspects. It's deceptively quiet. As they round the corner, gunfire erupts, nearly striking Powers. Nia takes hold of his tactical vest and yanks him out of the fray.

Powers positions himself against the wall. "They've got plenty of fucking ammo, that's for damn sure."

"Looks like two gunners by the window. And I clocked gunfire from that office. We'll have to be on the lookout for a possible fourth." Nia eyes the branch manager's office. "If we clear that office, we might be able to take cover in there."

"I say we unload on the fuckers," Powers says. "Drive them into the corner."

"We won't stand a chance against their firepower."

"Then, I'll have to get close," he says. "Won't hit shit at this range."

"Understood."

"Aim and spray, Adams. Don't stop until I get that office cleared."

"Got it."

"On my count," he says. "One . . . two . . . three." Powers leaps from the staircase while Nia fires at the suspects near the window. She hits one man. His body slams against the glass and slides to the floor. Blood smears the pane. The other takes cover as Nia continues her assault.

Powers ducks and rolls. Once he's beside the office's entryway, he crouches and aims his Mossberg. The door is slightly ajar. Nia can see a suspect moving inside.

The end of a long-barrel rifle appears and nudges the door open wider. Nia makes eye contact with the gunman. He's dressed in black military fatigues. Plucky eyes, a rabid grin.

Powers remains crouched, out of sight.

Wait for it.

Wait for it.

The suspect aims his weapon at Nia. She mouths "Go" to Powers, who pushes off the wall, angles his body, and fires a slug into the suspect's chest. The suspect drops his weapon and falls backward into the room. Powers charges in with his shotgun poised and ready.

"Clear!" he shouts a moment later.

Nia advances across the room. The other suspect has taken cover near the windowsill. She can see a black combat boot sticking out from behind a long executive desk. She concentrates her barrage on the desk, tearing through particle wood and metal. The computer tower and monitor are ripped apart.

"Fucking bitch!" The suspect cries. "I'm going to kill you, *puta*!"

The suspect pops up clutching the semiautomatic rifle Nia glimpsed from the street. She doesn't hesitate. Before he can take a shot, she fires a burst of bullets. They enter the suspect's chest and stomach. A single bullet penetrates his eye, blots out the socket, and exits through the back of his head.

Nia stands over the lifeless man. He's young, no older than twenty-five, she thinks. His face is tatted: tears dotted below where his eye once was, skull and crossbones on his cheek. Buzzed head, eyebrows shaved, and more tattoos on his neck. Street bangers outfitted with cartel guns.

Three down.

"Adams?"

"I'm fine," she says. "Let's keep moving."

They reconvene and advance toward two offices at the end of the room. Doors are closed. Lights off. Powers motions Nia to the door. She turns the knob, leans in with her shoulder, and crouches.

The room is empty.

The relief doesn't last. They move on to the next office. Nia turns the bloody door handle and pushes it open.

"I got movement," Powers says, aiming his shotgun at a suspect on the floor. He's dressed like the others in black fatigues. A green bandanna is tied around his forehead. He's bearded. Looks older. He could be the ringleader, Nia thinks.

"Put it down!" Powers orders.

The suspect's pistol slips from his grasp. "I give up. Don't shoot." He's sitting in feces and blood.

"How many of you are there?"

"Four," he says. Blood gurgles in his throat and spills out the corner of his mouth. "Just four of us."

"You better not be lying to me."

"I'm not, man. Please, I'm hit. I need help."

"Yeah, I see that."

Nia pulls out her cuffs from their holster, grips the chain, and approaches the dying man.

"Wait," Powers says, his arm keeping her back.

"What? We need to take him into custody."

"Hey, hombre," he says. "Pick up the gun."

"Nah, man."

"Do it!"

"Powers?" Nia asks. "What's happening?"

"Stand down, Adams."

"I said do it," Powers repeats to the suspect.

"You don't need to do this, man," the suspect says. "I'll work with you . . . I know shit. I can tell you everything."

"You don't look like a rat."

A tear rolls down his cheek. "Please, man. Anything you want to know."

"Pick it up," Powers says. "Don't keep me waiting."

The suspect weeps softly.

"Pick it up, asshole."

The suspect grabs the gun and slides his finger into the trigger guard.

"Raise it," Powers says.

The man's hand turns rigid as he lifts the pistol. He knows what comes next—he's docile and accepting of his fate.

Bang.

The cacophony shakes the room. An alarm goes off in Nia's head. She thinks her legs might give out. She steadies herself and tries to focus. *Calm down. Get a grip.* She looks at the dead suspect. Smoke spirals out of the wound; a softball-size hole at the top of the sternum. Chunks of blood and mangled tissue resemble ground pork—puffy and pink.

She can hear heavy footsteps. SWAT has arrived. They're shouting commands. She can't make out what they're saying . . .

A SWAT member calls out: "Hands up!"

Powers drops his weapon. Nia's mindful enough to do the same.

"We're Rangers!" Powers says. "SRT!"

SWAT officers march closer. "Turn and face us," the commanding officer says.

The Rangers turn around slowly, their hands high above their heads.

What a clusterfuck.

"Give the all clear," Powers says calmly. "We got 'em. It's over."

• • •

A paramedic assesses Nia's cuts and bruises in the back of an ambulance. The medic lightly presses the injured skin on her chest. Nia flinches. It's tender—hideous shades of purple and gray over her breastbone.

"You really should go to the ER," the medic says.

"And wait five hours for an ice pack? No thanks."

"Suit yourself."

The FBI is on-site. Forensic investigators in blue jackets with yellow lettering move about collecting shell casings, reconstructing the scene, and creating a timeline of the events. Agents haven't made their way over to talk to Nia, but she knows it's coming. Powers has been jabbering with the feds for thirty minutes. Periodically, he looks over at Nia, smirks, and keeps talking.

It's shaping up to be a long night.

Lieutenant Mitch McCann gets out of a white Ford sedan and starts walking in the direction of the ambulance. He's fair-haired with a country-boy tan. There's an awkwardness to him: he tends to stare; allows too much space between sentences. Nia's gotten used to it, but others on her team call him *weirdo* and *creep*. Doesn't matter. He's a good cop—a Ranger's Ranger—who does things by the book.

McCann taps the medic on the shoulder and flashes his badge. "Mind if I have a word with her?"

The medic leaves to assist other injured cops.

"How is it?" McCann's eyes focus on Nia's chest. "Anything broken?"

"Contusion."

"Well, it looks bad."

"I'm alive, that's all that matters."

McCann sighs. "It's a fucking mess, isn't it?"

"Yes, sir."

"FBI has their work cut out," he says. "They'll reconstruct what went wrong here, but I prefer to hear it from you."

"There were aspects of the situation that weren't clear to us," she says. "We should've been better prepared."

"Is that what you'll be writing in your report?"

"I intend to provide a full, detailed accounting of the events, sir."

"Two team members are dead, and one is in critical condition."

"Yes, sir," she says with a tinge of shame. "We experienced serious failures. People lost their lives because of it."

"And you'll get the Medal of Valor," he says. "Despite the piss-poor communication and tactics displayed today, you and Powers saved lives."

"Sir, I don't know what to say . . ."

"Don't say anything. Powers will talk enough for both of you."

"About Powers, sir . . ."

"What is it?"

Nia swallows hard and whispers. "The last suspect was attempting to surrender. I was prepared to cuff him when Powers ordered the suspect to grab his firearm. Then Powers shot him."

McCann stares as if he sees through Nia—as if she's become translucent. He clears his throat and slips his hands into his pants pockets. "I see," he says. "Even if I were to believe such a thing, what outcome are you expecting?"

"I don't know. But it happened."

"People died at the hands of these animals. These piece-of-shit bangers come up from the cesspools of LA, New York, Phoenix, and Chicago. They flood our good state with their dope and filth and murder. Frankly, I'm tired of it."

"I understand that, sir, but what Powers did—"

"Enough," he says sharply. "You don't mention any of this to anyone. Not a word to the FBI or HPD. Understand?"

"Yes, sir," she says.

"Now, get home," he says. "I'm putting you on leave until you recover."

"But, sir. I'm fine . . . really."

"You need rest, Adams. It isn't up for discussion."

Nia looks over McCann's shoulder and locks eyes with Powers. She would never have ratted out her squad leader if she had given it more thought. But hours ago, she stared death down and survived. Maybe it's righteousness or wanting to go home with a clean conscience . . .

Her home is in Sugar Land. Twenty miles away, where she lives with Sharon.

Sweet Sharon. What is she going to tell her? How the hell does she explain all this?

Nia imagines the drive will feel endless. Heavy thoughts can slow time, but there won't be any escaping them. Some cops lay it out for priests and pastors. Others confide in mistresses and pole dancers. All she has is Sharon's altruistic ear, and in Nia's most doubtful moments, she wonders for how long.

CHAPTER TWO

DESMOND

Vietnam is 9,018 miles from Houston, but Desmond Bell is never far from the bush—never far from the war. He's been living for months at a boardinghouse in Little Saigon, the city's Vietnamese and Indochinese community. As a Black man in a homogeneous enclave, he draws attention, which is why he stays in, mostly, except when his work forces him out.

The news plays on a small TV. Desmond is half paying attention. He's busy preparing. A 9mm SIG and an assault rifle rest on his single bed with ammunition and a portable gas-powered buzz saw. There's a state map, blueprints, a box of ping-pong balls, foil, a tactical vest, and a latex mask made to look like George Bush that he purchased at a Halloween store last October.

He perks up when the news anchor speaks of the failed robbery at the downtown Central Bank of Texas. He knows the bank well. He robbed the same branch five years ago. It was the last time he stole money from a bank, and for good reason. The recon, the logistics, the manpower, the transport—it wasn't worth the hundred-thousand-dollar score, which he immediately gave to his handler, Marco.

There's a knock at the door. He turns down the TV's volume and walks across the creaky floor wearing a T-shirt and sweatpants. He looks through the peephole.

"Yes," he says.

Linh stands holding a tray with a large clay pot, a bowl, and a spoon like a mini ladle. She's Vietnamese. Early to midthirties, he thinks. But she carries herself as though she's lived a lifetime.

"Sorry," Desmond says. "Is the TV bothering you? I'll keep it down."

"No. It's fine. I thought you might like some pho. Tripe and brisket. Extra sprouts like you like."

Desmond opens the door slightly, so he doesn't reveal his cache. "*Cảm ơn*," he says, accepting the tray. "Smells good."

Linh seems to consider a smile but holds to her placid expression.

"There was a leak in the bathroom," he says. "Under the sink."

"So sorry. I'll have it fixed."

"Won't be necessary. I repaired it. Just needed tightening and some epoxy."

"You didn't have to do that . . ."

"It wasn't any trouble. I was happy to do it."

"Thank you, but you shouldn't have to repair things. I'm the one charging you rent, remember?"

"It's a big house. You're one person."

"Wasn't always that way. It was my grandmother's home," she says. "When I was a child, it seemed so much larger."

"Perspective . . ."

"Yes," she says. "Funny how it changes things."

Desmond isn't unaware of the home's history. He checked the property records at the tax assessor's office before inquiring about renting a room in the six-bedroom boardinghouse. He needed a place to lay low that wasn't on anyone's radar, which meant no defaulted property taxes or liens. He didn't want people coming around, especially county workers. He learned that Linh inherited the home a decade ago from her grandmother, an exceptional cook who converted the first floor into a café known for its Vietnamese coffee, sandwiches, and pho. After her grandmother's death, the café closed; Linh turned it into a banquet hall and began renting the rooms by the month. A stay includes three meals a day, use of a community bathroom, and access to the backyard, a large lot shaded by magnolia trees.

Prices are reasonable, and she requires rent to be paid in cash. He's seen only two other tenants: a student from a local university and an older woman whose dentures click when she speaks. The first week in the home, when the woman spoke, the noise pestered him so much that he ignored her and refused to greet her. He's since grown used to the sound. Tenants are exclusively Vietnamese or, in Desmond's case, fluent in the language and customs.

"There will be a small party tomorrow tonight," she says. "A friend of a friend is getting married on Sunday."

"A bachelor party?"

"They promised to keep the noise to a minimum. I explained how you like your quiet. If you like, I can bring your dinner to your room around seven?"

"No need. I'll be out of town."

"Oh," she says. "Taking a trip? Business or pleasure?"

"Neither."

"Okay. I won't hold you any longer. I'm sure you have things to do."

He wants to tell her she isn't any trouble and he looks forward to their chats, but he can't get the words out.

"Enjoy the soup," Linh says. "Leave the tray outside your door when you're done, and I'll collect it."

"All right," Desmond says before closing the door.

He stands for a moment, hand tight on the door's handle, feeling like a *người đần độn*—an idiot, a dunce. He's never been much for mingling. Hates small talk. But maybe he should've said more. Asked about her day or interests. Too much isolation has diminished his competence with banter. He's a poor socializer, and his aloofness has never served him well with women.

Maybe it's for the best, he thinks. What good could come from knowing Linh better?

He's certain of one thing, though: she's too young to be so tired. It's what his mother used to tell him when he'd come home from a long stretch working on fishing boats in the gulf. This was before he enlisted in the Marines, before the war, before finding purpose.

He pulls a duffel bag from under the bed and begins loading it with the items. The rifle and ammunition are the last things in.

A gray maintenance jumpsuit hangs in the closet. He tosses it on the bed and takes out a pair of boots. In the corner of the room are a small desk and chair. On the desk sits a framed photo of Desmond—younger, with a killer's vacant eyes, dressed in his Marine Corps uniform. He stands with his unit. An M16 hangs on his shoulder, a cigarette dangles from the corner of his mouth.

He taps the image of another man, who is short, heavy, and dark-skinned. "Semper fidelis," he says softly. "See you soon, brother."

• • •

The Toyota pickup—midnight blue, ordinary—whines when Desmond shifts into second gear. A bumper sticker reads "MARINE VETERAN" in bright orange letters over black.

The tank is full. Even though it is more than a decade old, the truck gets thirty-five miles to the gallon, so he won't have to stop for gas during the three-hour drive to Waxahachie.

Desmond rolls down the window and lights a cigarette. George Michael plays over the radio; before that was Luther Vandross. Smooth R & B and jazz—the good stuff.

He rolls through channels until he hears Teena Marie. She sings like a sista, he thinks. She's soulful and can hold a note like his mother. He doesn't like thinking about his mother, but lately, his mind has been on family.

He merges onto I-45; the dusty highway parts the flat earth. The route to Waxahachie is a straight shot north: Madisonville, Buffalo, Fairfield, Corsicana, and so on. Traffic is bearable, but far more cars are on the road than usual. Tonight's the Republican National Convention in New York, but politicians have parties planned all over town. He's happy to be out of the city. There'll be fireworks—fireworks put him on edge.

A full pack of smokes, a jug of water, and two foil-wrapped pork belly banh mis are on the passenger seat. His duffel bag is in the cargo bed under a tarp. He considered covering the bed with a shell but thought it too suspicious. Covered cargo beds draw attention; it's how smugglers transport people and drugs across the Mexican border and into the state.

It's a war they'll never win, Desmond thinks. After three tours in Nam, he knows a losing battle when he sees it. Even if Texas and the US won't admit it, they've become reliant on the cheap labor illegal immigration brings, and the narcotics cater to America's appetite more than anything else.

Desmond finds an open lane. Drops the truck's speed to sixty-five. He rolls through more channels until he finds classic rock and oldies, and then loses the radio station's signal.

The sun's beginning to set. He switches on the headlights, unwraps one of the banh mis that Linh made yesterday, and takes a bite. Knowing he'd get hungry on the long trip, he saved the sandwiches instead of eating them for lunch.

The driver of a Japanese sedan in the next lane looks annoyed by the traffic. Smacks his palms against the steering wheel. A checkered tie is loosened around his neck, sleeves rolled to the elbows—

Desmond knows what the end of a shitty day looks like. He had plenty in theater. But even his worst day in combat didn't measure up to the shitty days most people experience on a square job. Cubicle life is a death sentence. Some say Nam was too, but at least he felt the measure of his worth, and his efforts were significant. No one was there for the paycheck. No paper-pushing or watercooler conversations or sucking up for promotions. Layoffs and pink slips: a fucking rat race.

People kill themselves working jobs they hate—it's a long suicide.

Desmond knows the empty look; he's recognized it on the faces of bank tellers, branch managers, and security guards that he's ordered into vaults at gunpoint. Most of them don't like that he's robbing the bank, but few are invested in stopping him. People want to believe they matter to their company and that their loyalty is reciprocated. Their co-workers are like family, and customers are friends, not acquaintances. But that isn't the truth: the workers are cogs in the machine. Numbers. Replaceable. And if they weren't standing there with arms up at gunpoint, someone else would be.

Most people—smart people—want to return to their families, but those looking to be heroes get no rewards: only cracked noses, shattered collarbones, broken femurs, arms yanked out of their sockets. It's painful and ugly, and Desmond prefers things not to get physical, but when tested, he obliges.

A black Camaro with a white hood and light bar rides his bumper. Seconds later, blue-and-red lights flicker in his rearview.

"Damn," he says, steering the pickup onto the shoulder and cutting off the engine. He takes his wallet from his pocket and pulls out his driver's license. The name reads Martin Chambliss, one of his many aliases.

He lowers his window, places his hands on the steering wheel, and waits.

The trooper exits the Camaro, walks to the driver's side window, and shines the flashlight into the car. He's a towering white man whose signature brown uniform clings to his love handles.

"Evening," he says, right hand on his hip. "License and registration."

"Sure." Desmond slowly opens the glove box, takes out his registration, and hands it to the trooper, along with his license.

The trooper inspects the fake credentials. According to the driver's license, Martin Chambliss lives in Austin and is an organ donor. But the real Martin Chambliss, or "Marty Chambers" as he was known within the circle, has been dead for a decade. Desmond knows this because he shot him to death and disposed of his remains off the coast of Cuba. It wasn't unwarranted. Chambers would've killed Desmond first if he'd gotten the chance.

"Mr. Chambliss," the trooper says. "Long way from Austin."

"Coming from Houston, visiting my sister."

"Your tarp is flapping around. Doesn't look secure," the trooper says. "Wouldn't want it flying off and blinding another motorist."

"Ah, hell," Desmond says. "I knew I should've used more tie-downs."

"There's a rest area at the next exit. I suggest you fix it. I'm warning you this time, but you get stopped again, and it's a citation."

"Much appreciated, Trooper."

"You're a Marine?"

"That's right, sir."

"I was too young to go to Nam," the trooper says, handing Desmond back his license and registration. "But I would've been there if I could."

"Desert Storm, then?"

The trooper gives an affirming nod. "I think most people have forgotten about it."

"Why's that?"

"It was too damn short," he says. "Nothing like this war on terror. What's that say about us as a country if the only wars we remember are ones we can't win?"

"Don't know."

The trooper slaps the pickup's roof. "You're good to go," he says. "Get that tarp fixed."

Desmond waits until the trooper returns to the Camaro, then he pulls into traffic and continues down the interstate.

He exits onto a two-lane street and pulls into a gas station adjacent to a busy diner. A window advertisement touts a blue plate special: soup or salad, meat loaf, and mashed potatoes. Smoke pumps from the diner's roof. The salty scent of charred beef and fries taints the air. If there's ever been a uniquely American smell, that's it—burgers, fries, and deep-fried meats. That's what he fought for. That's what they told him freedom smelled like.

Time's wasting . . .

He gets out of the car and checks the tarp. It isn't as loose as the trooper made it seem. He tucks it in more but knows he needs to make up for the twenty minutes he's lost because of the traffic stop.

He just needs to get there. Once he's in Waxahachie, he can relax, clear his mind, and keep it focused on the job.

Back on the road, traffic hasn't died down any. It might even be worse. Desmond's restless, stomach tight. It isn't hunger, but he eats the other banh mi sandwich anyway and smokes a cigarette. He tunes the radio, finds a talk station, and figures it'll keep him awake—lots of outrage over the economy, the war, and the president. Not much is being said, but there's plenty of shouting. He tries other stations and lands on a bass-heavy rap song. The disc jockey calls it southern hip-hop—"Straight Outta Cashville." Admittedly, Desmond doesn't listen to rap or hip-hop but understands it. It's scrappy music with heart and emotion, but his ear isn't suited for the words—they come too fast, too hard—reminding him of a drill sergeant he had in Nam who only shouted when he spoke, minus the rhyming. Still, they've been songs he's failed to comprehend beyond words. He doesn't understand how some songs about shooting and killing is entertaining. He's been surrounded by death, communed with it, and nothing about it has ever amused him.

• • •

It's after ten o'clock when Desmond arrives in Waxahachie. He finds a truck stop a mile from the interstate and parks for the night. He winds a small alarm clock, sets it to ring at 5 a.m., and places it on the dash. His 9mm SIG is on his hip. A blanket covers his body and the gun.

He shuts his eyes, but there won't be much sleep. Four hours if he's lucky. He's done jobs with little sleep before. Sleep comes later, when the job is finished. It needs to be earned.

• • •

He wakes before the alarm clock sounds. It's still pitch-black; thousands of stars glow brightly.

A yawn, a stretch; he knuckles into his sore shoulder. Sleeping in a pickup gets harder as he ages. He climbs out of the truck and heads into the restroom to change into the jumpsuit, stepping over a used condom and three press-on nails that he at first mistakes for french fries.

Years ago, a sex worker, someone long haulers call a lot lizard, solicited him. She was in her early twenties, with glitter makeup and violet eyeliner. She wore a Prince concert tee commemorating his 1981 Dirty Mind Tour in Dallas. He declined her offer, and for the rest of the night, he thought about his baby girl and his hopes for her. Fathers should fear their daughters becoming lot lizards, he thought; they should fear most things for their kids.

The restroom smacks of shit; it's splattered on the ceiling and walls. Blood, too. He tries not to touch anything, quickly changes into his clothes, then pisses in the urinal. The soap dispenser is empty; he rinses his hands with hot water and leaves.

Outside, he gets a whiff of marijuana and hears a woman's sensual moans. Someone's paid for an all-nighter. It's odd to hear after 4 a.m., and it's five-thirty. Most truckers need rest unless they're doped up on speed or coke, and sweating over bargain cooch and snorting powder are activities that bring cops around.

It's best to get going, he thinks.

He returns to the truck, starts it up, and drives out of the parking lot. Twenty minutes in, he smokes a cigarette, keeping his speed below the highway's posted limit. He's got dozens of robberies and burglaries under his belt. Some days, he can't remember them all, and still, his stomach is doing that thing it does right before a heist: his belly turns to Jell-O, and every nerve fires at once. The menthol helps; he takes easy drags, exhaling through his nose—smoke steams as if he's got a bull's snout.

Fifteen more minutes of open highway, and he'll be there. . . .

• • •

He pulls into the parking lot of the Colonial Trust Bank of Texas and cuts the engine about twenty feet from the entrance.

It's six o'clock.

He reaches under the passenger seat and takes out a shopping bag. Inside are aluminum foil and ping-pong balls. He crushes the balls in his hands until they look like broken eggshells and packs them inside the foil.

More vehicles park: a Ford Expedition and a Chrysler Sebring. Moments later, a black Lincoln Town Car polished to a showroom finish pulls into the spot designated "Bank Manager." A plaid-suited white man gets out and begins walking toward the entrance. Two others join him with bouncy steps and toothy grins: a tall, dark-haired man in a navy sports coat and a woman with golden hair teased high, wearing a loose-fitting blazer.

It's six-fifteen. Early bird customers will arrive soon.

He puts the George Bush mask on and looks in the visor's mirror. The rubber chin is too high; the nose is crooked, too. He makes modifications and adds his black cap.

Time to move.

He hops out of the truck, grabs the duffel bag from the rear, and walks fast, eyes glued to the ground. He enters the bank, never slowing his stride.

Mounted in the ceiling are video cameras. To the left are stairs descending to a vault.

Three tellers—two women varying in age and the man in the navy suit—tend to their stations. A gray-haired woman roves the bank manager's office while the manager, the Lincoln owner, sits behind a long desk talking on the phone. The weary security guard, a hefty Black man with burn scars along his neck, approaches Desmond.

"Can I help you with something?" the security guard asks.

Desmond strikes the guard hard across the face with an open hand. His jaw juts forward. The guard staggers and then drops. Desmond removes the guard's handcuffs, forces his arms behind his back, and locks the cuffs tightly on his wrists.

People scream.

"Anyone hits the alarm, and I kill every last one of you!" Desmond shouts.

The older woman in a dated skirt suit comes out of the manager's office, along with the manager, who asks, "What the hell is going on here?"

Desmond locks the door and removes the rifle from his duffel bag. "Everyone on the floor!" He points the weapon at the tellers. "Get over here." The tellers shuffle from behind their stations. They join the manager and older woman lying down, their cheeks and noses pressed against the cold marble.

"You," he says to the older woman. "Get up!"

The woman slowly gets to her feet. Bad knees, maybe. Could be a hip replacement.

"Everyone listen carefully," he says. "You'll move into the vault when I tell you to. Any deviation from my orders will be met with repercussions. Understood?"

Murmurs follow.

Desmond studies the hostages. "Now, get up," he says. "Into the vault."

The tellers and manager get up, hurry down the steps, and enter the vault. The older woman lags.

"You," he says to her. "How long have you been working here?"

"Me?" she asks.

"Yes, you. How long?"

"Twenty-eight years," she says. "We don't keep very much money here. We're a small, older branch. More of a novelty."

"You have access to the storage closet?"

"I do."

Desmond orders the other hostages deeper into the vault. More panic, followed by loud shrills as the vault door closes.

"They can't breathe in there for long," the woman says.

"Worry about yourself. Take me to the storage closet."

Desmond looks at his watch. Based on his calculations, the vault has enough oxygen to sustain the hostages for forty-five minutes, longer if they stay quiet.

"It's this way," the woman says as she walks upstairs to the main floor. "We barely use it these days. Nothing's kept in there but boxes of old records."

He follows her to a door at the end of the hallway. "Open it," he says.

The woman produces a long brass key from her pocket. Unlocks and opens the door. She turns on a light to reveal stacks of banker's boxes. "See," she says. "Old records, like I told you."

Desmond lays the gun on the floor and takes a zip tie from his duffel bag. "Hands behind your back."

"Is this necessary? I won't be any bother."

"Do it."

The woman turns around, placing her wrists against the small of her back. Desmond applies the zip tie and proceeds to move the boxes.

He tosses them into the hallway until a small safe appears mounted into the wall.

"What the devil . . . ," the woman says. "How'd you know that was there?"

The safe is old—a late eighteenth-century Mosler—B-rating with minor corrosion. He puts his ear to the steel door and turns the combination dial, listening.

"No one's seen your face," the woman says. "And you haven't taken anything . . . yet."

He rotates the dial and keeps listening for the sound . . . *tick, tick, tick.*

"I promise, if you leave now, I'll make sure nobody speaks of this to the police. You've got my word."

Tick, tick, tick.

The safe is too old. It'll take too long to crack, even with its simple locking mechanism. He removes the buzz saw from the duffel bag and rolls up his sleeves, exposing a tattoo on his forearm: a crude skull wearing a ballistic helmet. On each side, a bleeding rose and an M16 rifle.

Desmond cuts into the metal. Sparks fly. The woman stays clear, keeping against the wall, still trying to convince him to leave.

The safe opens to dust and cobwebs. A leather book and a loincloth satchel are inside. Desmond brushes dirt from the book's cover and evaluates the pages. He opens the satchel, looks inside. Satisfied, he places the items in the duffel bag.

He reads his watch—seven minutes have passed—leaving him three minutes to exit.

"Please, let me go, Mister," the woman says. "You've got what you wanted."

Desmond pulls a switchblade from his pocket. "Turn around," he says to the woman. She complies. He cuts the zip tie from her wrists. "Get to the vault."

The woman walks to the vault, a few paces ahead of Desmond. As they near the vault door, he reaches into the duffel bag and removes the foil pouch packed with crushed ping-pong balls. He flicks his Zippo and lights the crushed plastic on fire. White smoke pours from a small opening in the foil.

He tosses the pouch into the lobby. "Let them out when I'm gone," he says. "Not a second sooner."

The woman nods.

The smoke fills the lobby—innocuous, theatrical—a rolling vapor. Desmond heads toward the bank's rear, slams against an emergency door's push bar, and exits to an alarm.

Outside, he removes his mask, throws the duffel bag over his shoulder, and peers around the side of the building. Two customers are gathered at the entrance, pounding on the door's glass. "Fire! Fire!" they shout.

The smoke is a useful distraction. He walks quickly to the pickup, gets in, tosses the duffel bag on the passenger seat, and starts the engine.

The bank's door opens. Hostages spill out, trailed by smoke. They cough and brace their hands against their knees.

Desmond drives out of the parking lot, down a street, and turns left into traffic.

• • •

He arrives at a shopping center off Highway 77 and parks outside a Whataburger. Teens in oversize shirts and baggy jeans kick-flip skateboards and puff cigarettes. Mike Jones's "Still Tippin" plays from a boombox. He wipes the truck's interior with a bleach-soaked rag, strips the truck of anything that could identify him, and tosses the rag into a garbage bag containing the vehicle's key, the dismantled rifle, the buzz saw, and the George Bush mask. He gets out of the truck and deposits the bag of evidence into a Salvation Army donation receptacle.

He walks into the Whataburger, orders a Coke and a cheeseburger with extra pickles at the counter, then eats it quickly. In the restroom, he puts the jumpsuit into the garbage bin and puts on a pair of jeans and a checkered shirt.

Afterward, he walks half a mile to a Greyhound Station, a relic of the 1950s, and buys a one-way ticket to Houston. He sits in the lobby for three hours, watching the news on a television bolted on a bookshelf. There's no mention of the robbery. He isn't surprised. The bank would never admit to having looted Spanish gold and a slave manifest in its possession. It's the sort of thing that would land the bank on the cover of *TIME* magazine and be broadcast on *60 Minutes*.

When it's time to board, Desmond takes a seat in the rear of the bus. An older white man with a sun-blistered nose stares him down. Desmond fights the inclination to meet the man's scowl with equal hostility. Looking at anyone for too long increases his risk of being identified if it ever comes to that. Besides, it's a look he's endured his entire life. He knows what the man sees—coal-black skin, budget clothes, and an all-day stink. He'd never believe that hours ago, Desmond robbed the oldest bank in Texas of two million dollars in Spanish gold and a slave manifest implicating the Duchamps, one of Texas's wealthiest families, as profiteers in the transatlantic slave trade. Maybe the man would laugh out of spite—call Desmond a liar, spit in his face for speaking ill about the beloved Duchamps, whose supporters are known to be fanatical. And with Corbin Duchamp preparing a run for the White House, the nation's gotten a crash course in the oil baron's politics and old-money pedigree.

The Duchamps have managed to keep the sordid details of their formidable years a secret. As far as the world is concerned, the bank is currently owned by a group of investors—a big-money conglomerate that's shielded the Duchamps from scrutiny, preserving their status as the epitome of the American dream.

Desmond tries not to look at his scores as anything other than jobs and ways to make a living, but Corbin Duchamp is a puppet of his megalomaniacal father. The younger Duchamp is privileged in a way most Americans will never understand, yet they cheer for him with his Kennedy looks and good-ole-boy politics. But Desmond knows a con artist when he sees one, and if Corbin Duchamp were to become president, it would be bad not only for the country, but for the world.

• • •

It's after nine—night's fallen. The bus pulls into a busy rest area three hundred miles from Houston. Desmond estimates that if the bus keeps its pace, he'll arrive in the city around midnight.

He purchases a large coffee and a turkey sandwich from a vending machine located near the men's restroom. He drinks half of the bland coffee, walking the sidewalk to get his blood pumping, then returns to the bus.

The white man with the stink-eye never deboarded, which doesn't strike Desmond as peculiar until he notices a gold badge on the man's hip, slightly obscured by his shirttail. US Customs and Border Patrol? FBI, maybe? Local police? It could be nothing, Desmond thinks. Coincidental. An officer traveling for work . . .

Desmond returns to his seat and bites into the cold, stale sandwich stuffed with wilted lettuce, sour tomato, and dry turkey breast. *Three hours*, he reminds himself. Just three more hours, and he'll be home.

• • •

It's 11:15 p.m. when the bus enters Houston. Desmond's delighted to see the downtown skyline. The city's beacon, the JPMorgan Chase Tower, is stacked up to heaven. He's seen taller buildings in other cities—Chicago, New York, and LA—and plenty throughout Asia, but a tower in the Texas flatlands makes an impression. The bus maneuvers the narrow streets, pulls into the depot on Main, and parks.

The driver, an older dark-skinned woman with fuchsia fingernails, eases from the driver's seat and addresses the riders: "Please remain seated. Federal agents will be boarding the bus." The words are monotone. Slightly shaky. Rehearsed.

The passengers' chatter grows, accompanied by befuddled stares that turn to worry in a few blinks. Desmond looks at the man with the gold badge. He's adjusted himself so his hips are square, and his legs are angled toward the aisle. He's got cutthroat eyes and is calm as a high-stakes gambler. A burnished black pistol is on his hip. Glock, maybe... something that'll put a nice-size hole in somebody.

This lawman's operational, but who's the target?

Desmond focuses on the passengers, taking in their faces. He's careful not to observe too long but long enough to read their expressions—see what's behind their eyes. He notices an older man with a face like crumpled paper, rough bronze skin, creased and saggy. He's wearing a gas station trucker hat—a cheap plastic snapback with a flimsy bill.

Border agents board the bus with their guns drawn. The lawman jumps up like something's bitten him, pulls his weapon, and aims it at the man in the trucker hat.

"Manuel Ruiz. You're under arrest," he says, spit flying. "Hands where we can see them!"

The old man looks too tired to put up a fight; he raises his bony arms over his head. His palms are riddled with scabs, some fresh cuts, as if he's wrangled barbed wire.

"Get up, slowly."

Ruiz stands up and shuffles toward the agents. The lawman grabs his arm, throws him over the seat, and cuffs his wrists.

Gasps and sighs.

There's no telling what Ruiz did, but he's too frail to be thrown around like a sack of potatoes. "Doesn't look like he's putting up a fight," Desmond says. "All that necessary?"

"Mind your business, boy," the lawman says. "Or you're coming with him."

Desmond's tired and isn't thinking straight. Minding his business is usually what he's best at, aside from thievery.

The lawman escorts Ruiz off the bus. When all the agents are gone, the passengers' chatter returns. Desmond rubs his eyes. He's certain they're bloodshot.

"Y'all can deboard now," the bus driver says.

People hurry and pile into the aisle. Desmond waits until the bulk of passengers are off before making his way to the front of the bus.

Outside, the passengers form a crowd around an attendant snatching luggage from the cargo hold and piling it on the sidewalk. Desmond walks past the crowd and stands under a sign hanging by chain-link marked "TAXI." A yellow cab flashes its lights; a hand waves him forward.

Desmond gets in and sets his bag on the seat.

"Address?" the cabbie asks.

"5233 South Emanuel Street."

"Little Saigon?"

"That's right."

• • •

The house is unexpectedly busy. It takes some time, but Desmond remembers why. Linh rented out the café for a bachelor party. It was still going on despite the early morning hour. A young Vietnamese man with wet hair and tattooed arms loiters on the porch, smoking a cigarette. He's drunk, punching the air—left hook, right cross, an uppercut. "Who the fuck are you?" the man asks as Desmond approaches. "It's a private party."

"I live here."

"You? Here? This ain't your neighborhood."

"Where's Linh?"

The man shrugs. "Who the fuck is Linh?"

Desmond goes inside, leaving the man to box a ghost. Six men are drunk in varying stages of consciousness. Empty beer bottles roll across the floor; rice noodles are stuck to the walls. A thick-necked man with a mullet and tattoos stands on a chair, gyrating his hips and singing "Tiến Quân Ca," the Vietnamese national anthem. His mouth is too close to the mic—feedback, static—Desmond's ears ring.

The other five men are slumped in corners and face down on tables, mouths covered in sticky rice.

Broken teacups are on the floor. Pho trickles from a table's edge, forming a puddle. It's a shit show, and he knows it's not what Linh agreed to.

Desmond goes upstairs and knocks on Linh's door. "It's me," he says.

She unlocks the dead bolt; the door opens.

Linh emerges from the dimly lit room; her head hangs low. Struggling to see her eyes, Desmond brushes the hair away from her face. She's been crying, and her collarbone is bruised.

"I'm sorry, Desmond," she says. "I begged them to leave . . ."

Desmond examines the purple lesions along her neck's dainty curve. "Did they pay you?" he asks.

Linh nods.

"Keep the door locked until I come back." He steps across the hall and enters his room. The single bed with the worn mattress has never been so inviting. Showering, then sleeping—that's what he should be doing. But the men downstairs have shifted his priorities. He opens the safe and puts the stolen goods inside. Once the gold and manifest are secured, he removes a rattan stick with an end wrapped in boxer's tape from a dresser drawer and proceeds downstairs.

Two men who appeared conscious before are no longer alert. The thick-necked man has swapped patriotic hymns for 50 Cent's "P.I.M.P." He's nearing the end of the song when Desmond unplugs the karaoke machine.

"Get the fuck out," he says. "All of you."

The drunk entertainer steps off the chair and dangles the mic in his hand. He's shorter than Desmond, and aside from his swollen neck, he's solid in the places that count—arms, chest, shoulders. Desmond holds the Arnis stick behind his back. He doesn't want to escalate things unless he has to.

"I paid for the night," the man says.

"Night's over."

"Ah, fuck off . . . I'm going to enjoy my last night of freedom . . ."

"*Freedom*?" Desmond grins.

"You got a problem with that, Pops?"

"How many times have you hit her?"

"What?"

"Your soon-to-be-wife," Desmond says. "How many times?"

"Who do you think you're talking to? You don't fucking know me."

"I know you're weak . . . *yếu đuối*," he says. "And that mark on Linh's neck, you did that, didn't you?"

"It's called dancing, *homeboy*. Ain't nothing wrong with a little bump and grind. You know what I'm saying?" The drunk pokes Desmond's chest. Training takes over. Muscle memory. Desmond grabs the man's wrist, twists it into an unnatural angle, then bashes the Arnis stick against his skull. The drunk's eyes buck. He tenses up—still not sober but alarmed enough to put up a fight.

"Get your friends and leave," Desmond says. "I won't tell you again."

The man touches his head where the stick made contact. Blood smears his fingers. "You mutherfucker . . ."

Desmond ducks a hook, then levels the stick against the man's knee and sweeps his leg, sending him to the floor. "Huy!" the man screams.

The café door opens. Huy, the boozy boxer from the porch, enters and charges Desmond, screaming in Vietnamese. Desmond pivots, shoves the stick's tip into Huy's ribs, then elbows his jaw. Huy collapses on the floor next to his comrade—*người bạn*.

Linh appears on the stairs: "Enough!"

Desmond lowers the stick and steps away from the battered men.

"Gather yourselves and go," Linh says. "And never come back."

The drunken men get to their feet. Spit blood and stumble around the room, waking those who have passed out.

"Hurry up," Linh says, holding on to the banister. "I want you out of my sight."

As Huy and the future groom wake the last of the sleeping men, Desmond observes with the stick braced against his shoulder. After the last man scampers through the café door, Linh comes down to assess the damage.

"I can help you clean," Desmond says, laying the Arnis stick on the table.

"You've done enough."

"Please," he says. "I won't be able to sleep knowing you're doing all this alone. Besides, what if they sober up and come back?"

"They won't."

"I think it's better if I stay, just to be sure."

Linh walks over to a closet and removes two parlor brooms with wooden handles and straw bristles. She hands one to Desmond. "This will take some time . . . Coffee?"

"Yes. Thank you."

She touches his shoulder; he trembles. "No. Thank you," she says, then goes into the kitchen.

CHAPTER THREE

NIA

Water dampens sound. Makes the world quieter. Helps Nia think. As a child, she could hold her breath at the bottom of the family's pool for three minutes, sometimes longer, before surfacing for air. She's older now, and three minutes seems like forever.

Sharon enters the bathroom dressed in a navy power suit with white pinstripes and two-inch high heels, a conservative height for a judge. She's home from the courthouse earlier than expected. She says something Nia can't make out. Her voice drones like an overworked air conditioner.

Nia comes up for air.

"Do you have to do that?" Sharon asks, leaning over the tub. "You look like a drowning victim. Scares me half to death."

"Sorry."

"You get to the store yet?" Sharon takes the hairpins out of her bun, unraveling her freshly permed hair down her back.

"No," Nia says. "Got sidetracked."

"We're out of milk." Sharon wipes the blush from her cheeks with a tissue. "Actually, we're out of most things, and the steaks didn't thaw for dinner."

"I meant to take them out . . . Slipped my mind."

"Uh-huh."

"We'll order in. Pizza?"

"Sure." Sharon sighs. "Why the hell not?" Heavy sarcasm.

"Okay."

"That's all you have to say?"

"What else is there?"

"It doesn't have to be this awkward," Sharon says. "You can talk to me."

"I'm talking to you now," Nia climbs out of the tub. "Are we not communicating?"

"You know damn well that's not what I mean."

Nia snatches a towel from a brass bar and binds it around her body.

"Just when I think we're past the worst," Sharon says, "something happens, and you go right back to shutting me out."

"That's not what I'm doing . . ."

"Then talk to me, for goodness' sake." Sharon snatches another tissue from the box and rubs away lipstick. "Tell me what's going on in that head of yours."

Nia moves behind her, presses her chest against Sharon's back, and rests her chin on her shoulder. Gestures like these are how she says, "You're right, and I need you," but Sharon will never hear those words. Nia isn't built that way—the share-your-feelings way. She grew up believing showcasing feelings was for the weak.

On her block in Queens, shedding a tear was the mark of death. It wasn't until her family moved to Texas that she felt she could breathe. But by then, New York had left its mark—boys in school called her "ice queen" because she wasn't interested in them. Nia was attracted to girls and had been since she was six. After seeing a pretty curly-haired blond dancing on the Mickey Mouse Club, she contemplated writing the performer a letter confessing her feelings, and she fantasized that they'd fall in love and share an ice cream cone the way she'd seen in movies.

She doesn't tell Sharon these things, but maybe she should try.

"Don't worry," Nia says, arms around Sharon's waist. "It's just with what went down in the bank..."

"It rattled you. I get it."

It did more than that, Nia thinks. She was party to a suspect's execution by a fellow Ranger. Nothing about that sits well with her, and it shouldn't.

Nia's cell phone vibrates on the nightstand.

"Gotta love the timing," Sharon says. "Go ahead."

Their eyes meet in the vanity mirror. Nia looks away—she always looks away.

She marches into the bedroom and answers the phone. It's Lieutenant McCann.

"Hello?"

"Adams, what's your status?"

"I'm home, Lieutenant," she says, "What's up?"

"I've got something I'd like for you to look into for me."

"Okay," she says.

"I'll discuss further at headquarters."

"I'll head there now."

She hangs up.

"McCann so soon?" Sharon asks, huddled in the bathroom doorway.

"I'm needed in the field."

"You're supposed to be recuperating."

"I'm fine."

"Damn you, Nia. They're going to use you until there's nothing left, and you're going to fucking let them."

Nia sucks her teeth. "I need to go..."

"What about dinner? I was hoping we could talk."

"I'm sorry, it'll have to wait."

Sharon's eyes fall flat. Emotionless. She's heard it all before.

This is the job, and there isn't anything Nia can do about it. Breaking dinner plans, missing special occasions, long nights away from home—it should've been written in the fine print when she applied to join Houston PD, then Ranger School, but it was something she learned later. And it didn't bother her until she met Sharon—that's when showing up mattered and when she started breaking promises.

"I'll make do for dinner," Sharon says. "You should go."

Before Nia can respond, Sharon shuts the bathroom door. Nia gets up and takes hold of the doorknob. She wants to go in, explain herself . . . make Sharon understand. But Nia doesn't have time to soothe her reservations and doesn't know what to say, anyway.

Right now, she needs to work.

• • •

"Why isn't the sheriff handling it?" Nia brings her chipped coffee cup to her lips and drinks.

She can't keep her eyes off the wastebasket next to McCann's desk. Looks as though it hasn't been emptied in days—burger wrappers, cola cans, and microwave dinner boxes have nearly toppled over the brim. He eats like a man without a family. It's easy for cops to get hooked on the euphoric rush of junk food. Nia despises sugar and trans fat, but she understands their attraction. Thinking you may not see tomorrow means living for the day. *Eat what you want—it might be your last meal.* The chocolate glazed donut from Shipley's sitting on McCann's desk further illustrates this point.

"The sheriff believes you could shed light on some things," McCann says. "*Illuminate* was the word he used."

"And the bank hasn't accounted for what was stolen?"

"The only thing they're sure about is that a safe was opened, and whatever was inside is gone." A fly circles his donut. He swats at it, coming close to batting it down.

"Waxahachie," she says. "And where the hell is that?"

"Out a ways," he says before biting into the donut. Shards of chocolate glaze accumulate on his top lip and in the bristle brush he calls a mustache.

Nia's amused.

McCann smacks his lips, sweeping the crumbs deeper into the coarse hair. "Like I said, you were requested for your expertise."

"A little town like that? When's the last time a Ranger set foot there?"

"Word spreads quickly about what you pulled off at Central Bank. People think it was a damn miracle. It won't do any harm to check it out."

"So, this is a new assignment?"

"Yes, your new marching orders."

"I haven't been cleared by medical yet."

"Don't worry about that. I'll deal with it."

Nia sighs.

"What do you want me to say?" McCann asks. "You've become a celebrity. People commend what you and Powers did."

"Then they should've asked for Powers."

"They did," he says, striking the fly with his palm. The broken insect lands on his desk, still buzzing. "He's spending time with his family."

"Family time . . . *right*."

"Don't act like you were soaking it up at home," he says, cleaning the fly's remnants from his hand with a napkin. "We both know you can't sit still for a minute."

McCann is a yuk, quick with the wisecracks, but he's hit a truth. Nia tends to be jittery and generally unsettled, and lately, it's been worse at home. Her skittishness tormented her throughout elementary school so much that her teachers thought she had an attention disorder. Her father believed she lacked focus and confidence and thought the cure was to teach her useful skills. He started with firearms training—safety first, then speed loading and manipulations, and when it came time for her to shoot, he made sure her grip was tight and that she didn't pull the trigger but squeezed it until the *surprise break*. Finally, he taught her never to miss a target, even if it was moving. Her father was seasoned in all instruments of violence, and it wasn't until Nia's seventh birthday that she learned why.

"It's a long drive," McCann says, "you better get going." He tosses the napkin cradling the dead fly into the wastebasket.

"I'm supposed to leave now? What about the Central Bank case?"

"Feds have assumed full authority. It's not our circus, Adams."

McCann is wantonly cavalier, and Nia no longer finds the humor in him chewing like Mister Ed, the talking horse. She liked watching reruns of the show with her father, who explained that peanut butter was spread along the horse's gums to make it look as though he was talking.

There's no defying McCann. There's an unspoken agreement that exists between them. She does what she's told and doesn't push back, and he'll treat her with respect. Reporting what Powers did could have jeopardized everything she's worked for, and while McCann would never say it, Nia's important to the Rangers—to their ranks and public image. She's the first Black woman sworn into the law enforcement body since its founding in 1823. Marie Reynolds Garcia and Cheryl Steadman came before her but neither shared Adam's skin color. All of them faced scrutiny and harassment but refused to quit.

Despite the hell she was put through, Nia doesn't regret joining the fraternity of lawmen with a blood-soaked legacy. Plenty of innocent Mexican Americans were struck down by Rangers' bullets, but the Rangers were cast as protectors charged with banishing evil. It was Old Testament shit. And still, she pursued the circle-star badge, knowing the world she'd inhabit.

Sharon likes to remind Nia that she chose to be a Ranger—not that she needs reminding. "No one made you become a Ranger. No one forced it on you," Sharon says, to which Nia invariably replies, "And no one can take it from me either."

• • •

Nia arrives in Waxahachie around 10 p.m. and checks into the two-star motel in the center of town. She calls the sheriff on her cell. After a minute of pleasantries, they agree to meet at the bank at 8 a.m. the next day.

She calls Sharon. "Thought I'd say goodnight," Nia says.

"You sound exhausted."

"It's been a long day."

"You should go to sleep, then. I'm surprised you had the energy to call."

Nia can still hear some saltiness in Sharon's voice.

"You're right," Nia says. "I have to be up in a few hours, anyway."

"Of course, I am . . . I'm always right."

Nia groans as if someone's poking her in the ribs with a screwdriver. "I'll call again when I can," she says. "The morning will be busy, but I figure things will wrap up by noon."

"Okay."

"Talk to you later."

"Be safe, Nia . . ."

Nia never knows how to respond when she hears those words. She doesn't need anybody reminding her of what she already knows. She's been a cop for decades and a woman forever. Safety is never far from her thoughts.

She ends the call and turns off the lamp.

• • •

Nia wakes at 5:30 a.m., thirty minutes before her alarm is set to buzz. She's well rested and has no memory of dreaming. She prefers it that way. Dreams have a way of sticking with her. After her father went to prison, she dreamed about him behind bars at least twice a week for a year. It was a siren song. No matter the bliss she'd conjure in her mind, it would always end with her reliving the fourteen and a half minutes it took for Texas Rangers to serve a felony warrant, arrest her outlaw daddy, and disappear into the night.

The trajectory of his life always seemed to suggest prison would be the outcome. Her father had grown up in Texas and had left to pursue the fast life in New York, landing in Queens, where he met her mother. Years later, the fast life came to a halt when her father crossed the wrong people, and they were forced to flee to his humble home in Houston, where he continued his life of crime.

Nia knew her father was a criminal at seven, when she found blueprints and a notebook detailing a bank robbery he planned to commit. She was thirteen when he went to prison.

It wasn't until she enrolled at St. Mary's University that her rigorous class schedule and entangled social life took precedence over her father's ruin. She thought less about her father and his predicament and more about her studies and career choices. Police science and criminology were the only subjects that held her attention.

Nia looks out the window into the darkness. It's a ghost town. Nothing like Houston, whose faint pulse beats until dawn.

She starches and irons crisp, hard lines into her white oxford. After a shower, she gets dressed and goes downstairs to the lobby, where the motel's continental breakfast bar displays fruit cups, mini cereal boxes with milk, and an assortment of muffins.

After drinking two cups of watered-down coffee, she walks outside, gets into her white Ford Explorer, a replacement for the Blazer she drove into Central Bank, and proceeds down Main Street to Colonial Trust. Nia muses to herself. Nearly every town and city in Texas has a Main Street with a bank. History teaches slaves were sold on Main Streets. She figures the same goes for other cities across Texas . . . and America.

• • •

The parking lot is empty; she's ten minutes early, which Nia considers to be on time. The bank is unassuming, the way she'd imagined, a 1930s time capsule that seems an unlikely target for a robbery.

She has no idea why McCann has sent her to the sleepy town, and given Texas's mounting crime rate, especially in Houston, she could be investigating less insipid crimes. The gang responsible for the Central Bank robbery hasn't been brought to justice.

A white Ford pickup pulls into the parking lot. The word *SHERIFF* in large brown letters stretches across its side, stacked above *ELLIS COUNTY*. A potbellied man in uniform gets out: green shirt, navy pants, and a beige cowboy hat. He slams the truck's door, then leans against its side, studying Nia's Explorer.

After a moment, he tugs on his Sam Browne belt, hikes up his pants, and walks toward the bank's entrance. He greets the manager with a handshake and dawdles the way cops do, hands over his belt buckle, weight shifted to his gun leg.

No point in wasting time. The sooner she can liaise and resolve the case, the sooner she can get back to Houston. She gets out of her vehicle and walks toward the men engaged in friendly banter, which ends when Nia's within speaking distance.

"Morning," the sheriff says. "We wondered when you'd join us. Adams, right?"

"Ranger Nia Adams."

"Nia . . . it's got an exotic ring to it."

"*Adams* or *Ranger* is fine."

"All right." The sheriff looks to the bank manager, who frowns. "I'm Sheriff Clifford Rowe. This is Don Silvestri, the bank manager. Welcome to Ellis County."

"How was the drive?" Don asks.

"Uneventful. Got in last night."

"You're staying in town, then?"

Nia focuses on Don's pocket square. Flower-printed silk. Intricately folded. It sweetens an otherwise drab suit. "Staying at a motel," she says.

"You came alone?" the sheriff asks. His wide neck flares like fish gills, and his nose looks as though it's been flattened with a shovel.

"Is that a problem?"

"No," he says. "Just thought McCann was sending a team or someone more—"

"Older?" Nia says, heading off what she's sure would be an offensive remark. "I get that a lot."

"I bet you do." The sheriff pushes his thick-framed glasses up the bridge of his blotchy nose. "Don was present during the robbery."

"Not sure we can call it a robbery," Don says. "We don't know if anything was stolen."

Nia turns to Rowe. "Sheriff?"

"Don has his theories. I, on the other hand, am worried this might've been a dry run. Some professional testing out our response time and capabilities."

"Which are?" Nia asks.

"Deputies were on the scene within ten minutes of getting the call, but the perpetrator was long gone by then."

Nia takes a notepad and pen from her pocket. "I'd like to see the safe."

"Sure," Don says. "I mean, you drove all this way . . ."

A sign on the bank's door reads "CLOSED." Nia follows the men inside.

Much like the exterior, the lobby suggests that the bank may be one of the oldest in the country, which adds further perplexity about why someone would target it.

"Right here is the detonation site." Don points to the floor where charred foil and ashes are scattered.

"Detonation?"

"Ping-pong balls wrapped in aluminum," Rowe says. "From what we can tell, the suspect lit it on fire as he fled. Probably as a distraction."

"A smoke bomb?"

"Old-school, I know. But it had a handful of customers thinking the bank was on fire. Dispatch prioritized sending the fire department, which accounted for our delay getting to the scene." Rowe clasps his fingers over his belly and rocks on his heels. "One of them managed to dial 911 from a pay phone."

"You get many bank robberies in Ellis?" Nia asks.

"Two or three . . . a decade."

"Did the suspect have a firearm? What did they look like?"

"Mrs. Maynard got a look at his arm. Says he might've been a Black fella. As for the gun, he carried a rifle," Rowe says. "Sounds like military-grade, based on witness accounts."

"I'm terrible at identifying guns," Don says. "But it made quite the statement. Put the fear of God into us."

"The robber wore a mask," Rowe says. "President Bush."

"Junior?" Nia asks.

"Nope. Senior."

"You think those masks are selling in costume shops these days?"

"Probably got it off the internet."

"Or it's old," she says. "Could check suspect files. See which ones wore those masks during commissions of crimes."

"Oh, almost forgot . . ." Don digs into his pants pocket. "Mrs. Maynard did this sketch for us." He hands Nia a folded sheet of paper. "It's a tattoo she said was on his arm."

She unfolds it like a letter: a crudely drawn human skull wearing a hat.

"Mean anything to you?" Rowe asks.

"Can't say it does. Looks military, though. Is it all right if I hold on to this?"

"Sure," Rowe says. "We Xeroxed plenty."

"The safe is this way," Don says.

Nia follows him to the bank's rear, down the short flight of stairs, and through the hallway to the storage closet.

"I can't fathom how the suspect would know a safe was even here," Rowe says. "Don's been working at this branch for almost twenty years and didn't know it was here until, what? Five years ago?"

"That's right." Don stares at the safe, accusatory, as if it had conspired against him. "I came across some old blueprints in the basement and had me a little treasure hunt. Not much of a mystery, though. Took me an hour to realize the safe was in this storage closet."

"The blueprints," Nia says, examining the empty safe in the wall. "Anyone else have access to them?"

"Hard to say. It's an old branch. One key opens most doors around here, including access to the basement. But they'd have to know what they were looking for."

"And you've got no idea what was being kept here?" she asks.

"I'm all out of guesses," he says. "It's a shame you made the trip, but not a dime was touched. We've already requested additional security from corporate, and they've agreed to add more cameras."

"Where was the security guard during the robbery?"

"On the floor bleeding," Rowe says. "Took an ugly shot to the kisser. Lost a tooth."

"As if that wasn't bad enough, the suspect bound him with his own handcuffs," Don says, shaking his head, disgusted. "Such a shame Fletch had to endure that."

"It's plain old disrespectful to treat a vet that way," Rowe adds, "no doubt about it."

Don nods in agreement. "It wasn't Fletch's finest moment, but at least no one was killed."

"You say his name is Fletch?"

"Hakeem Fletcher. He's been our guard since January."

"Was he armed?"

"No," Don says. "Corporate didn't want to pay for an armed guard considering this bank is low-risk—was low-risk."

"I'll need a list of everyone in the bank that day and files on all the employees, including addresses and how long they've worked here."

"Right," Don says, "I have everything you need in my office." There's plenty of sweat on his brow. Nia thinks his pulse must be racing. "So, this is really happening? I mean, a *formal* investigation?"

"How about you just get me those files," she says. "And I'll worry about the investigation."

"Right. Right. I'll get on it." He traipses down the hallway in his polished loafers.

At first, Rowe's chuckle sounds like he has rocks in his throat, then he clears it and says, "I know what you're thinking, Ranger. And I'm not sure you want to bark up that tree."

"Excuse me?"

"Inside job," he says. "Simplest explanation. How someone might've come across those blueprints and learned about the safe."

"You've considered it?"

"I have," he says. "And I would have pursued it if there was cause."

"This isn't cause enough for you?"

"A man lost a tooth, and a smoke bomb went off. Can't say that deserves the Spanish Inquisition."

"What does it deserve?" Nia asks.

"Well, if I find out who did it, I'll arrest them for assault and mayhem."

Don returns with a box of manila folders tucked under his arm. "I also made a list of all the employees in the bank during the robbery," he says, handing Nia the box.

"Security footage?" she asks.

"We have it down at the station," Rowe says. "We've been reviewing it. You're welcome to come by. Check it out for yourself."

"I'll do that. Thank you for your time, gentlemen." Nia carries the box toward the lobby.

Outside, Nia loads the files into the rear of the Explorer. The sheriff saunters toward her, sucks in his gut, and flashes a crooked grin.

"Is there something else?" Nia asks.

Rowe stammers. "I was wondering if you'd like to get dinner later. We've got some decent barbecue here in Ellis. Nothing like Houston, I'm sure, but—"

"I'm a vegetarian."

"A vege-what?"

"I don't eat meat."

"Oh, I see. I'm sure we can rustle you up some stewed green beans or collards . . ."

"I'll take a rain check, Sheriff."

"Interesting accent you've got there."

"Excuse me?"

"Not a native Texan, are you?"

"Does that make me an outsider?"

"Well, not exactly. Seems like you've been here long enough to know your way around towns like ours, but it is rare . . ."

"What is?"

"The Rangers taking in a Yankee."

"I've been here long enough to consider myself a Texan, and I earned my spot just like everyone else."

"Sure, sure. I'm not implying—"

Nia climbs into the Explorer and starts the engine. "If you wouldn't mind bringing the surveillance tape by my motel, I'd be grateful."

"Well, all right. I do hope you change your mind about dinner."

He removes his hat and brings it to his chest, an act of courtliness. The budding sun bounces off his bald spot. Nia's never been attracted to any man besides Usher, whom she's seen in concert twice, and while she wouldn't call Rowe ugly, his looks have neared an expiration date. And his abecedarian approach to criminal investigating assures her they'd have little to talk about over a fair-to-middling meal.

"Call the station if you need me, and I'll get that tape to you ASAP," Rowe says.

"You know where I'm staying?"

"Sure," he says. "It's the only motel in town."

"Of course it is." Nia gases the Explorer and pulls off.

• • •

Back in the motel room, she calls McCann and rehearses her talking points, filtering out the curse words while waiting until he picks up.

"McCann here." He's groggy, more so than usual.

"It's Adams."

"Thought you'd be calling," he says. "You make it to Waxahachie all right?"

"I'm here. Not sure why, though."

"What's the trouble? Rowe working your nerves already?"

"You know this guy?"

"From decades ago," he says. "Doubt he or the town has changed much."

"I'd like to know why you sent me down here. Nothing about this supposed crime merits Ranger involvement."

"I thought it'd be good for you—"

"In what way, sir? These people aren't even sure a crime was committed. Seems to me the bank manager prefers to drop the entire matter."

McCann is silent.

"Sir, are you there? Did you hear what I just said?"

"I heard you fine, Adams."

"Shoot straight with me, sir. What am I doing here?"

He sighs. "Ah, dammit."

Nia's heard the phrase plenty growing up. Her father routinely uttered it on the precipice of learning something dreadful, and afterward, once the revelation sunk in, he'd fire off more *Ah, dammits*, along with other words her mother would chastise him for using in Nia's presence.

"Sir?"

"They want to investigate you. Powers, too."

"Public Integrity Unit?"

"Yes," he says. "There's a growing consensus that SRT should have waited for the FBI."

"And let more people die?"

"And there's something else . . ."

"Lord have mercy. Go ahead."

"The family of the suspect Powers shot is requesting an independent autopsy. They've raised considerable funds and have retained an attorney."

"I told you what happened in that room, sir . . ."

"I know," he says. "And I should have listened. But you stipulated to everything Powers said in his report, and if we all want to keep our jobs, there's no going back. We need to stick with Powers's story."

"How long do I have to stay here?"

"Long enough for the next crisis. Maybe then people will forget about the Central Bank."

"That man's family isn't going to forget."

"In the court of public opinion, the Rangers are heroes. That's what matters."

There's a knock at the door.

"Someone's here," she says. "I better go."

"It might not seem like it, but I sent you to Ellis for your own good," McCann says. "You've got a bright future ahead of you, Adams. Remember that."

"Understood, sir," she says before hanging up.

Another three heavy pounds on the door. It must be Rowe. No matter the agency an officer belongs to, all cops have a common knock.

She walks to the door and looks through the tiny peephole. A white film is accumulated on the pin-size window, and she can barely make out Sheriff Rowe standing awkwardly, holding a VHS tape to his chest like a bouquet of flowers.

Nia opens the door enough to see him dampened with sweat from his face to midsection.

"Mama always said never knock on a woman's door empty-handed," he says.

She takes the videotape from his hand. "Thanks."

"Everything all right?"

"Just peachy." Nia proceeds to close the door.

"Just so you know . . . ," he pipes up, "the offer still stands."

"Offer?"

"Dinner at the barbecue joint . . . The Smokehouse."

"That's original," she says.

"People aren't too creative around here."

"Well, like I said, it's not really my cuisine."

"That's right—the no meat thing." He slaps his thigh, recalling their exchange. "I bet we can get you fixed up with some sides, though. You eat cornbread, don't you?"

Nia tolerated most cornbread recipes. Nothing came close to how Sharon made it. She might've started with a box mix, but she'd doctor it up with a can of creamed corn, grated honeycomb, and whipped butter that slid off the crusty edges and was quickly absorbed by the moist yellow center. It was more like a dessert than a side dish, but Sharon hadn't made cornbread in months. In fact, Nia couldn't remember the last time they shared a proper supper.

"I plan to order in," she says. "There's a good number of files I'll need to get through."

"Well, all right then. I'll let you be." Rowe drops his chin and softly says, "I know how to accept defeat."

"Here's my card with my cell number," she says, handing him the basic business card. "Call if there's any developments." She shuts and locks the door, then collapses onto the springy mattress. "Why me, Lord?" she says in a cringy shrill. "Of all the damn cases..."

She cycles through the box of files. Lays them on the bed. Eleven employees. Not too bad, she thinks. Depending on how thorough the files are, it should take her a few hours to get an initial read on everyone present at the robbery.

She looks at the clock: 10:30 a.m.

Best to get started...

• • •

Nia borrows a VCR from the motel's manager, who requests a sixty-dollar deposit in case she fails to return it in proper working order. It's a dusty machine with buttons that require a strong thumb press. The videotape is eight minutes of grainy footage showing the suspect wearing the George Bush mask Rowe mentioned and carrying a duffel bag. She watches Fletch's assault, which seems unnecessarily brutal. As Don said, Fletch is unarmed but doesn't try to protect his face, even when the suspect's hand barrels toward him.

• • •

Hunger peaks around noon. She digs two granola bars out of her purse, devours them and a banana she took from the motel's lobby, and returns to reading the employee files. The files aren't out of the ordinary. Aside from two employees—a chronically late bank teller and a janitor with a drinking problem—Don hasn't terminated anyone in more than a decade. Still, they're worth looking into. People who've been fired hold grudges, but enough to want to rob the bank?

Revenge-motivated robberies are generally impulsive, driven by emotion. They aren't about stolen money or goods. It's the act that matters—justice-seeking. Smiting for alleged transgressions. A double-barrel shotgun an inch from the offending supervisor's chin, the one with the tousled hairpiece who doled out the pink slip two weeks earlier. That's what revenge is about, and while Nia doesn't condone it, she understands it.

But this robbery is different. Something else compelled the suspect to target the bank. He's dispassionate, advertent, calculating—nothing like the stupid criminals Nia's put away over the years. There have been some outliers. She recalls a joint operation with California's Department of Justice to catch a Dallas gang transporting fifty tons of empty beer cans into California. Their goal was to cash in on California's lucrative recycling industry. They would have cleared nearly one million dollars had Nia and the DOJ failed to intervene.

Then there's Fletch. On paper, he's an exceptional employee. Military background. A graduate of Pinnacle Security Training Academy. Don's notes read: "well-trained, accommodating, trustworthy."

Is this an inside man? He's worth a look.

Nia writes Fletch's address in her notebook, grabs her keys, and heads out.

• • •

Fletch's home is modest: cut lawn and pruned hedges. Staked on the front lawn is a realtor sign advertising foreclosure.

Nia gets out of the Explorer and crosses the road. She walks the driveway toward the front door, passing a pit barrel smoker blackened and warped.

She looks up toward the roof, where a section of failed rain gutter dangles by a strip of rusted metal. Careful of its precariousness, she stands clear and presses the doorbell.

Her stomach growls. She should've eaten a proper lunch. Sharon usually scolds Nia for missing meals, but it's easy to skip eating when she's hounding a case.

The door opens, and a young Black woman stands there, already looking perturbed. "Yes?" she says. "Can I help you?" Nia notes her smooth brown skin. She's young, maybe a decade younger than Nia.

"Ranger Nia Adams," she says, pointing to her badge. "I'm looking for Hakeem Fletcher."

"You a Texas Ranger?"

"That's right."

"Let me see that."

Nia unclips her badge and holds it up for the girl to see. "Damn," she says. "You're for real one of them?"

"Miss, is Hakeem Fletcher here or not?"

"Nope."

"Do you know where I might find him?"

"He ain't lost," the girl says. "He's still in the hospital getting his jaw set."

"May I ask who you might be?"

"Do I have to answer you?"

"No, but it would be helpful." Nia realizes she isn't twenty-something, but a churlish teen masquerading behind lipstick and rouge, squeezed into a tube top, baggy jeans cinched around her waist.

"Uh-huh." The girl crosses her arms. "Whatever. Fletch is my daddy."

"Is your mother home?"

"Nah, she's at work."

"I see the foreclosure sign out front."

"Guess your eyes work, then."

Nia sighs. "Which bank is it?"

"You mean which cutthroat bullshit institution is ruining my family's life?"

"Sure."

"Colonial Trust. Who the hell else."

"I'm sorry for what your family is going through . . ."

"*Sorry* ain't going to pay what my daddy owes. So, you might as well keep them *sorrys* to yourself."

"Can I ask one more thing?"

"Go ahead, but make it quick," the girl says. "I've got things to do before my mama gets home."

"Which hospital is your father at?"

"The only one we got. Ellis General."

"Where is it?"

"Main Street. Where everything is that's worth a damn." She shuts the door hard, and Nia heads back down the driveway to the Explorer. A conspicuous gray sedan sits at the corner—an American big-body with tinted windows and aftermarket wheels.

She glances at the driver. The facial features are nearly undistinguishable through the reflective windshield, but he's a white man, bald—possibly some facial hair, but to be sure requires a long stare, and it's best not to overcommit in these situations. Nia keeps walking and remains relaxed until she's back inside the Explorer.

She watches the car idle in her rearview. The vehicle is out of place on the street but not in the way a lost motorist might be. It's waiting with purpose.

She scribbles the plate number on her notepad. The car pulls away from the curb, and she shrinks into her seat as it drives past.

• • •

The county hospital looks more like a DMV than a medical facility—three stories, red brick, eight-pane windows, and signage with large painted arrows directing visitors to the main entrance and emergency room. Some may find the town's provincial flavor charming, but Nia is not one of those people. Old counties like Ellis are monuments to a horrific past. Sharon, who fancies herself a local historian, aptly reminds Nia that Houston also has a long, sordid history of intolerance, not just the small country towns Nia takes issue with. Still, Nia has never feared her city the way some rural counties make her flesh crawl, especially after sundown.

Nia enters the lobby through a sliding door that squeaks as though the track needs oil. An attendant, a blond woman with Tammy Faye Bakker eye shadow, does a double take.

"Hello, sir—"

Given the large-brimmed hat, slacks, and men's sports coat, it's no longer surprising when people presume Nia's a man. By the time they spot her badge or she's announced herself as Ranger Adams, they're either apologetic or on the verge of a conniption.

"Hello," Nia says, her badge visible on her waist. "I'm here to see a patient."

The attendant stares at her computer screen. "Name?"

"Hakeem Fletcher."

"Fletcher," the attendant repeats, fingernails rapping the keys. "I see him here. It's going to be room 216."

"All right."

"You'll need a visitor's pass. Left wrist, please." The attendant nervously puts a yellow bracelet around Nia's wrist, pressing the sticky ends together. "Please spell your name."

"It's Ranger Adams. A-D-A-M-S."

The attendant writes the name on a sticker slightly larger than a business card. "Here you go." Her breath carries a hint of spearmint. Nia notices lime-green chewing gum wedged in her teeth. "You'll want to keep that visible. Maybe there?" She subtly reaches toward Nia's left breast to place the sticker, then quickly retracts her hand when inner panic sets in. "Well, I'll let you do that."

Nia takes the sticker from her hand and slaps it on her jacket.

"Elevator's down the hall."

"Thank you." There are many eyes on her and some scowling faces as she passes.

The elevators are situated between drinking fountains on both sides of the lobby. Nia is certain the layout is a carryover from the segregation era. One elevator and fountain for Black folk, the other reserved for whites.

The elevator opens. She rides it to the second floor.

She steps out into a busy hallway and approaches the nurse's station. A nurse with a bleary expression cradles a phone to her ear.

"Room 216?" Nia asks.

The nurse points at the busiest end of the hallway, crowded with people in scrubs and lab coats. Nia maneuvers past patients in wheelchairs, clutching walkers, and lying on stretchers, and is careful to avoid clipping a doctor's arm as he brushes past her, racing to a call.

Outside Fletch's room, she looks through the small observation window and sees he's alone. She gently taps the door twice, barely loud enough for anyone to hear. It's for the sake of decorum and a watchful nurse who can't take her prying eyes off Nia.

Nia steps inside and shuts the door behind her. She stands like a sentry at the foot of Fletch's bed. He shoots up, his back at ninety degrees. His mouth is fixed shut, and his jaw sags as if he's got a paperweight for a tongue.

"Name's Ranger Adams." She takes out her notepad and pen. "Are you Hakeem Fletcher?"

He nods reluctantly.

"I'd like to ask you some questions about the bank robbery." She offers him the pad and pen. "You can write down what you've got to say on here."

Fletch attempts to speak, but there are only mumbles. Maybe it's muscle memory, having to remind his brain that his jaw is busted.

"As I said, the notepad is best."

He takes the pad and pen from Nia's hand and begins to write. The pen moves across the paper slowly as a toddler tracing a broken line. Afterward, he hands the pen and pad back to Nia.

She reads. "You don't remember anything?"

He beckons for the writing tools again; she obliges. Fletch writes more. She reads for a moment. "Memory loss? Partial recall."

Fletch shrugs and hands her back the pen and pad for good.

Nia puts the items in her jacket pocket and hands him her business card. It's customary, but she doubts he'll call. "In case that memory starts working again."

He sets the card on the tray next to his bed, shimmies under the bedsheet, and closes his eyes. The interview is over.

Nia's worked cases with roadblocks before. Some even dead-ended investigations. But this case is working against reason. Neither the bank manager nor Fletch is forthcoming.

The door opens to a tall, dark-haired man in a lab coat, who shuffles into the room wearing Velcro sneakers; a stethoscope hangs from his neck. "Mr. Fletcher," he says, "let's take a look at that jaw." He looks up from a chart and sees Nia. She smiles, pretending her visit with Fletch was pleasant. "Oh, I didn't know you had a visitor, Mr. Fletcher." If he's surprised by the cop in the room, he does well to hide it. "I'm Dr. Sadeghi."

"Good afternoon, doctor," Nia says.

"I hope I'm not interrupting anything."

"We were just finishing up. Fletch isn't in a talkative mood." She smirks, then nudges the doctor's shoulder. "A little hospital humor."

"Oh, yes," he says with a chuckle, "that's quite clever."

Dr. Sadeghi's laughter wanes to silence as Nia leaves the room.

• • •

Nia drives down Main Street, headed in the direction of the motel. Maybe it's time to return to Houston to face the investigation and the hell that comes with it. Sure, the operation got messy, but Nia saved countless lives. She put an end to the assault, which is what she was trained to do: assess and respond. If anyone should be investigated, it's Powers; he's dirty and a walking lawsuit.

Driving past the sheriff's station, she sees parked the big-bodied sedan that sat idle outside of Fletcher's house. Nia U-turns and then pulls into the station's parking lot.

She parks the Explorer next to the sedan and gets out. Digging into her jacket pocket, she pulls out the notepad and flips to the page where she'd written the license plate. Nia walks to the rear of the Buick Century—the plates match. She wonders whether the sheriff has put a tail on her, but the Texas plate isn't exempt, which rules out any law enforcement or government agency.

Nia knows she should go back to Houston. There's no good reason to enter the sheriff's station. But she's curious. That's the thing about cops; curiosity is no small thing. There's more to the bank assault than recon or some pissed-off employee. There are better targets: larger, more lucrative banks. Why bother with a novelty branch? Unless the branch is hiding something. And the likelihood that some vindictive ex-employee carried it out is looking less likely. All she's got is Fletch and a mysterious Buick Century.

• • •

Nia's been in more than a dozen police stations, and none look as sophisticated as the division Eddie Murphy strolled through in *Beverly Hills Cop*. Most stations are utilitarian, tired as a pair of old running shoes. They'll function if the soles are intact, and the sole of the Ellis County Sheriff's Station is a one-story building where white men sit in glass-partitioned offices chewing dip behind desks.

"Can I help you, ma'am?" a redheaded woman behind the front desk asks. It's been a long while since Nia's seen an adult with an abundance of freckles, and while she knows freckled children grow up, she finds the woman's looks childlike.

"Sheriff Rowe, please."

"May I get your name?"

"Ranger Nia Adams."

"A Ranger?" she says. "Well, I'll be . . ."

"You'll be what?"

Freckles blushes until her face and hair are matching crimson. "Oh, nothing—it's just that I've never seen a female Ranger before."

"Well, now you have."

"Yes, apparently so . . ." She speaks in a whisper, "I didn't mean anything by it. I think it's really cool."

"No offense taken. I'd like to see Sheriff Rowe now."

"Oh, right. Is he expecting you?"

"I'd be surprised if he isn't."

Nia follows the woman toward a large office at the rear of the building. Rowe is holding court with a tall man: bald, black suit and tie, and matching cowboy boots. Likely snakeskin. She isn't a Johnny Cash fan, much to Sharon's disappointment, but a man in all black looks like he's wearing a costume. An all-black wardrobe should be reserved for Mr. Cash or an undertaker, and the bald man doesn't fit either bill.

"Speak of the devil . . . ," Rowe says, summoning Nia into the office. "Ranger Adams, let me introduce you. This is Mr. Bartholomew Katz."

The name sounds fictional but somehow fits the big man with a head nearly as pointed as a football. Nia notices the Star of David around his neck, the gold gleaming against the emptiness of his black wardrobe.

"Mr. Katz represents Colonial Trust. He's come to help augment our investigation."

"I didn't think the investigation warranted augmenting," she says. "I was thinking I'd head back to Houston once I cleared something up."

"Is that right?" Rowe says. "What's on your mind?"

"Did you know Hakeem Fletcher's home was being foreclosed on?"

"I did not. However, you care to explain the relevance?"

"Glad to," she says, "the bank that holds his deed is Colonial Trust."

"Well, damn. I knew you were a crack detective..."

"Save the sarcasm. Why wouldn't you look into it?"

"We've known Fletch for years, and to be honest, he's always had trouble holding down a job on account of his issues. These vets got a lot going on upstairs..." Rowe points to his temple, grins cockeyed, and rotates his finger. "Kind of cuckoo, but God bless him."

"Doesn't mean there isn't a motive."

"What? Steal from the bank that's threatening to foreclose on you? Even if I think he'd have the balls for it, why pick the branch you work at?"

"I don't know," she says. "Maybe the key is what was taken. It could've been worth more than whatever cash his accomplice might've been able to carry out of there."

"And what about his jaw?" Rowe asks. "As you said, he's the only one injured in the whole ordeal. Seems a little overkill to smash a jaw, don't you think? A gut punch would've been as effective."

"Maybe that's the point? Overkill to avoid suspicion. Incapacitate. Keep him from talking."

"Interesting theory, but there's no need to press further," Katz explains. "My employer takes this sort of thing very seriously, which is why they've sent me here."

Nia can't place his accent. It's foreign and familiar. Middle Eastern, maybe—or a poor imitation.

He continues: "That branch is one of the oldest banks in Texas and has been in my employer's family for centuries. Such a treasure should be preserved at all costs, wouldn't you say?"

"And who exactly is your employer?" Nia asks.

"I'm not at liberty to say, but they've sent me to ensure no harm comes to that bank."

"You mean to the people in the bank?"

Katz nods. "Yes, of course. Our priority is keeping everyone safe."

"Then you've seen Hakeem Fletcher?"

"No . . . I hope to see him once he's been released from the hospital."

"From what I hear, that should be this evening," Rowe says. "My ex-wife is a nurse on Fletch's floor. She's been keeping an eye on him while he heals up."

"How kind of her."

"She's got her moments," Rowe says. "But I'm still glad I'm not married to the broad."

"I'm not a native Texan, as you may have guessed," Katz says. "But the spirit of Ellis—the unparalleled sense of community. It's something to marvel at."

"Indeed, it is," Rowe says, "and we intend on keeping this community safe from any nefarious outfits that may have set their designs on that bank."

"What exactly is your plan, Mr. Katz?" Nia asks. "What can you provide that the sheriff and I can't?"

"I'm sure you and Sheriff Rowe have much more important business. I'm here so you both can get back to your regular duties. I will safeguard the bank and make sure everything remains status quo, and if someone dares attempt something, I will notify the sheriff immediately."

"Your plan is to patrol the bank alone?" Nia asks.

"Correct," Katz says. "Given the square footage, this is not a monumental task."

Rowe takes a cigarette from the soft pack tucked in his uniform's breast pocket. He offers one to Katz, who declines. "I already know Miss Vegetarian here doesn't touch these things."

Nia rolls her eyes. "Mr. Katz, how long do you plan on staying in Waxahachie?"

"As long as necessary."

"I'm sure we can make it comfortable for you," Rowe says. "Mr. Katz was just telling me about his past gigs. He was a bodyguard for Justin

Bieber and the Backstreet Boys. A few weeks in Waxahachie ought to be a cakewalk."

"That's right," Katz says. "It'll be like a vacation for me. Ribs and real music. What more can I ask for?"

"So, when does this operation start?" Nia asks.

"I'll begin surveillance tonight." He postures like a soldier: shoulders rolled back, chest out, and arms pinned at his sides.

"Don't worry, Ranger Adams, Colonial Bank is in good hands," Rowe says, his sleazy charm turned up to the max. It makes Nia long for a hot shower.

"Until this person is caught, all I've got are worries," Nia says.

Rowe tips his hat and heads out to smoke, with Katz following behind.

CHAPTER FOUR
MR. KATZ

Bartholomew Katz dines alone—always alone. This is not by choice but by necessity. There isn't any room in his life for banality, and most people he encounters bore him before opening their mouths. There's a frivolous aspect to human beings that he's never understood. Though he's studied them and adapted their mannerisms, accents, and ways of speaking, he stopped seeking meaning in human existence long ago. Most people live without purpose. They are without nuance, lacking fascination. But he found a calling long ago that keeps him interested—their complete and utter ruin—and like every great artist, he's always looking for a muse.

"More tea?" the waitress asks. She's young, pretty, Mexican—could be his type if he had a type.

The diner is practically empty, and she's given him more attention than warranted. He finished his cheeseburger ten minutes ago, and she's refilled his sweet tea twice.

"Water is fine," he says, having abandoned his faux accent.

She tops off his glass mostly with ice. "What's your name?" she asks. "Never seen you in before."

"Bart."

She giggles. "Like the Simpson's character?"

"I guess that's right—sure, like Bart Simpson."

"Cute."

"It is?"

"I've never met a Bart before."

"Because you've never met a Bart, you think it's cute?"

She splutters, trying to get her words out. "I mean, yeah? I don't know. Just trying to be friendly, Mister."

"Do I look like I need a friend?"

"You are sitting here by yourself," she says. "That plate of fries turned cold half an hour ago."

"I value my alone time."

"I get that."

"You do?"

"Yeah," she says. "I think best when I'm alone. Got a nice thinking spot, too. I lie in my brother's truck bed, look up at the stars, and just let my mind wander."

"And what is it a girl like you thinks about?"

"Stuff," she says nonchalantly. "Like what I'd do if I ever got out of this boring-ass town."

"And?"

"I'd go to New York or Miami . . ."

"Overrated."

"Maybe just someplace new. Austin seems cool. Good music. Good food. Might meet someone."

"Or it could be indisputably horrible."

"Well, shit. Talk about a dream-killer. There's nothing wrong with hoping for better, Mister."

"That's the thing about hope. It tends to fall short."

"But it's worth a try. You can't live life being scared all the time."

"Sure you can. That's how humans have lasted this long."

"You're just a ray of fucking sunshine, aren't you?"

"People don't like hearing the truth."

"Okay, then, what about you?" she asks. "Since you seem to have all the answers."

"What about me?"

"What is it you think about? Or are you at the height of contentment?"

No one has ever asked him the question. It deserves more than a brush-off answer. But the thoughts that populate his mind haunt and thrill him equally. Sharing them would send her to the kitchen to call the police.

"Nothing important." He stares at her collarbone. Wondering how many pounds of force it would take to shatter it—she's an itch he can't scratch. It's best not to stare into the face of temptation. "I better go, or I'll be late."

"A night job?"

"I do my best work at night."

"You want to take the fries to go? I can pack them up for you."

"Won't have much time to snack." He drinks from the glass of water until only the ice remains.

"Well, if you're ever back in Waxahachie, come and visit us," she says, picking up his plate. "Maybe try the meatloaf, it's to die for." She lays the bill on the table. "That'll be ten bucks."

"Return to this place? Doubtful." He reaches into his wallet, pulls out a twenty, and places it on the table.

"Gimme one sec and I'll get your change," she says.

He places his hand over hers; his thick machinist fingers are blistered and dry. "Leave it," he says, slowly letting up. "You've earned it."

"I did?"

"That smile you've got made my night. I'll be thinking about it for a long while."

"Uh, thank you," she says, uneasy. "Good luck with whatever you've got going on tonight."

"I do hope you leave this place," he says, sliding out of the booth. "A girl like you deserves to see the world and all it has to offer." He towers over the petite server, staring at her as though she holds a secret. And she does, he thinks. All the young, pretty girls do . . .

• • •

Upon returning to Fletch's home, he parks across the street. And just as before, he watches the house, keenly focused on movement inside.

Attached to the mailbox are three foil balloons that read "GET WELL" in large shiny letters. Hakeem Fletcher has come home to recover.

Mr. Katz puts on a pair of leather gloves. Pops the trunk, then steps out of the car. The night's air is cool, but he's comfortable in his suit. A diamond-plated steel toolbox is inside the trunk. He unlocks the box and removes a small-caliber pistol, suppressor and magazines, a bowie knife, zip ties, and a flashlight. A jar of smelling salts and laboratory-grade chloroform spray is already in his pocket. He closes the toolbox, removes it from the trunk, and walks across the road to the Fletchers' home.

He rings the doorbell. The porch light turns on, and the door opens.

Fletch's daughter stands in the doorway, her twig-like frame far from imposing. "Yes?"

A woman's voice calls from a bedroom: "Fontaine, who's at the door?"

"I don't know," Fontaine says. "Some man."

"Is Fletch home?" Mr. Katz asks in the ambiguous accent he's perfected. "I heard about the unfortunate situation at the bank, and I'd like to see him."

"Who are you?" Fontaine asks.

"A friend from the service," he says. "From our Nam days."

"Vietnam? Didn't know Daddy had any white friends from the war."

"Really? Hard to believe he's never mentioned me."

A plump woman with a caramel complexion and bone-straight hair nudges Fontaine aside. She's dressed in business attire: a pressed gray suit, blouse, pumps, and pearl earrings. "And who are you?" she asks.

"Mr. Katz," he says. "A friend from Nam. Thought I'd drop by and see Fletch."

"You served with Hakeem?"

"Yes, ma'am."

"What's your first name?"

"Bartholomew, ma'am, but you can call me Bart. Like the Simpsons."

"Fontaine, go and get your father."

The teen shrugs, then walks down the hallway. "Daddy! Some white man here to see you."

"You mind if I wait inside?" Mr. Katz asks. "It's been a long drive, and I need to rest my legs."

"What's in the box?"

"Oh, this?" He shakes the toolbox. "Old photos from our war days. I thought he might want to stroll down memory lane."

"You thought *my* husband would want to reminisce about Vietnam?"

"Well, yes—"

"Hakeem hated Nam. All that . . . whatcha call it? Agent Orange they pumped into the air. It left him with terrible migraines. Sometimes he can't even sleep or eat because they're so bad. And now his jaw is smashed to shit."

"I understand his suffering . . ."

"That goddamn war was senseless."

"Same could be said for all wars, really."

"Funny, he's never mentioned you." She glares skeptically, focused on his gloved hands. "Which tour did you serve together?"

"You seem like a sweet woman," he says. "Hakeem was lucky to have you."

"Whatchu mean *was*?"

Mr. Katz shoves the bowie knife into the woman's abdomen, seals his hand over her mouth, and breaches the doorway. He gently closes the door with the heel of his foot, while keeping a tight seal over her mouth.

Sometimes it's hard to contain the rush and stay clear-headed. But he's disciplined his mind to think through every scenario. Without knowing the layout of Fletch's home, he must act quickly. He's certain that Fletch is in the house somewhere, and there could be additional occupants. Fletch is a veteran and a Texan—no question he has firearms within reach—which is why Mr. Katz must be careful not to alarm him and give him time to retrieve a weapon.

The woman moans as he drops her to the floor. She's choking on blood and suffering without purpose. She holds no contractual value; he's only interested in what Fletch knows.

He pulls the knife from her stomach and slices her throat, ensuring the blade cuts through the aortic valve.

When Fontaine returns, he takes her from behind and sprays the chloroform into her mouth. Seconds later, she collapses, and he quickly drags her and her dead mother to a corner of the dining room. He removes the pistol from the toolbox, screws the suppressor into the muzzle, and waits.

Fletch appears from the hallway and pauses when he sees blood on the entry tile. He screams through his broken jaw. The wires fastened to his jawbone stretch and rip. Mr. Katz steps out of the darkness and brings the pistol to Fletch's chest. "Quiet," he says. "Your wife is dead, but your daughter doesn't have to be if you do as I say."

Fletch tries to speak amid the blood and drool; the words are broken: "Do . . . Don . . . Don't hurt her."

"Answer my questions, and I'll leave. Lie to me, and you and your daughter die. Understand?"

Tears stream down Fletch's face; he nods.

Mr. Katz pulls a chair from the dining table. "Sit."

Fletch sits in the chair, feet from where his wife and daughter lie. He closes his eyes, then slowly opens them and sobs.

"You are not dreaming, Mr. Fletcher. This isn't a nightmare in the logical sense. I'm going to make this easy for you. One finger means yes. Two fingers mean no. Simple enough?"

Fletch nods.

"Were you involved in the Colonial Trust Bank robbery?"

With a quiver, he raises one finger.

"Did you share the blueprints with the thief? Is that how he knew about the old safe?"

Another lone finger . . .

"See. Easy," Mr. Katz says. "Now, give me the name of your accomplice."

Fletch's knees knock. He retains enough composure to motion for something to write with.

"You'll write on the table." Mr. Katz takes hold of the back of Fletch's neck, forcing him out of the chair to the floor. "Use her blood," he says, pointing to Fletch's dead wife.

Fletch's breathing is erratic; heavy gasps sustain him.

"It can all be over. Just give me the name."

Fletch grovels at Mr. Katz's feet; he pleads in whimpers. Tears drip onto the killer's snakeskin boots.

"You're wasting time." Mr. Katz presses the gun into Fletch's temple. "Now move."

Fletch splays his fingers and slowly extends his hand toward the open gash in his wife's neck. Overtaken by dread but unable to scream, he bites through his tongue, working his fingers across his wife's severed neck.

"Good," Mr. Katz says. "Start writing."

Fletch rises to his feet, then drops into the chair. He works his fingers like a paintbrush, stroking the wood grain.

Fontaine's narrow chest faintly rises and falls. "She's lovely," Mr. Katz says. "Unrefined, but that could be said for many Texan belles, can't it?"

Fletch looks into the murderer's eyes, which reveal his virulent desires. He knows what Mr. Katz is capable of and knows he can do nothing but bleat from the inescapable torment.

"Hurry it up, Mr. Fletcher. She'll need to wake soon."

Red letters span the length of the table. Fletch continues to write.

Mr. Katz's eyes are still on Fontaine. "She's coming into her own, isn't she? Blooming into a wildflower, and with that kind of beauty, she'll have men doing anything she asks."

The blood is almost dry when the name appears: Al Bouchard.

"Who the hell is Al Bouchard?" Mr. Katz doesn't wait for an answer. He presses the suppressed barrel to Fletch's head and squeezes the trigger.

He goes into the family room, pulls out his cell phone, and dials his business partner, a man known only as Dice. "It's me," he says. "Run the name Al Bouchard along with any aliases . . . There could be some connection to the Marine Corps . . . Call me when you've got something."

Mr. Katz hangs up, looks at the unconscious Fontaine, and beams . . .

CHAPTER FIVE

DESMOND

Desmond speaks into a large satellite phone that allows him to call anywhere in the world: "What's the next move?"

"You'll bring the goods to me." The man's voice is polished and sophisticated, like a radio announcer's. "We'll discuss payment then."

"And the next job?"

The man rudely ends the call.

Desmond paces. He hasn't left the boardinghouse for days. Lying low is best regardless of the heat a score brings, or the lack thereof. But knowing that doesn't stop him from going stir-crazy. He craves fresh air, sunshine, and a break from the confinement of four walls.

Knock. Knock.

"Yes?" Desmond says.

"It's Linh."

He opens the door. "Something wrong?"

She wears a flowered sarong. Linen, he thinks, and a white blouse and sandals. Her hair is different: wavy with a sheen. He's never seen her without a ponytail, often shoved under a ball cap or woven sun hat.

"I wasn't sure you were home," she says. "Haven't seen your truck in a few days."

"It's in the shop."

"I see . . . Do you need anything?"

He looks perplexed. "Me? No, I've got everything I need."

"I mean . . . ," she prattles and looks away nervously. "Have you eaten?"

"No."

"Okay. Would you like to get dinner with me?"

"Tonight?"

"Say in an hour?"

Desmond hasn't showered in a day, maybe longer, but his odor hasn't propelled Linh to flee. "I'll need to get changed," he says.

"All right," she says, noting his tank top and work pants. "Might I suggest a collared shirt?"

"I can do that. Give me an hour."

"Perfect. I'll make a reservation."

"Okay, then."

Linh smiles, and Desmond can't help but reciprocate with a slight grin.

Desmond closes the door and quickly goes to the mirror to inspect his jawline speckled with coarse, black hair. He takes out his shaving mug, brush, and razor and works up a lather from cheeks to chin.

In his closet are a pair of charcoal slacks, a white short-sleeve shirt, and a checkered blue polo. His "work clothes," as he refers to them, are three mechanics' shirts, Dickies, and a stonewashed denim jacket. The oldest item in his closet is a pair of black loafers with a patched right heel. He likes how they cradle his feet and can't bring himself to part with them, even though they've seen better days. Rarely has he worn his only pair of slacks more than once a year. On occasions when he needs formal attire, he's invariably found high-end three-piece suits and sports coats at thrift stores bordering wealthy, predominantly white neighborhoods.

• • •

Linh arrives at his door at ten minutes past the hour, and together they walk downstairs, both smelling of their best fragrances.

Desmond: sandalwood and cedar; Linh: plum blossom with notes of peony and vanilla.

He typically reserves cologne for special occasions, like his wedding day and, years before, his junior prom.

"I'll drive," Linh says, pulling keys from her purse.

It's his first outing with a woman since his wife's death, and he's unprepared. Tasking a woman with driving on a first date seems unconventional. Though he considers himself a modern man, having Linh drive makes him uncomfortable. He's been told his entire life that men should never let women drive, especially on dates or at night. Not because they're poor drivers but out of respect and consideration.

"Everything all right?" Linh asks, unlocking her 2001 Toyota Corolla. "You look bothered."

They get into the car. Desmond clicks the seatbelt across his waist and fidgets. "I don't sit in the passenger seat much . . ."

"Does it trouble you?" Linh asks. "Me driving?"

"I wouldn't say that."

Linh grins. "It's fine, Desmond," she says. "I was going to suggest we go Dutch, but if it makes you feel better, you're welcome to pay for the evening."

"Gladly," he says, relieved.

Linh laughs, then looks away as if to spare Desmond's ego. The gesture reminds him of something Audrey Hepburn might've done in *Breakfast at Tiffany's*. Not that he's ever watched the film in its entirety, but it was shown on base one night to a room of Marines with little to do but drink and smoke cigarettes and talk about what they'd give for a date with the quirky actress.

• • •

When they arrive at Sweet Mary's, one of the oldest barbecue restaurants in town, their reserved table is ready. The host, an older man with whiskers and hair sprouting from his ears, seats them at a table near the window. Desmond pulls the chair out for Linh, and she sits. He sits across from her, facing the door. He's never gone out so soon after a score, but it feels right. The old bank was a low-risk target, and he didn't take money, so the feds or any other agency with teeth won't be after him.

Besides, he's good about covering his tracks and couldn't miss an opportunity to spend time with Linh. In a few days, he'll move to another city, use a new alias, and plan the next heist, which means his outing with Linh will be the last, so why not savor every moment?

"So," she begins, "I've been wanting to know something . . ."

"Yes."

"How is it you speak Vietnamese so well? Your dialect is formal, as if you had a proper teacher."

"Her name was Mai. She taught children in the province."

"And she just decided to teach you out of the goodness of her heart?" Linh teases as she peruses the menu.

"I can be persuasive," he jokes. "I suppose it was me who suggested mutual lessons. I helped her with English, and she taught me Vietnamese."

"How long was she your teacher?"

"Six years," he says. "Sometimes I think she's still teaching me now."

Linh sets the menu aside. "I don't understand."

"We fell in love and were married. Had a little girl. Then I lost them."

"My God," she says, "I'm so sorry."

"It was a car accident . . ." Looking at the empty water glass, he's transported back to the fateful night—a cold rain, pitch-black road, death in the air. He remembers how the windows blew out, glass cut his face, and how the car tumbled down the highway and finally rested in a ravine. "It all happened so fast . . ."

Linh reaches for his hand. "Desmond, I don't know what to say—"

The server, a teenage boy with a high-top fade, arrives and fills their glasses with ice water. "Any questions about the menu?"

"Still looking," Desmond says, still lost in the memory. "Give us a minute."

"Let me tell you about our specials," the boy says, disregarding Desmond's request for more time. "We've got beef ribs, hot links, and candied yams topped with pineapple."

"Pineapple," Linh says. "That's different."

"Like they say, don't knock it till you try it." The simpering teen rambles with enthusiasm. "My brother here knows what I'm talking about."

"How's that?" Desmond asks.

"Oh, well, you know . . ." The server smirks through his abashment. "How about I give you two a few more minutes to decide?"

"You should do that," Desmond says, sharply.

The boy leaves, carrying the water pitcher to another table.

"You know, we don't have to talk about it," Linh says.

"It's all right. Talking about them makes me feel good . . . like they're still a part of me."

"Because they are, and that will never change."

Desmond nods. "Yes," he says. "I'm thankful for that."

• • •

Good food can be disarming, and for two hours, Desmond talks about his life in and out of the military. He keeps the details vague and speaks mostly about his three tours in Nam, the men he served with, and the brotherhood they formed. He listens to Linh recall her family's migration to Texas from the Philippines, having fled to Manila from Vietnam at the start of the American occupation.

"All that pain and death," he says. "And nothing gained in the end."

"I like to think everything happens for a reason," she says. "It's how we're here right now—enjoying this meal together."

Unsure of what to say, Desmond bites into a hot link and chews longer than necessary.

"Do you still keep in touch with your military brothers?" she asks.

"Just one is still living. I'm helping him out of a jam."

"What kind of jam?" She spoons the last of her candied yams into her mouth.

"A while back, he got sick. Started getting headaches really bad. Doctors said it was PTSD, but it wasn't. The shit we breathed over there was poison. Agent Orange was just one of the things we were exposed to. Some of us got headaches and cancers; our bodies just didn't work right. The doctors prescribed Fletch medications that helped enough, and he was able to get back on his feet. But all that time not working, he'd missed mortgage payments, and the bank gave him thirty days to come up with the money, or he'd lose his house."

"That's terrible . . . What were you able to do?"

"Got him a job. One day of work, and he could keep his home. Wasn't easy, though."

"Sounds lucrative. Can I ask what it was?"

"Something that required his unique skill set," he says coyly.

"Well, it's nice you were able to help him. I'm sure he's grateful."

Desmond sips his coffee. "I don't have many friends, so I look after the ones I've got."

"The way you looked after me the other night with those drunk fools?"

"Yes."

Linh blushes. "So, what type of work do you do? I don't mean to pry, but it's been racking my brain. First, I thought you were in construction or a landscaper—"

"Or a fugitive?"

"The thought did cross my mind, but you don't strike me as the type."

He had prepared for the question, settling on a lie hours ago while shaving. "I'm a treasure hunter."

Linh laughs so loud it startles patrons at a neighboring table. "Oh, goodness. I'm so sorry." She covers her mouth with a napkin. "I wasn't expecting that."

"It's all right. I know how it sounds."

"You do? Because you're basically telling me you're Indiana Jones."

"Minus the six-shooter and bullwhip."

"Please explain."

"I travel around the world procuring things for people."

"Rich people?"

"They have voracious appetites for priceless rarities."

"And then what?"

"Once I have the item, I deliver it to them, and they pay me."

"You make it sound so simple, but there's a reason they'd want a Marine veteran doing this, right?"

"Transferable skills," he says. "The things I secure aren't always in the possession of the nicest people. It takes negotiation, and I'm a very good negotiator."

"Desmond Bell, you may be the most fascinating person I've ever met."

The server arrives table-side. "Will y'all be wanting anything else?"

"Just the bill," Desmond says.

High-Top drops the bill on the table and gathers their empty plates. Desmond looks the bill over quickly, reaches into his pocket, and takes out his wallet. He pulls out cash, including enough for a 10 percent tip, and lays the money on the table.

"Shall we?" he asks Linh.

She nods, and Desmond gets up and pulls out her chair. "Very gentlemanly of you."

"It's how Mama taught me."

"And where is Mama these days?"

He pauses, then delivers another lie. "Unfortunately, she's dead."

"Shit," Linh says. "I keep putting my foot in my mouth. I'm sorry."

"It's fine. People die. Wish it wasn't the case, but it is."

"Still hurts, though," she says. "I think about my *bà ngoại* every day."

"Can I show you something?"

"All right."

They exit the restaurant and get into Linh's car. Desmond's nervousness is gone, replaced by a warm, bubbly feeling in his stomach. It's new, or at least it's a feeling he hasn't experienced in a long while.

"So, where to?" Linh asks, turning the ignition.

"You know how to get to Uptown from here?"

"I think I can manage it."

• • •

They arrive at a park near Williams Tower, a massive skyscraper that's become a Houston landmark for no other reason but its size. They get out of the car and walk a concrete path past oak trees and greenery until they reach a stunning fountain shaped like a horseshoe.

"This was one of the first places I visited after I got out of the service. Not sure what it is, but being near this water, listening to it, helps me think."

"It's beautiful," Linh says. "Huge, but beautiful. How much water do you think this thing pumps?"

"I heard it's something like eleven thousand gallons a minute. They call it a water wall."

"I can't say I've ever seen such a thing, but now that I have, I'm happy it was with you." She takes Desmond's hand. "Thank you for agreeing to dinner."

"Thank you for knocking on my door and asking me."

She pulls him closer and kisses his cheek.

"There's something I need to tell you," Desmond says.

"Is it going to ruin this moment?"

"I don't think so . . . Well, I don't know, really. But it's the truth . . ."

"Can it wait, then?"

"Yes," he says. "I guess it can."

"I trust you, Desmond. If it can wait, then let's just enjoy this."

"All right," he says, moving closer to Linh. He takes her by the waist and kisses her as if nothing else matters, and in the moment, nothing else does.

• • •

After sundown, they find a small cocktail bar and enjoy drinks. They sit close and don't talk much, watching the light crowd laugh, smile, and shuck and boot-scoot to soul and country tunes.

When they arrive at the boardinghouse, Linh leads him through the café and upstairs. She kisses him in the hallway under the dim light of a dying bulb, then enters her room, leaving the door slightly ajar. Fear sets in. Desmond wonders whether he's making a mistake. He's setting a dangerous precedent, he thinks. But happiness doesn't come easy; it doesn't come cheap, either. And while he's resigned himself to living a nomadic life of solitude, it isn't what Mai would have wanted for him. She'd want him to be happy; she'd want him to know love again. And as much as he wants to believe he's worthy of Linh's affections, he isn't. He's a killer, a thief, a liar . . .

"Are you coming?" Linh calls from inside the room.

Desmond looks through the crack. She stands nude. The moonlight shines against her back; clothes are piled at her feet.

"Yes," he says going into the room and shutting the door behind him.

CHAPTER SIX
NIA

Nia prepares to check out of the motel at noon. She's almost finished packing her suitcase when her cell phone rings.

"Hello?" Sheriff Rowe is on the other end; he's talking fast. "Slow down, Sheriff," Nia says.

"You need to get over here to Fletch's place," he says, nearly out of breath. "We've got a situation. It's bad, Adams. Real goddamn bad."

It takes Nia ten minutes to drive to Fletch's home. She parks across the street behind a row of sheriff's vehicles. Rowe's truck is parked in the driveway, along with unmarked sedans. Crying neighbors stand at the edge of the lawn, congregating near the mailbox. Deputies hold a line.

"This is a crime scene, folks," a deputy says, motioning with his arms to keep a nosy neighbor at bay. "Let us do our work. Otherwise, you'll be hauled into the station for interfering in deputy matters."

Nia shows her badge to the deputy. "Rowe's inside," he says. "He's been waiting for you."

She tips her hat and walks up the driveway to the front door. Another deputy, standing watch, moves aside, allowing her to go in.

Inside, she walks around the pool of blood in the entryway. More deputies move about, along with medical examiners and the county's forensic team. Nia follows Rowe's voice to the rear of the house and finds him standing in the hall near the doorway, white as a sheet and with dampened brow.

"Adams," he says. "You came . . ."

"Where's the bodies?"

"Inside the master bedroom." Rowe points to the king-size bed saturated with blood where Fletch and his wife have been discarded and piled on each other like a heap of garbage. "The in-home nurse found them. Back door was unlocked. Killer probably exited from there."

"I see," Nia says.

"No one has touched the bodies yet," he says. "The team is still collecting evidence. I had the right mind to call the FBI but thought if you were still in town . . ." He searches for the words. "It's just that this is beyond me. Why would someone do this?"

Nia moves closer to the bodies for a full view. "He was shot, close range," she says. "I think the female's method of execution was similar. Close. Intimate."

"Her name's Keisha. She was his wife."

"Keisha," Nia says somberly, moving closer to the body. "Her throat was cut with a very sharp blade. It's almost surgical."

"No signs of forced entry," Rowe says.

"Because they opened the door." Nia stares at the hole in Fletch's head. "They didn't recognize the danger until it was too late."

"There's something else," he says.

"The daughter? Where is she?"

"She was found in her bedroom. Strangled on the mattress. We believe she was sexually assaulted. Possibly while unconscious. There are no defensive wounds." He grimaces as though he smells something rotten. "What kind of sick fuck are we dealing with?"

"Depends."

"On what?"

"Where's your friend, Mr. Katz?"

More color drains from Rowe's face. "Good Lord . . ." He fans himself with his hat. "You're thinking . . . ?"

"He's the missing piece," Nia says, turning and leading Rowe down the hallway. "There was never any intention to investigate the bank robbery or act as security. He wanted to find out what your department knew. Did you even bother checking with the bank to see if they actually sent him?"

"Well . . . no," he says. "We didn't see the need."

She sighs. "Right."

"So, you're telling me he did this to Fletch and his family?"

"I'm certain."

"That fucking death-dealing piece of shit brought this madness to our town." Rowe wipes his forehead and neck with a handkerchief, still looking as though he's on the verge of vomiting. "I invited him to eat ribs . . ."

"It's cause and effect," Nia says. "The robbery precipitated his arrival. The question is who sent him." She goes into the dining room and analyzes the blood-soaked carpet under the table. "It all happened in this room." She directs her attention to the bloody name scrolled on the table. "He forced Fletch to write this but didn't bother wiping it. Does that seem odd to you?"

"Maybe he ran out of time? Got occupied with the girl?"

"No," she says. "He wanted you to see it. He's having fun with you now. He knows you're out of your depth, Sheriff."

"Excuse me?"

"There's no place for ego. Katz, or whoever he is, is a professional killer. Do you have someone running his name?"

"I'll get on it," he says. "And we'll put out an APB. Get people searching the county."

"Don't bother," she says. "Katz is long gone by now. Probably hundreds of miles between him and Ellis. Use the manpower to canvass the neighborhood. Go door-to-door; see if people saw or heard anything. Collect as many statements as you can. We might be able to piece together what happened here . . . and find out who the hell Al Bouchard is and why a dead man wrote his name on a table."

"I thought you were going back to Houston?" Rowe puts his hands on his hips, jutting his neck forward like a bobcat catching wind of prey. "I mean, we can have the FBI down here in a jiffy."

"No, you can't . . . You need me, and if you don't see that, then you shouldn't be wearing that badge."

"You've got some fucking nerve."

"What I have is a desire to help you, and seeing as Katz did this knowing a Texas Ranger was in town, he sent a message not only to you but to me as well."

"What's the message?"

"That he fears nothing. Who knows how long he's been doing this? Might have more bodies under his belt than we've got fingers and toes."

"And you think you can stop him?"

"Sheriff, I don't have a choice."

• • •

Technicians from the Office of the Coroner arrive to remove the bodies from the home. They carry them out in bags strapped to gurneys. No matter how many times Nia has seen deceased victims removed from crime scenes, it never feels routine. Only a few hours ago, they were breathing, living their lives—and now, erased.

The forensic team collects blood samples and dust for prints. Nia knows they won't find any belonging to Katz. He's no amateur.

Her cell phone vibrates. It's a text from McCann. Five minutes later, she receives one from Sharon. Nia leaves the house and walks past a deputy smoking a cigarette while guarding the perimeter. At the foot of the driveway is a young Latino wearing a 2Pac T-shirt and a Houston Rockets cap broken off, worn at an angle, like he's from uptown Harlem. He's seven or eight, straddling a bike intended for a much younger kid.

"Is Fontaine all right?" the boy asks.

"Hello. What's your name?"

"Tomás."

"You know the Fletchers?"

"Fontaine watches me sometimes when my parents go out to eat and come home late. Is she okay?"

Nia bends low so she's at eye level with the boy. "I'm sorry," she says. "But Fontaine isn't all right."

"So, it's true? Somebody killed them?"

"Is that what you heard?"

"Everybody's talking about it," he says. "Mr. Willoughby thinks it's a serial killer."

"What do you know about serial killers?"

"Only what I've seen on TV."

"Well, I don't believe it's a serial killer, so you have nothing to worry about."

"Oh, I wasn't worried," he says. "Our house is like Round Rock Armory. My dad said he wished the killer would've knocked on our door."

"Can I ask you a few questions? It could help with my investigation."

"Okay."

"Did you hear or see anything weird last night? Maybe someone screaming or yelling? They might've been running or making a lot of noise on the street."

"No."

"What about dogs barking? You hear any of that?"

He pauses and looks up at the sky to think. "I did hear the dogs next door barking a lot."

"You know what time that was?"

"Maybe around nine," he says. "I was supposed to be asleep, but Mr. Willoughby's dogs were going crazy."

"Nine o'clock. Got it."

"So, are you a Ranger?" he asks.

"I am."

"Have you ever . . . like, shot somebody?"

She hesitates, then answers: "Yes."

"Oh, shit," he says. "That's crazy. So, when you catch the bad guy, what if he doesn't want to go to jail? Do you shoot him then?"

"Hopefully, I won't have to."

"Yeah, but what if he gives you no choice?"

"Then, yes," she says. "If there's no other choice."

"Damn! You think I can be a Ranger one day?"

The boy is young, but Nia wonders if his interest in guns and shooting people is a natural curiosity or something else. "You can be whatever you want. Just make sure whatever it is, you're doing it for the right reasons."

"Cool." The boy turns the bike in the opposite direction and pedals down the street. He shouts, "Bye, Ranger Lady."

Nia thinks about Powers and what sort of upbringing his kids may be receiving. What type of lessons does a man like Powers impart to his children? Perhaps they're the same lessons Tomás has been receiving in his household, and if so, she can't help but worry about the future and the next generation of law enforcement.

She gets into the Explorer and dials McCann.

"Sir," she says. "It's Adams."

"Quite the mess down there in Ellis. Rowe called me about an hour ago and filled me in."

"He did? What exactly did he say?"

"That they've got an entire family dead. He did express the need for you to remain in town."

"I can't say they've got the experience to handle this sort of thing."

"You have my clearance, Adams. It's a horrific thing that's happened to that community. They don't deserve it. No place does. Having a Ranger present will send the right message."

"And what's that?"

"That whoever killed those people will be brought to justice."

"I'll do what I can, sir. From what I've been able to piece together, the suspect might've killed the two adult victims earlier in the evening, assaulted and strangled the daughter, then left around nine o'clock. Which means he was likely in the home for an hour or more."

"Christ All Mighty. Absolutely horrific."

"Does the name Al Bouchard mean anything to you?"

"Can't say it does."

"You mind looking into it? I'm unsure how long it'll take on the sheriff's end, and time is of the essence."

"I'll see what I can dig up."

Nia ends the call and dials Sharon. She anticipates a short conversation. She's always less talkative when she works on cases, especially perplexing ones.

The call goes to voicemail. "Hey, it's me," Nia says. "Got your text. Just giving you a call back. I hope you're doing all right. Not sure when I'll be home. I'll call again when I can." She ends the call guilt-ridden because part of her is relieved Sharon didn't answer.

Nia rests momentarily, her eyes closed, mentally preparing to return to the carnage inside. Then she collects herself and goes back into Fletch's home. Deputies and the forensic team are still processing the scene. They concentrate their efforts in the dining room, where Fletch and his wife met their fates, but Nia's interested in the small space in the rear of the house that looks to have served as an office and guest room. A twin bed, a small desk, and a file cabinet are against the walls. Nia opens the cabinet. It contains hanging folders organized by subject: home repairs, banking, taxes, mortgage, medical/health, and a folder without a tab. Nia removes the folder marked "Mortgage" and sifts through the documents—mostly bank statements that show overdue balances and letters from Colonial Trust Bank threatening foreclosure. The "Medical" folder contains bills for procedures: CT scans, postvisit summaries supplied by neurological specialists, and trips to the VA hospital. She removes the unlabeled folder. Inside are three black-and-white photographs of Fletch in uniform, his discharge paperwork, and his last will and testament. Nia studies a photograph of Fletch posing with another soldier: shirtless and broad-shouldered, an M16 hoisted over his shoulder. Identical tattoos are on their arms. She remembers the drawing the bank manager's secretary did and pulls it from her back pocket. She compares the drawing to the ink on the soldiers' forearms—a near-uncanny match.

She looks at the back of the photograph. Inscribed there is "Thicker than blood: Me and Al."

Al Bouchard is more than a name written on a table. He's a Marine, maybe still is, and likely served in Fletch's platoon. But if he's out there, he's in danger. And if Nia is to find him before Katz does, she'll need to work fast.

CHAPTER SEVEN

MR. KATZ

Mr. Katz spends the night at a Dallas motel, forty miles from Waxahachie. He knows putting more miles between him and Ellis County is best, but he needs to see his mother. When morning comes, he drives to the two-story home he was raised in and pulls into the driveway.

The house hasn't been updated in twenty years. The grass is overgrown, and so are the shrubs. His middle-aged, slender, blond sister walks out of the front door with a tie-dyed fanny pack riding her hip. She used to keep her stash in it: blow and smokes. These days, it holds their mother's medicine and her cell phone.

He can already tell that she's in a mood, walking fast and yapping like a lap dog.

"What are you doing here, Richie?"

"Nice to see you too, Mary Beth."

"Cut the shit," she says. "I told you not to show up like this."

"I was in the area. Wanted to see how she was doing."

"She's fine, which I could have told you over the phone if you ever bothered to call."

"Don't talk to me like that!" He flirts with rage. "You've got no idea how hard I've been working these past few months, and there's no telling how you've been using the money. For all I know, you've snorted every cent of it."

"Fuck off, Richie. Mom is being taken care of."

"Then you shouldn't have a problem with me seeing her."

"But it's breakfast time," she whines as she did when they were kids. "She needs to eat."

"So?"

"Last time, she didn't finish her food. Even after you left."

"It's not every day her favorite child comes to visit," he says. "She gets excited."

"Oh, fuck you."

"I'm not leaving without seeing her."

"Dammit," she says. "Make it quick."

They walk through the garage, passing a 1972 Buick station wagon. It hasn't run in years. He's urged his sister to sell it, but she refuses, believing their mother will drive again one day. The last time his mother walked without the aid of a cane was in 1995. She'll never leave her wheelchair short of a miracle, and those aren't real.

Inside, the furniture is outdated. Antique pieces from the '60s, when Scandinavian-designed swivel chairs were popular and people sat on couches zipped in plastic.

He looks in the kitchen. Water boils in a pot on the stove. "What's for breakfast?" he asks.

"The only thing she'll eat is oatmeal."

Mary Beth leads him through a sliding glass door and into the backyard, where his mother sits in her wheelchair facing a large oak tree. She's wrapped in a thin blanket he recognizes from ten years ago. Her legs, swollen to elephant-size, are squeezed into house slippers.

"You just left her like this?" he asks.

"She's bird-watching."

Magpies clamor and squawk from the treetop. "Nobody fucking cares about crows," he says.

"She does."

"How the hell would you know?"

"Look at her. She looks happy," Mary Beth says. "It's something she has to look forward to."

He takes a knee in front of his mother. "Hi, Mom. It's been a while."

The old woman's smile is jagged; stained teeth poke up from blackened gums. Her skin is riddled with boils and age spots. Looks like borderline leprosy, but he'd never say it aloud. There's no joy in getting old, he thinks. It's lonely and dull and miserable.

She reaches for his hand and mouths words without sound.

"Told you," Mary Beth says. "She's fine."

"She looks thin."

"You try getting her to eat anything besides oatmeal and grilled cheese."

"It's fine," he says. "As long as she's eating."

"Ran into Christy Robach the other day in Walmart. She asked about you."

"How is she?" he asks, rubbing his mother's dry, fragile hand.

"She looked good. I mean, she's got to be thirty-something now. Had a couple of kids with her. Didn't see a ring, though."

"That's nice," he says, half-listening. "Good for her."

"She asked what you were doing these days."

"And what'd you tell her?"

"The truth," she says. "I've got no idea what you do or why the hell you're dressed for a funeral, and since when did you become a Jew?"

He'd forgotten to remove the Star of David from around his neck. "It's nothing."

"It sure looks like something."

"Leave it alone, Mary Beth."

"Fine. Whatever floats your boat," she says. "Anyway, Christy gave me her number. Told me to tell you to call her."

"Not interested."

"And why's that? She not your type?"

He looks at his watch. "I need to make a call."

"Um, yeah. Go ahead," she says, "but it'll cut into your visiting time."

He leaves his mother's side, goes into the house, and sits in the den. He calls Dice.

"What did you find?" he asks. "Tell me you've got something."

"According to military records, Al Bouchard is deceased."

"Fucker's dead?"

"Car accident in 1986. Looks like his wife and daughter perished, too."

"It doesn't make sense," he says.

"Maybe Fletcher was lying?"

"I know when someone's lying."

"I've got a last known address in Austin."

"Give it to me."

"1568 West Plano Parkway."

"Have you heard from the clients?" he asks.

"Yeah, Big Ed has called twice and would like to know what's taking you so long."

"Tell that rich fuck to relax. The job will get done."

"Richie, are you sure—"

"No, don't tell him that," he says. "Tell him I'm making progress. It won't be long until the items are back in his possession."

"Time's up," Mary Beth says, stomping into the room. "I need to get moving on her breakfast. She's hungry, and you gotta go."

"Just give me a second, will you?"

"Nope," she says. "We agreed. Time's up."

"God, you're a pest."

"It's my house. Mama left it to me, and I say how things go around here."

He mumbles, "You always were an intrusive cunt."

"What the fuck did you say?"

He ends the call. "Fuck it, I'm leaving!"

"And don't bother coming back." She follows him to the front door. "You're fucking nuts, you know that? Next time I see Christy Robach, I'll tell her the truth."

"Yeah, and what's that?"

"You're a freak. Always have been and always will be."

"Fuck you."

The screen door squeals open; he stumbles off the porch with Mary Beth on his heels.

"You come back, and I'm calling the law," she says. "You can keep your shitty money. We'll make it just fine without you."

He gets into the car, shoves the key into the ignition, and waits. He's fuming. Can't think straight. It isn't like when he's working. That's when he's in control. He bangs his fists against the steering wheel, bombarded by visions of pain and blood.

Without more thought, he exits the car and enters the front door. He finds his sister in the kitchen, pouring the quick oats into hot water.

She screams. "What are you doing? I told you to leave!"

He snatches her by the throat and yanks her to the floor. The pot spills from the stove, splashing hot water against her skin.

She screams louder.

"I should fucking kill you," he says. "The only reason you're breathing is because Mama needs you." His mouth is inches from her ear, so close he could chew her lobe if he wanted and tear it from her skull. "Otherwise, I'd cut your throat and let those fucking crows pluck out your eyes. Give Mama a real show."

"Please, Richie? Please?" She's too petrified to cry. Tears well up in her eyes and remain trapped. Her lip trembles, but her body is still. She's powerless to do anything but pray.

Once the seething ends, he releases her neck and stands with his fists clenched. "Expect me every month from now on. And if I find out you're spending the money I send for her on blow, I'll move her into a facility, and you'll be the one in the fucking wheelchair."

The most hate he's ever held for anyone has been toward family. First, his father, a malevolent narcissist; then, his sycophantic, drug-addled sister. It's the closest he's ever come to killing her, and just as quickly as he'd come in with a thunderous rage, he leaves, gets into the car, and speeds away.

• • •

He drives forty minutes to Al Bouchard's last known address and parks in front of an abandoned farm. The only thing that remains is a decaying barn next to a horse stable. He gets out of the car and approaches the structure.

"Fuck," he shouts, stepping into a reservoir of mud. "Damn it all to hell."

He looks at the termite-ridden barn, with a third of its tin roof missing, and conceives his misfortune.

It's a dead end.

Time isn't on his side.

"FUCK!" His howl seems to echo for miles.

CHAPTER EIGHT

DESMOND

Desmond cracks two eggs into a bowl, beats them lightly, then pours the yolks into a buttered skillet. He works the eggs over low heat until firm. Once the eggs are done, he spoons them onto a plate with two slices of maple-glazed bacon and toast. He grabs a napkin and fork from the drawer and carries the plate upstairs to Linh's room.

"I've got breakfast." He enters the room, balancing the plate in his palm like a seasoned waiter. "Toast is extra crispy, as you like it."

Linh's sleeping gown is an oversize University of Austin T-shirt hanging off her left shoulder. "Are you sure that's how I like it, or is that just how you make it?"

"Good question," he says, setting the plate on the nightstand.

Linh props a pillow behind her back, sits up, and takes a bite of eggs. "Perfect," she says. "I could get used to this."

Desmond could get used to it, too. He was supposed to have vacated the boardinghouse a day ago but hasn't been able to break the news of his leaving to Linh. It took him a little introspection to know why. It's been a long time since he's had a reason to wake up in the morning that didn't revolve around carrying out a job, and for the past two days, he's been smitten by the thought of staying in Houston and seeing how things go with Linh.

She bites into a piece of bacon. "Wow," she says, chewing loudly. Desmond finds it endearing.

"Told you it was delicious," he says. "Pork fat and dry toast."

"God bless America . . . So, what do you have planned today?"

"Headed out to Clear Lake to see a friend."

"But what about your truck? It's still in the shop."

"I'll take a cab or something."

"A cab? No way," she says. "Just take my car."

"I couldn't, Linh. It's fine. Really."

"A cab is too expensive, and the bus will take an extra hour." She licks the bacon grease from her fingers, gets out of bed, and grabs her car keys off her dresser. "I insist," she says, handing them to Desmond.

"Okay," he says, putting the keys in his pocket. "I'll bring it back with a full tank."

"You better," she jokes. "See you tonight?"

"It might be kinda late."

"I'll be up," she says, then kisses him. "Thanks for breakfast."

He licks the bacon grease from his lips, left behind from Linh's kiss. "See you later."

• • •

Desmond stops at a liquor store for cigarettes, bottled water, and a prepaid phone. He lights a smoke and calls Fletch from the burner. When no one answers, he tries again. He suspects Fletch isn't answering on account of his injured jaw, which Desmond still feels guilty about. It was never his intention to hit Fletch as hard as he did, but it needed to look real to avoid suspicion. Given the money Desmond intends to wire him, a broken jaw is a small price to pay.

He finishes his cigarette, doesn't try Fletch again, and gets into Linh's

Corolla. It's far more comfortable than his old truck, and the upholstery smells like her, which makes him giddy, like a teenager. He won't mind thinking about Linh during the hour-long drive, and the sooner he can conclude his business, the sooner he can return to her.

• • •

Driving into Clear Lake, Desmond feels as foreign as he did in Vietnam. He has little in common with the people who occupy the expensive lakefront homes. Even with their money and privilege, their lives seem needlessly complicated. All he's ever wanted has been simplicity: his family safe and money in the bank. But it comes with caveats. This time, things will be different. A life with Linh is possible outside of crime and nefarious dealings. He has plenty of money—enough to last three lifetimes. They'll want for nothing, and maybe, just maybe, he can have a family again.

He pulls into the driveway of a two-story home: a wraparound porch, a brick facade, and Grecian columns. It stands out among the other homes, and Desmond wonders whether that's the point. He parks the car, gets out, and makes his way to the front door, carrying the gold coins and slave manifest in an aluminum briefcase. When he's a few feet from the door, it opens, and Marco, a jovial man pushing sixty, spills out. He's shirtless, wearing sunglasses and a visor; it's a new style, along with an accent Desmond hasn't heard him use before. Six months ago, Marco was dressed like a Wall Street broker, speaking like a Brooklynite, sporting Armani and a handlebar mustache.

"My friend, what took you so long?" Marco asks.

"Traffic."

"You look thin," he says. "Have you been eating?"

Desmond plays along. "Laying off the booze." He pats his belly. "And the pork rinds."

"All right. All right." Marco puts his arm around Desmond. "No matter. I made your favorite dish."

"You did?"

"Of course. Anything for my dear friend."

Desmond whispers, "Rubbing it on thick, aren't you?"

"Just get in the house." Marco ushers him inside and slams the door behind them. Annoyed by the charade, he removes the sun visor and tosses it to the floor. "Nosy neighbors think I'm a retired Costa Rican golfer."

"You're not dressed like a golfer. More like a washed-up tennis pro."

"It's the best I could do. Just open the case."

Desmond walks into the living room, nearly bare save for a card table and two chairs. "Nice place. I love how you get a villa, and I get a room without a shitter." He places the case on the table and opens it.

Marco puts on a pair of cotton gloves and removes the satchel of coins. "Exquisite," he says, inspecting one with a magnifying glass. "Thought to be destroyed in the Mexican-American War. They were found in what is now South Pasadena, California, in one of the last adobes from the era, and somehow ended up in the possession of the Duchamps."

"Stolen?"

"Likely, and later sold or traded."

"They belong in a museum."

"Naturally," Marco says. "But until then, they're leverage." He reaches into the case, removes the slave manifest, and carefully places it on the table. "But this beauty changes everything."

"You really believe the Duchamps will pay five million to keep all this a secret?"

"There's a reason it was hidden in a safe for more than a century. But it isn't about the money. It's about the compliance it buys. We want Duchamp's son to suspend his political campaign."

"Plenty of people in Texas, hell in this country, aren't going to care about the Duchamps' past. Slave owners or not, they like the message and eat it up."

"Privately, yes," Marco says, reading the names on the manifest. "They may not mind a family that profited from enslavement. But publicly, most people want to pretend they're decent, or at least project that they are to the outside world. Politically correct. Upstanding. That's most people. And that's the Duchamps. These days, they've branded themselves friends of military veterans, reserving jobs for those who've seen combat. But in fact veterans are cheap, hardworking labor. These men dig crude for pennies. And before them, the Duchamps exploited sharecroppers. Decades earlier, hundreds of enslaved Africans worked their plantations from Texas to Louisiana. How many people do you think have died for the Duchamps to triumph?"

"Too many to count," Desmond says. "I get it, though. People like that should be kept in check."

"Autocrats with bright smiles who profess they're on a God-given mission to save America."

"Save it from what?"

"The future. What else? Which is where we come in."

"Then, who's a check against us? Power corrupts absolutely. Remember?"

Marco tenses up. "Can't recall you sounding so disillusioned. What's gotten into you?"

"Nothing. It's been a long week, that's all." Desmond squeezes the bridge of his nose. "Can I get the money now? I need to wire Fletch his half."

"One sec," Marco says, slipping the manifest into a plastic sleeve. "This Fletch guy, you really trust him, don't you?"

"I never would've involved him if I didn't."

"But he isn't one of us. This thing of ours . . ."

"Easy, now," Desmond cuts a smug grin. "You're starting to sound like Michael Corleone."

"He's an outsider who doesn't know our ways."

"Trust me. I vouch for Fletch. Besides, I owe him."

"Ah, yes, Vietnam. The hell that unites us all." Marco removes a painting from the wall: an oil landscape set in a copper frame. He places the painting on the marble floor to reveal a wall safe the width of a shoe box. He turns the combination knob left, then right, and left again. "I suppose I shouldn't curse that godforsaken jungle. After all, it's where I found you." The safe opens, and he reaches in. "My prodigy."

Desmond shrugs. "You know how I feel about all that. It's an agreement. Nothing more."

"Well, it's the truth. I taught you everything I know. Poured into you more than any other apprentice, and you've proved yourself a masterful thief. But there's one lesson I failed to teach you."

"What's that?" Desmond says.

"To lie better." Marco spins on his heel and points a .22 Beretta at Desmond.

"What the hell, Marco?" Desmond's hands reach above his head. "What gives?"

"You aren't wiring any money to Fletch."

"The hell I'm not," he says. "That's what we agreed on."

"You never should've involved him. How could you have been so stupid?"

"Come on, Marco. Talk to me. What's this about?"

"There's nothing to talk about. Things have been set in motion."

"What things? What the hell is going on?"

"Your actions have brought this on . . ."

"I haven't taken any actions except the ones I cleared with you," he says. "Now, put the fucking gun down and tell me what's going on."

"You don't know?"

"Know what?"

"Fletch is dead, and so is his family. It's been all over the news, which you're supposed to be monitoring."

Desmond's stomach tightens; he doubles over, recalling their last meeting. "Oh, God," he says. "Dead? No. That can't be."

"How the hell can you not know this?"

"I haven't seen the news," he says, reflecting on his time with Linh. "I've been preoccupied. I should've been paying attention."

"Well, I know you didn't kill him. So, who did?"

"I don't know," Desmond says, his mind racing. "I was just trying to help him." His legs feel anchored to the floor. He braces his palm against the wall. "I'd never hurt Fletch or his family."

"That's the trouble, isn't it? Because somebody did. And that got me thinking . . ." Marco keeps the gun aimed at Desmond. "Someone out there knows he helped you, which means it's only a matter of time before they come for me, and that puts this entire organization in danger."

"The Duchamps?"

"They've got the money and resources," Marco says. "I suppose I didn't give them enough credit."

"Look, Marco. I'll always be grateful for what you've done for me, but maybe this is a sign."

"What sign?"

"Let this be my last job—a clean break."

"You want to walk away now?" Marco laughs. "After you've dumped this steaming pile of shit in my lap?"

"I'll clean it up," Desmond says. "Find out what happened to Fletch and his family and make it right."

"You don't have a choice. Otherwise, that life you've got planned, the one you've been dreaming about, isn't going to happen. I see that look in your eyes." Marco steps closer to Desmond, glaring suspiciously. "Who is she? The woman who's convinced you of a second chance."

"You want to talk, then put the gun down, and we'll discuss it like grown men."

Brakes squeal in the driveway. A ticking engine goes silent. Marco goes to the window and peeks through the curtains. "Fuck. They're here," he says.

"Who's here?"

"Sit down and keep quiet."

Seconds later, the doorbell chimes, followed by pounding. Marco slips the gun into his pocket and heads for the front door. Desmond remains seated.

Three men enter the house dressed in designer golf attire: khakis, tucked-in polos, and sun visors. A toothpick-chewing blond man accompanied by two brutes. It'd be peculiar if Marco wasn't playing the role of a golf pro. These men are committed to the ruse as much as he is but clearly have never set foot on a course. Like Desmond and Marco, they're members of the Fraternal Order of Thieves, also known by its more archaic title, *Ordo fraternus furum*. He's heard rumors of tribunals; sit-downs where a man's actions are weighed and judged, a punishment is rendered, and the man is never heard from or seen again. Even if someone were to survive a tribunal, what condition would he be in? Missing limbs, tongue detached? In a permanent coma, living the rest of his life in a vegetative state?

The Fraternal Order of Thieves has existed for centuries but sounds more farcical than clandestine. Desmond finds its cloak-and-dagger qualities hokey, but he's never doubted their importance to those higher in its ranks.

"Is this him?" the blond man asks. "Is this the man they call Desmond Bell?"

"Yes," Marco says. "But I've made a mistake. I shouldn't have involved you."

"You're not one to make mistakes, Marco. What's changed?"

"I drew conclusions without all the facts. Desmond had no knowledge of the murders in Ellis."

"That's interesting," the blond man says. "Yet, you called me believing he had jeopardized this organization, and as you know, nothing is more important than our secrecy."

"Yes, not even friendship," Marco says, looking to Desmond.

"A news anchor called it a slaughter. The work of the 'Ellis County Butcher.'"

"You know the news, if it bleeds, it leads. Right?"

"Are you saying the killing of the family isn't as bad as it's been portrayed?"

Marco begins to sweat. First his brow, then under his arms. "It's just that Desmond and I've talked, and I was presumptuous. His recruitment of the Marine veteran appears unconnected to the killings. A tragic coincidence. Nothing more."

"You sounded so certain of his involvement on the phone."

Desmond sucks his teeth. "Dammit, Marco," he says under his breath.

Marco shushes Desmond as though he's a child speaking out of turn.

"Wait," the blond man says. "I'd like to hear from Mr. Bell. What do you have to say for your actions?"

"Marco advised me not to involve Fletch. He said it was creating unnecessary risk, but I believed I'd taken all precautions."

"What are you doing?" Marco asks. "It's a fucking tribunal."

"These men came all the way here, then they deserve the truth."

The blond man pulls the toothpick from his mouth and flicks it at Marco. "Let him finish," he says. "And what is the truth, Mr. Bell?"

"I questioned Fletch's loyalty," he says. "I doubted if he could withstand a police investigation, so I took matters into my own hands."

"You're responsible for these murders?"

Desmond lowers his head. He never fathomed lying about his best friend, but he tells himself that Fletch would understand. The mission always takes precedence. Still, it doesn't assuage the guilt of tarnishing his brother's memory.

"And the girl?" the blond man says, still probing. "You raped and strangled her?"

Desmond looks at Marco and shakes his head in disbelief. "Fontaine was raped?"

"Enough! You didn't kill the Fletchers." The blond man reaches for the pistol on his hip. "You're wasting my time."

Before the blond man can squeeze the trigger, Marco pins the Beretta to his rib, aims at the man's head, and fires, shooting him in the collarbone. The blond man shrieks and collapses. The other men scramble to draw their weapons from holsters clipped to their belts.

Desmond catapults from the chair, takes hold of the legs of one of the brutes, and pulls him to the ground. He wedges the gun out of the man's hand, takes control of the barrel, and jams it into his right eye, rupturing the socket. The brute bucks and kicks. Desmond softens him with a hard knee to the groin, then fires a bullet through his skull.

Marco shoots the other man, then puts another bullet in the blond for good measure.

Blood and tissue dot the walls and ceiling.

Desmond aims the gun at Marco. "Hold up."

"You're going to point that thing at me after what I just did for you?"

"What's your play here, Marco?"

"Play? There is no fucking play. Look around you," he says, pointing to the dead. "It's over."

Desmond lowers his gun. "I didn't want it to come to this."

"Then you should've kept your fucking mouth shut and done your job."

"I'm sorry."

"Not as sorry as we'll both be."

"So, what do we do?"

"Killing fraternal members is inexcusable." Marco puts the Beretta in his pocket. "We've started a war, but I suppose it's fitting."

"How's that?"

"I plucked you out of a war zone," he says, sitting in the folding chair. "It's what you know best, and that spirit of death and carnage follows you wherever you go, doesn't it?"

Desmond doesn't want to believe he's cursed, but the thought has crossed his mind. "We should get moving."

"No." Marco rests his head back and looks up at the blood splatter on the ceiling. "This is my last stop."

"You're not serious."

"The fraternity's reach is limitless," he says. "There's no outrunning them."

"We can try to talk to them," Desmond says. "Exercise diplomacy."

"Who the hell do you think these people are? The United Nations? They alter history, birth, and end the careers of politicians, dictators, and CEOs. Cripple corporations. Fund militias. Actions that have influenced the governance of countries across the globe, including this one. And they'll never forgive us."

"The marionette . . ."

"So, you do remember?"

"That night in the bar when you offered to get Mai and me out of Vietnam, you asked me if I thought it was better to be the puppet or the puppeteer. But I'd been a puppet my whole life and was tired of the strings."

"You never stop being someone's or something's puppet," Marco says, getting to his feet. "I offered you wealth, enterprise, and a purpose beyond dying for a country that will never accept you. And in return, you did everything I asked, and you did it well."

"A fair exchange?"

"I believe so."

"Mai would disagree."

"I never said there wouldn't be losses."

Desmond looks at his watch. "The police will be along soon or another tribunal. Either way, if you stay here, you're dead."

Marco reaches into his pocket, takes out a rolled cigar, puts it in his mouth, and lights it. "I'm too old to run. I'm ready for whatever comes next."

"Don't be stupid. We can make it out. There's enough time to get—"

"No," he says. "Put daylight between you and them, and maybe you'll have a shot."

"Just hear me out, Marco . . ."

"I've heard enough," he says. "Your objective now is to stay alive. Take the money from the safe, the case, and go."

"I can get us to the border and to a safe house from there."

"I said go, goddamn it!"

"All right, Marco. All right." Desmond removes the bills from the safe, puts them in his pockets—fifty thousand in C-notes—and puts the slave manifest and coins back in the case.

"You know what to do," Marco says, smoke curling from his lips. "Leave and never come back. You understand me?"

Desmond walks to the door. "Goodbye, Marco."

Marco's eyes are hauntingly vacant. "I'll give Mai your regards."

Outside, Desmond opens the passenger door of the van. A transistor radio is mounted in the console. A torn piece of notebook paper is on the floor. Written in blue ink is Linh's license plate number. He walks to the van's rear and opens the hatch. A sheet covers a wooden crate containing an AK-47, three magazines, and night vision goggles.

He removes the crate, puts it and the case in the trunk of Linh's Corolla, and gets in the car.

Marco stands in the window, smoking, as Desmond reverses out of the driveway. When he looks again, Marco is gone.

• • •

Desmond returns to the boardinghouse to find Linh watering the lawn in flip-flops and her sun hat. She waves, bubbly and jovial. He thinks it may be the last time she greets him warmly.

She walks over as he gets out of the car. "How'd it go?" she asks.

"I need to show you something."

"Okay."

Desmond opens the trunk, showing the rifle, ammo, and goggles he confiscated from the dead men.

"Wow," she says. "Did you stop at a gun convention?"

"No," he says. "It isn't mine."

"Look, Desmond, I don't really allow guns in the house. It's in the lease agreement."

"It's for protection."

"Protection from what? A grizzly bear?"

"I haven't been honest with you . . ."

"Oh, God," she says. "I was right, wasn't I? You're on the run—a fugitive."

"Listen," he says, taking her by the arm. "I need you to leave Houston."

"Say what?"

"The people who are coming for me ran your license plate. They could know your name and this address by now."

"This isn't funny, Desmond."

"I'm not joking, and my name isn't Desmond."

Linh's hand flutters against her chest. "I can't breathe."

"Relax," he says, trying to comfort her. "Take it easy."

"Don't tell me to relax." She bats his hand away. "I mean, what else are you lying about? And why the hell do you need a gun? What could you have possibly done to need this thing?"

"My job," he says. "That's all I did, but I'm done with it."

"You aren't a treasure hunter, are you?" She buries her face in her palms. "Jesus, just saying those words sounds fucking ridiculous. How could I have ever believed—"

"I don't buy things for rich people. I take things from them."

"You're a thief."

"The things I take, they shouldn't have anyway."

"And these things, what do you do with them?"

"Before, I'd give them to my handler, who'd pay me."

"And what does he do with them? Turn them over to the police or government?"

"No," he says, studying vehicles as they pass. "He exposes their existence to the public unless he's paid large sums of money or they do what he wants."

"So, blackmail?"

"It's more complex than that."

"Doesn't sound complex. Pretty straightforward if you ask me."

"These aren't good people, Linh."

"And you . . ." Her voice cracks. "Are you a good person, Desmond? Or whatever your damn name is."

"It's Al," he says. "My name is Al Bouchard, but I haven't gone by that name in decades."

"Like it matters . . . You're a liar and a criminal."

A white truck slows down in front of the property, idles for a moment, then speeds past. "We should go inside," he says, watching each passing vehicle with the acuteness of a hawk.

Linh hisses, then marches toward the front porch. Desmond walks behind her, carrying the gun crate and the briefcase of stolen goods.

She goes upstairs to the hallway; he follows.

"You'll need to pack for at least a week." He sounds more like Al Bouchard: hardened and commanding.

"Do I even have a say in this?"

"No," he says. "It's for your safety. Where will you go?"

"My aunt's place near San Antonio."

"I'll need her phone number and address."

"What about the residents here? I need to tell them something and explain what's happening."

"I'll take care of it. Start packing."

Linh goes into her room and slams the door, leaving Desmond to ponder the weight of his life without her. He lost Mai to the hazards of his profession, and soon, Linh will be gone, too.

He goes downstairs and waits for her on the porch. Ten minutes later, she comes out of the house carrying a duffel bag, walks past Desmond, and goes to her car.

"Hold on a second," he says, double-timing to keep up. "I have something for you."

"What is it now?"

He pulls five hundred dollars from his pocket and offers it to her. "Please, take it."

"Why?"

"Please, Linh . . ."

"No," she says. "I don't know how things work in your world, but money doesn't make everything all right." She opens the rear car door, tosses her duffel bag onto the seat, gets behind the wheel, and shuts the door.

Desmond taps the window, gesturing for her to lower it. "I never wanted to hurt you," he says. "You have to know that."

". . . and yet, here we are." She hands him a Post-it with writing on it. "My aunt's phone number and address."

"I'll call you when I can."

"And if you don't?" She reads Desmond's silence. Eyes wet, she rolls the window up before a tear can fall and backs down the driveway.

Desmond watches as the Corolla travels north toward the highway, then disappears.

He goes inside the boardinghouse and knocks on the old woman's door. When she answers, he explains that the home will need to be treated for termites and that Linh is busy arranging the treatment. "I believe this should cover the inconvenience and your time at a hotel." He presents the woman with one thousand dollars, and she agrees to leave in an hour.

After, he informs the college student, who nearly faints when presented with the money. "My *ông* is very sick," he says. "I need to return to Dong Nai. This is truly a blessing."

The boy hugs him. Desmond isn't one to be touched by strangers, but he surrenders to the embrace. It's a small kindness, an interlude from guilt over the damage he's done.

He can only hope that Linh will understand and forgive him one day.

CHAPTER NINE
NIA

"Sharon," Nia shouts. "I'm home." The house is as she left it. Shy of tidy, but it's to be expected. Neither she nor Sharon enjoys housework. Sharon has suggested a housekeeper, but Nia's too mistrustful to have a stranger in her home.

She drops her duffel bag and gear by the front door and sifts through a stack of mail on the coffee table. "Honey, I'm home," she says, giving her best Desi Arnaz catchphrase. "Where the heck are you?"

She ignores the mail to search, checking the kitchen, bedrooms, and bathroom. Sharon has been known to hold a grudge, but never for more than a day. But things have been unusual between them lately: strained and contentious. It's possible she's still upset about their tiff from days ago.

Nia goes into the garage. "Baby, what's going on?"

Sharon kneels on the pavement, shoves her hands into a bucket of sudsy water, comes up with a sponge, and vigorously scrubs the hood of her Lincoln LS.

Nia approaches. "What happened?"

Sharon's eyes are red and puffy. Nia knows the look; she's been crying for some time. Likely for hours.

"Look what they did," Sharon says speaking through a clenched jaw. "Goddamn animals."

Written on the car's hood in white paint are slurs: *Dyke, Queer, Whore*.

"Who did this?"

"I don't know," Sharon says, dipping the sponge back into the bucket. "Came out of the courthouse and found it like this."

"The courthouse? But there's security all over that place."

"Like that matters?"

"Someone had to have seen something, and there's cameras. Did you call the police? File a report?"

"No, Nia. I didn't dust for prints either."

"I'm just trying to cover the bases, all right?"

"Cover the bases? That's what you're concerned about? I mean, my God . . . can you for one minute recognize how utterly fucked-up this is? Do you know how it feels to see this at the place you work, no less?" She stands and tosses the sponge onto the ground. "How would you react if you came out of your headquarters and saw this? And you knew . . . I mean, knew in your heart that it was someone you probably saw every day. Maybe they smiled in your face and shook your hand and then went and did this."

"I'd be angry."

"Yes, Nia, you'd be fucking angry. Maybe you'd want to talk to someone who might understand this particular brand of pain."

"Baby, I . . ."

"But that person isn't around, and you can't tell your colleagues or even the police because then word might get out that somebody out there thinks you're a goddamn dyke! And just like that, you're not a victim. You're a sicko—an abomination who brought it on yourself."

Nia puts her hand on Sharon's shoulder. "Don't touch me!" She draws back, loses her balance, and stumbles to the ground, tipping over the bucket.

"Let me help you up," Nia says, extending her hand.

"I'm fine."

"C'mon, baby."

"Leave me alone!"

"But I'm here, Sharon . . . I'm trying."

"Only part of you," she says, still refusing Nia's hand. "You haven't been *here* in a long time."

"That isn't fair."

"You want to talk about fair?"

"I'm doing the best I can to keep this relationship together."

"Oh, please. If this is your best, I'd hate to see your worst."

"There's no winning with you, is there?"

"Don't worry about the car," Sharon says. "I'll deal with it the same way I always do . . . alone."

"I'm sorry, Sharon. Don't know what else to say."

"Just go."

"Can't we talk about this?"

"I said go!"

Sharon weeps as Nia quickly leaves the garage.

• • •

It's been three months since Nia last visited her father in the Federal Detention Center Houston, commonly referred to as the FDCH. The high-security prison has two housing units and holds about nine hundred inmates. Nia's father has served twenty years for his crimes and will be up for parole in 2023—that's if the world is still spinning by then and he's still breathing.

Nia waits in the cold concrete room while guards collect her father from his cell. She usually tells him a week in advance before visiting so he can shave and look presentable. It matters to him far more than

Nia, but she understands his need for decorum in a place that thrives on barbarity.

Joseph Turner shuffles into the room, wearing an orange jumpsuit and white slip-on sneakers. She's always thought of him as the most handsome with a five-o'clock shadow, but he gently rakes his face, perturbed by the stubble. He likes to tell Nia that she got her good looks from her mother, but her father's tawny skin, strong dimpled chin, and hazel eyes could make most women swoon. That's why he was such an effective bank robber. *Pleasant-looking* and *fine* were words often used to describe him in police reports. Some female bank tellers even admitted to writing their phone numbers on the tender before handing it over. So her father rarely relied on threats with a loaded gun; a smile and flirtatious banter proved most effective.

The guard pulls the chair from the table and shackles her father to the floor.

"Hi, Dad," she says.

"You didn't tell me you were coming, sweetheart . . ."

"Impromptu visit."

"Well, I'm not complaining. Surprises like this make my day."

She walks over and hugs her father. "I've missed you."

"I've missed you, too, darling . . . Everything, all right?"

She doesn't want the hug to end, but the guard is antsy. "Let's sit, Dad."

"All right," he says, easing into the chair. "So, what's going on? How's Sharon?"

"Things have been complicated lately. Feels like we're drifting apart."

"Relationships can be hard. Could be a rough patch. Plenty of couples go through that."

"Been thinking maybe it isn't meant for people like us."

"Don't ever say that, Nia. You deserve happiness, same as anyone else."

She touches her father's hand and allows herself to remember a time when he wasn't in chains. "And it's this case," she says. "Can't seem to get a read on it."

"Robbery?"

"Started that way, but it's become something else... something bigger."

"How much was stolen?"

"That's the thing..." Her fingers are tight on the bridge of her nose. "No money out of the vault, but an old safe was emptied."

"What was in the safe?"

"Can't be exactly sure, but it wasn't money."

"A bank robbery where no money was taken at all?"

"That's right," she says. "Then the bank's security guard who was present during the robbery is murdered, along with his family."

"Sounds like organized crime. Gangs, maybe?"

"Doesn't feel like it," she says. "The murderer had the guard write a name in blood before killing him. Seems careless to leave that behind. Not really the mob's MO, and gangs prefer drive-bys, not home invasions."

"Or it's a challenge..."

"That's what I thought."

"And the name?"

"It came back belonging to a dead man."

"Who?"

"Some Marine vet who died in the '80s."

Joseph taps his knuckles on the table in rapid succession. Something he does when he's thinking.

"What is it, Dad?"

"A name from the past just popped into my head," he says. "Bouchard."

Nia freezes; there's a lump in her throat. "Say that name again."

"Alan. Alfred. Can't remember exactly. But Bouchard was how most of us knew him. He'd been a Marine serving in Nam. A couple of tours from what I understood. Then he came back home and took up robbing banks. People say he'd made a deal with the devil, which was how he was able to bring his woman over from Nam."

"The things we do for love," she says. "Robbing banks? I guess Whataburger wasn't hiring?"

"I'm not making excuses for him, but it wasn't easy for Black soldiers coming home after the war. Strung out on dope. Shell shock. Bad economy. All I'm saying is that everybody makes choices in this life. Sometimes it's the wrong choice for the right reason."

"You sure you're talking about Bouchard?"

"We aren't so different, he and I. Both paid a price for our mistakes. Only he paid in blood. It's like I always tell you, we all have to bow out sooner or later."

"Paid in blood?"

"Orchestrated murder," he says. "I never worked a job with Bouchard, but I knew plenty who had. He was one of the best. Not even the cops could touch him. Then I started hearing things, like he'd stopped robbing banks and was going after people's things."

"Personal assets?"

"I'm talking things they kept close. Things they didn't want anyone to know about. Word around the campfire was that he'd stolen a priceless watch from the Denton County mayor. Fella had over fifty watches. Rolex, Piguet, LeCoultre—really expensive shit. Maybe a million dollars' worth. But Bouchard only took one watch."

"What was so special about it?"

"That, my dear, is a mystery. But when that mayor learned Bouchard was behind the robbery, he went after him. He ran Bouchard and his family off the road. Everyone died, including him and his wife and baby girl. A month after the Bouchards were buried, that crooked mayor was found hanged in his basement, surrounded by a bunch of Nazi shit from the war. Turns out, he'd been trading in the black market for years, and Nazi paraphernalia was his forte. Even had a collection of teeth from concentration camp victims."

"Jesus, Dad. That's awful. How do you know all this?"

"You learn things when you've been here long as I have. You want my thoughts on OJ?"

"I'll pass. Gotta go, Dad," she says, pulling out her chair.

"Where you off to now?"

"Depends on where this investigation takes me." She hugs her father and signals to the guard. "Take care of yourself."

"Thanks for stopping by, darling." The guard bends over to unshackle him from the floor. "Be careful out there, you hear?"

"Try not to worry about me."

"Baby girl, behind these walls, all I've got are worries."

• • •

Back inside the Explorer, Nia calls McCann on her cell. He answers on the third ring, sounding as if he's smacking something greasy. "McCann here."

"It's Adams," she says. "Any news from the Public Integrity Unit? Good or bad."

"Nothing much to speak of, but they interviewed Powers today."

"They did what? What reason did they give?"

"Actually, Powers volunteered."

Nia's been the only brown face in a department of white men long enough to know what that means. Powers is playing his good-ole-boy card. It means Nia's relegated to an outsider, which won't bode well for her credibility if the truth comes out.

"Tell them I want to go on record."

"You sure you want to offer yourself up like that?"

"What other choice do I have? If no one's going to take up for me, I've got to take up for myself."

"Easy now, Adams. You're presuming Powers sold you out."

"I'd bet a damn horse."

"The best thing for you to do is keep working on the Ellis case. It's garnered some national attention, and you can use that. No one's going to string up the Ranger who saved lives in Central Bank and brought the Ellis County Butcher to justice."

"String up?"

"Poor choice of words," he says. "But you know what I mean."

"Sure, I do. You want me to wear a cape."

"I've got faith in you, Adams."

Even when McCann is being supportive, she detects an air of condescension. He cares about saving his job far more than Nia; if that means burying her and Powers, so be it. "Any info on Al Bouchard?" she asks.

"Just came in. According to military records, he's dead. Even checked to be sure he didn't go under another name while enlisted. The only thing that comes up is a past address for a commercial peanut farm near Austin. Looks like it hasn't been operational for years."

She struggles to hear over a passing truck. "You said a peanut farm?"

"That's right. 1568 West Plano Parkway. Good acreage, too."

Nia writes the address in her notepad. "Is the land still in Bouchard's name?"

"It was put in a trust a while back."

"And the executor?"

"All that's listed is a law firm. Trillium and Boger. Hold a minute, I'll get you the address," he says, rustling papers. "Okay. I've got it here: 600 Commerce Street."

"Copy. Headed there now."

· · ·

Nia stands outside the door to the law office. "Trillium & Boger Law Office, LTD, LLP" is stenciled across bubbled glass. She's already knocked twice, and the place looks empty.

A Black man dressed in a janitor's jumpsuit stands holding a broom at the end of the hall. "Miss," he says, his salt-and-pepper hair in desperate need of a trim. "They left at four."

Nia checks her watch. It's after 5 p.m. "Figured it was a long shot."

"Ah, you're a Ranger," he says, looking at her badge. "Young, too."

Nia bucks. "Come again?"

"No, that's good," he says. "Means you've got more time to change things. See, I know all about the Rangers. Gave it a go myself back in the day. Things were different back then. Long before Lee Roy Young came on the scene."

"I see," Nia says.

"Way before they were letting women join. But enough of that," he says. "You're looking for the lawyers."

She nods. "Will they be back today?"

"Afraid not. They see most of their clients in the morning and keep those funny lawyer hours."

"Thanks. I'll try another time."

"Not a problem," he says, grinning.

"Have you worked here long?"

"Since '72," he says. "Plenty long in my book."

"You must be familiar with the area."

"Sure," he says, propping the broom against the wall. "Been here my whole life. I still love it . . . most days."

"Maybe you can help me," she says. "I'm looking for an old peanut farm off Plano Parkway. You know it?"

"Do I? That's Mimi Bouchard's old place. Back in the day, we used to have ourselves regular hoedowns in that barn until that sun started creeping."

"Any idea why it stopped being operational?"

"Time and circumstance, I reckon. Things got tough on the family when the boy went off to war."

"The boy?"

"Her son Alcott, which I don't reckon was a name he fancied much. People 'round here called him Al."

"And you're sure no one manages the land?"

"Far as I know," he says. "Mimi is the only person left to look after it, and I haven't seen her in years. She became a bit of a recluse when Al and his family perished in that car wreck. God rest their souls."

"Do you know where Mimi lives?"

"Well, she wouldn't like me telling her business like that. She always said I get too chatty with pretty ladies." He returns to sweeping trash into a tin dustpan. "But she's not too far from the farm. Like me, she's born and bred. Folks like us got no place else to go."

"Thank you for your time," she says.

"Certainly," he says. "And thank you for wearing that badge. Means more than you know to have it pinned to one of us."

• • •

Nia checks the road atlas again; she's in the right place, but it isn't what she expected. As she approaches, there's nothing that resembles a farm. She enters the property through a broken fence and parks in front of the old barn. It's desolate: overgrown weeds and dried soil.

She gets out of the Explorer and walks toward the decaying structure. It's a marvel that it's still standing. A sign posted on the door reads "NO TRESPASSING." A padlock meant to keep out vandals and squatters looks to have been broken for years. Nia opens the door and goes inside. The sawdust floor is covered in animal droppings; the place smells of urine. The wooden beams are riddled with small pin-size holes where termites have feasted. The barn is half the length of a football field and the width of four Cadillac Coupe DeVilles. Nia can picture people back in the day having a hoedown, packed in like sardines—drinking liquor from mason jars, boot-scooting and grinding all night.

She notices a few bats hanging from the rafters. They were likely drawn to the barn by the mice she's seen scurrying around. She's careful to avoid stepping in the droppings they've left. Sidestepping a pile of pellets, her boot heel rubs against a metal cover. Nia kicks away sawdust and dirt to reveal what looks like a sealed manhole. It could lead to a basement or storm shelter, she thinks. Nia knows opening the cover without reasonable suspicion or probable cause is a violation of the property owner's rights, but there's more to the barn. She feels it.

Besides, no one's around to take notice.

She returns to the Explorer, removes a crowbar from the rear, and goes back into the barn, leaving her hat behind on the passenger seat. Jamming the crowbar in between the ground and metal, she breaks the seal and works the cover free, then lifts it, and rolls it to the side. A short ladder leads into a tunnel. She takes her small flashlight from her belt's holster and shines the beam into the hole. The air feels cooler underground and smells of mildew. She steps on the top rung and climbs inside. Under normal circumstances, she'd call for backup, but nothing about this case is normal. When she reaches the last rung, she drops to the concrete and shines her light into darkness. The tunnel is narrow. Nia is certain it isn't an irrigation or a sewer system. There's no sewage, and, oddly, the tunnel is mostly dry. Someone with knowledge constructed it well, but for what purpose?

She walks forward, keeping the light ahead of her. The beam is unable to penetrate more than twelve feet, and with each step hissing cockroaches scatter. The tunnel seems endless, and after ten minutes of walking, she comes to another ladder extending from a covered opening. She takes hold of the rungs, pulls herself up, and turns the wheel lock until she hears a click. She pushes against the cover, but it doesn't budge.

"Shit," she says, realizing her only way out may be from where she came.

Holding on to a rung with one hand, she drives her palm upward, locks her arm, and grinds her teeth as she pushes harder. There's a small bend of light. She wedges the flashlight's handle into the opening, grips her hands on the cover, and pushes again until she can squeeze her arms through. Once both arms are through, she lifts herself out of the hole.

Just as she gets to her feet, an older woman, with bulky shoulders and forearms to match, stands holding a double-barrel shotgun. "Don't move," the woman says. She's dressed in a baggy T-shirt, jeans, and old-school Reebok sneakers, white and thick-soled. "On your stomach. Lemme see your hands."

"Easy, now." Nia rolls onto her stomach. "I'm a Texas Ranger."

"I don't care. What are you doing in my garage?"

Nia hadn't gotten a good look at where the tunnel had brought her. It's a large garage: wood beams and a tin roof. A tractor is parked beside her; there is shelving with garden tools, paint buckets, and mason jars holding an assortment of nails.

"I'm gonna ask one more time," the woman says. "What are you doing on my property?"

"I'm investigating a crime."

"Ain't no crime happening here, and even if it was, that doesn't give you a right to crawl through my bomb shelter."

"Bomb shelter?"

"Get up."

Nia gets to her feet, keeping her arms where the woman can see. "I made a mistake. I shouldn't have accessed your tunnel . . . I mean shelter."

"Damn right. Show me your badge."

Nia points to the badge on her hip. "Ma'am, I just need to know if you're Mimi Bouchard."

"That badge supposed to be real?"

"Please, ma'am," Nia says. "I believe your son may be in trouble."

"My son is dead."

"You and I both know that isn't true."

The woman lowers the shotgun. "Anyone else know you're here?"

"No, ma'am, I came alone."

"How'd you know about the access tunnel?"

"Lucky find, I guess."

"No one's been through there in half a decade or more. But the security cameras still work."

"Cameras?"

"That's how I knew you were coming through the tunnel. Got them fixed in the concrete walls. Infrared sensors pick up your movement. Usually, they go off for rats and critters that find their way in, so imagine my surprise . . ."

"I don't mean you any harm. I've come to talk," Nia says. "I'm hoping you can help me and maybe I can help you."

"Uh-huh . . ." She throws the shotgun over her shoulder. "You look harmless enough. But I've got more on me than this Remington. Get it?"

"Yes."

"What about you?"

"Not sure what you mean . . ."

"That pistol on your hip, is it all you're carrying?"

"That and a butterfly knife."

"Turn over the gun," she says. "The knife you can keep."

"I can't give you my firearm, ma'am. It's against policy."

"You want to speak to me, you do it without that gun. Besides, isn't you being here against policy?"

Nia unlatches the buckle of her Sam Browne with her gun still holstered and hands it to the woman.

"All right, then. Come inside," the woman says. "You like queso dip?"

"Haven't had it in years. It's hard to find a vegetarian version."

"What kinda Texan doesn't eat meat?" Ms. Bouchard asks. "Lord, honey, a little ground beef won't harm you none."

"Can't say I'm a true Texan. Wasn't born here."

"No kidding. How about I'll only put peppers in yours?"

"All right, ma'am. But you really don't have to trouble yourself."

"No trouble at all," Ms. Bouchard says. "The fact you walked through that tunnel means you've got a half-decent reason to be here. I'll hear you out, and then you can be on your way."

"All right, ma'am. Thank you."

Nia follows the woman from the garage, through the backyard where a small garden flourishes, and up a short flight of steps into a mudroom. While the home's exterior looks like something out of a period film set in the 1920s, inside, the house has been remodeled. Based on the lighting fixtures and flooring, it was likely upgraded ten or fifteen years ago.

"You'll have to take them boots off," the woman says. "Can't have you scuffing my floors."

Nia removes her boots. The butterfly knife is strapped to her ankle by Velcro. "So, Ms. Mimi," she begins, "how's it work?"

"Only my people call me Mimi," she says, putting Nia's Sam Browne into a cabinet. "You can call me Ms. Bouchard."

"Of course," Nia says. "I'd like to know what Al hopes to accomplish by hiding."

"What my son has or hasn't done is his business," Ms. Bouchard says, entering the kitchen.

Each appliance bears the brand name *White-Westinghouse* and was likely purchased new in the 1970s. The refrigerator and stove would be considered vintage, something a collector might find of value. Nia walks closely behind the woman. On the stove is a pot of white rice; in a skillet, red beans simmering with garlic and bay leaves. A pound cake cools on the counter next to a bowl of chopped lettuce, tomatoes, and cucumbers.

"You expecting company?" Nia asks. "Seems like a lot of food for one person."

"Kinda nosy, aren't you?"

"It's the job."

"Come on in and sit," Ms. Bouchard says, leading Nia into the living room. She takes a seat in a rocking chair and lays the shotgun on the floor. She points to the sofa, and Nia sits. "So, why all this interest in Al?"

"Second time you've talked about him like he isn't in the ground. Are you admitting he's alive?"

"For the sake of argument, let's say that he is."

Nia shifts her weight on the misshapen cushions, trying to get comfortable. "Okay, I'll play along. Let's say Al's recent criminal activity has upset some very powerful people with resources who don't back down when wronged. In fact, these people won't ever stop coming for Al. That means if they find out he's alive and he has a mother still living, they might decide to pay her a visit."

Ms. Bouchard grins at her shotgun like it's an old friend. "Sweetie, I pity the person who comes to this door looking to start some mess."

"I'm serious."

"I don't doubt that you are," she says. "But I am, too."

"Can you tell me where to find Al?" Nia asks. "That way I can help him—protect him, even."

"That boy doesn't need protection. Never has. In fact, if anyone needs protecting, it's whoever crosses him. Now . . ." she rises from the chair with a groan and picks up her shotgun. "I'm going to fix myself some sweet tea and get that cheese dip going."

"Okay, ma'am."

"Lemon in your tea?"

"Yes, please."

Ms. Bouchard returns to the kitchen with the shotgun.

"You really don't have to carry that thing with you," Nia says. "I'm here for information, not to make trouble."

"Don't take it personally. I haven't had anyone over in years," Ms. Bouchard shouts from the kitchen. "Just being careful. You can't trust everybody these days." She comes from the kitchen with two glasses of tea with lemon wedges on the rims and places one on the coffee table in front of Nia. "I'll be right back with the dip."

"Thank you, ma'am." Nia takes a sip of tea. It's perfectly sweetened. Reminds her of how her grandmother used to prepare it.

Ms. Bouchard carries a plate of tortilla chips and two dipping bowls of melted cheese to the coffee table and sets it down. For a woman who hasn't had visitors in years, Ms. Bouchard makes a delectable spread.

Nia dips a chip into the cheese and takes a bite. "This is delicious," she says.

"Nothing beats it."

Nia eats and drinks more tea. She hadn't realized how much of an appetite she'd worked up in the tunnel.

"Now, what other questions do you have for me?" Ms. Bouchard asks.

Nia's lightheaded; her mouth is dry. "It's got a kick to it," she says.

"Must be the jalapeños."

"I . . . I'm not feeling too well." Nia pushes the plate away and drinks more.

"Peppers don't always agree with everyone."

Nia struggles to get up from the couch but collapses back onto the cushions. "The cheese . . . You put something in the cheese." She's panting; sweat beads on her forehead. "What did you give me?"

"All that sugar in the tea, you probably couldn't taste it . . ."

"Taste what?"

"Don't worry, dear. It won't kill you. You're just going to take a little nap. Then, we'll have a real chat."

Nia tries to stand again but can't. She stumbles back onto the couch and closes her eyes.

• • •

Nia wakes up strapped to a twin-size bed. Her head throbs, and there's a sharp pain in her neck. The butterfly knife is missing from her ankle, and the taste of Ms. Bouchard's specially brewed tea lingers in her throat. The room is painted pink with a Barbie-themed wallpaper trim and a collection of dollhouses on a bookshelf.

A teen girl stands in the doorway holding a glass of water and a piece of white bread on a paper plate. Nia's been misled. The girl's copper skin and features suggest she's of Asian heritage and a descendant of the Black diaspora. Al Bouchard has orchestrated an enduring lie. Like him, his daughter is very much alive.

"Grammy," the girl says, "I think you gave her too much."

"It's fine, child." Ms. Bouchard steps into the room; a tea towel hangs over her shoulder, and she's holding a cold compress. "Go ahead and put this on her forehead." She hands the compress to the girl, who gently lays it across Nia's forehead.

"I don't know about this, Grammy. What if she really is a Ranger?" The girl looks eighteen but sounds younger; her voice registers high and airy, "This could be bad."

"Well, she broke about twenty laws coming on this property. What cop you know that dumb?"

"Plenty, Grammy."

"Now, I'mma have to seal those tunnel entrances before nightfall."

"People might be looking for her. What if someone sees her car?"

"What is it you want me to do, Amora? It's like I told you, we'll hold her until your father calls."

"Amora? That's a pretty name," Nia mumbles, then coughs. "Glad to see you're alive. Not sure for how long, though."

"What's that supposed to mean?" Amora asks.

"Oh, your grammy didn't tell you? Your father has some very determined enemies."

"Grammy, what's she talking about?"

"It's nothing, child," Ms. Bouchard says. "She's talking out of her ass, that's all."

Nia investigates the rope tied to her right arm and the straps over her legs. They are sophisticated knots. Something she'd expect to see done by a soldier or scout. "You tied this?" Nia asks Amora.

"Yes."

"Your father taught you how to do that, didn't he? When was the last time you saw him?"

"Enough with the questions," Ms. Bouchard says. "Give her the food and leave her be."

Amora hands Nia two slices of bread and a glass of water. "It should help with the headache."

"Your grammy's done this before."

"Anytime someone comes asking about—"

"Hush, child. There you go running off at the mouth again. Go downstairs and check on dinner."

"But Grammy, she's a Ranger . . ."

"I said get on down those stairs and don't make me tell you twice!"

"Yes, ma'am."

Amora leaves the room, and all civility goes with her. "Look here," Ms. Bouchard says, "I don't care if you're a Ranger. You want out of this house, then you do as I say. First, I want to know everything you know about my son's situation. Exactly what's he mixed up in?"

"Your granddaughter's right. People will come looking for me."

"We'll cross that bridge when the time comes. Right now, you need to answer my questions."

"All right. But before I tell you what I know, I've got a question for you."

"My Lord, you're a pain in the ass," Ms. Bouchard says. "Go ahead."

"You kept Amora hidden all these years? No interactions with other people. No school? No friends?"

"They tried to kill her once. I wasn't going to let them do it again."

"Sure," Nia says. "But you can't keep her here forever. At some point, she has to go out into the world. She's damn near grown. Doesn't she get to live a normal life?"

"This is normal for her. She doesn't know any different," Ms. Bouchard says, steadily losing patience. "And you ought to be more concerned with your own life. Stop worrying about my granddaughter, and tell me what you know about my son."

"I know he's a thief, and that's what got his wife killed and nearly Amora. And I know he's stolen something that someone very much wants returned. His Marine friend and his family are all dead because of it."

"A friend from the service? Who are you talking about?"

"Hakeem Fletcher."

"Fletch? My God . . ."

"I need to speak to Al before more people get killed," Nia says. "While there's still time to fix things."

Ms. Bouchard sits at the edge of the bed. "My son is not a bad man. The things he steals aren't from everyday folks. These people are the stuff of nightmares. They don't answer to the law or anybody. Hell, sometimes they are the law. So, he takes their secrets. Threatens to expose them if they don't pay."

"And when they do pay, he sends you the cash?"

"Take a minute and listen, will you? These aren't regular folk we're talking about. They're monsters. A man had a collection of women's pinky toes. Jars of them were stored in a basement safe for decades. Now, how do you think a fella would come into possession of such things?"

"There's no excuse," Nia says. "That's what the police are for. We could have helped."

"All those victims were Black and had been missing for years," Ms. Bouchard says harshly. "Police didn't care enough to look into that white man because he owned a petroleum factory near the gulf. Made money hand over fist in this state. Dined with the governor and senators. You ain't got to play blue blood with me, sister. You've seen enough wearing that badge to know people with money and power break all kinds of laws and get away with it, and the police don't bat an eye."

"Not all of us are like that—"

"You want to believe you're different? Look me in my eyes and tell me you've never done dirt or seen one of your own doing dirt while wearing that badge."

Nia is quiet, but her conscience speaks loudly.

"Like I thought and I bet you didn't do a damn thing about it," Ms. Bouchard says. "Now, I'll bring you some supper in a bit."

"How long are you keeping me here?"

"When I get word from Al on what to do with you, we'll talk about it. Until then, you're a guest in our home."

"Anyone ever tell you it's bad etiquette to tie guests to beds?"

"Either you're a guest or a trespasser I captured breaking in. Take your pick."

"This won't end well," Nia says. "You know that, don't you?"

"For whom? You're the one tied up." Ms. Bouchard leaves the room.

Nia manages to sit up in bed, takes a bite of bread, and chews. She looks around the room for something useful—sharp enough to cut the ropes—but there's nothing handy.

CHAPTER TEN
MR. KATZ

Mr. Katz is on his third beer, and there isn't much left in the bottom of the glass. He rarely drinks on the job, but today has been a special kind of fucked-up. Being in the biker bar might be a strange choice, especially when the walls are covered in Corbin Duchamp campaign posters, but Mr. Katz isn't bothered by the atmosphere, the tribalism: biker club flags, colored bandannas, and license plates are nailed to the walls. The jukebox plays Patsy Cline, the Allman Brothers Band, and Toby Keith. Despite his deep love for classical music, Mr. Katz's finds country songs amusing, particularly when they end in payback.

His cell phone vibrates. Another message from Dice, checking on things. Mr. Katz should call him back, but he can hold off until the gig turns around for the better.

"Another beer?" the bartender asks. He's an older white man with sun-burnished skin and a long beard like the wizards from *Harry Potter*, which Mr. Katz watched on a plane once.

"Keep them coming."

"One of those days, huh?" The bartender pours a dark ale into a frosty glass. "I had plenty of them in my day."

Mr. Katz notices the bartender's tattoos: an eagle on fire, a rebel flag, and a skull with fangs. Getting inked is risky, so he's avoided it. People remember tattoos more than faces; it's better to be forgettable in his line of work.

"It's a question of failure," Mr. Katz says. "No one wants to fail, yet it's sure to happen on a long enough timeline."

"And sometimes it's just about knowing when to quit. You know, like after four beers."

"I know my limit."

"Not so sure you do, pal. Time to close out. That'll be twelve, even."

Mr. Katz reaches into his pocket, pulls out his wallet, and removes a twenty-dollar bill. "Here," he says, sliding the money to the bartender.

"How much do you want back?"

"Keep it," Mr. Katz says. "We aren't long for this world."

"Speak for yourself, pal. I plan to live forever."

"Lofty goal."

"I'm talking eternal life, brother. But there's only one way to achieve that." He exhibits a tattooed cross on his forearm depicting a crucified Jesus—white skin, flowing blond locks.

"Fucking ridiculous."

"Say what?"

"Jesus wasn't Scandinavian."

"Doesn't matter what he looked like. It's about what he can do for you, brother."

"Are you trying to convert me at a bar? I don't know if I should laugh or be offended."

"Feel how you want, but you're my brother in Christ. Doesn't matter if you believe or not."

Mr. Katz reaches into his shirt and reveals the Star of David around his neck. "I'm taken," he says. "By the big bad Zionists."

"Well, I wish you wouldn't have done that," the bartender says. "How about you finish that beer and head on out?"

"Gladly," Mr. Katz says, gulping the ale. When he finishes, he slams the glass on the table. "Finito."

"Look, asshole. I'm not standing for any of your bullshit." The bartender reaches for the glass. Mr. Katz quickly wraps his fingers around his wrist and digs his thumbnail into the skin between the bartender's thumb and index finger.

"Ah! What the hell are you doing?" The bartender attempts to free his hand. "Get the fuck off me!"

"I'm applying pressure to a central nerve, and in a few seconds, you will lose control of your pelvic muscles and defecate."

"You're fucking crazy."

"And you're a despicable piece of filth. But we both are, aren't we? Only I own it." He presses his thumb deeper into the pressure point. "A few seconds more . . ."

"What the hell is your problem?"

"Your hypocrisy."

The bartender squirms and doubles over. "I'm sorry, man! All right, stop!" He brings his hand to his stomach. "Please, let me go."

"Say that you're filth."

"What?"

"Say it."

"All right. All right," the bartender says, exhaling through the pain. "I'm filth!"

"People like you are why people like me exist." He releases the man's hand. "Thank you for revealing yourself. It makes this next part more pleasurable."

"Hey, Smitty . . ." A bald white man approaches wearing a leather motorcycle vest adorned with white supremacist gang patches and insignia. "There a problem here?"

"No problem," Mr. Katz says. "I was just leaving."

"No, you keep your ass right here." The bald man rips the chain with the Star of David pendant from Mr. Katz's neck and throws it on the floor. "I think you got the wrong idea about this place," he says. "We aren't the tolerating type."

"You mean Texas or this roach-infested dive?"

"Both, dickhead."

"Fair enough." Mr. Katz drives his fingers into the man's eyes, then gives him a stiff kick to the groin. The man tumbles backward, collapsing into a table and barstools.

A long-haired member of the biker's crew charges with an empty beer bottle. Mr. Katz slaps the bottle from the man's hand, takes hold of his hair, pulls him to the floor, and stomps the back of his neck.

Mr. Katz looks around for more takers, but the beaten men deter others from joining. He picks up his chain and puts it in his pocket. His visit to the bar wasn't happenstance. The bar's a well-known haven for people who take issue with those of the Jewish faith and anyone not white and straight with claims to be Christian.

Coming to the bar was an occasion to release pent-up frustration so he could think clearly. And who better to use as punching bags than anti-Semites and Nazi sympathizers. Not that he hasn't worked for plenty of them in the past. He's certain the Duchamps have ties to white supremacist factions across the United States; that would make him a hypocrite, too, if he cared. Shallow differences such as skin color, spiritual beliefs, and culture mean little to him. His disdain is for all people, no matter what they look like, who they fuck and vote for, or what and how they worship. His victims are varied—fat, skinny, Black, white, gay, and straight—he's put them all in the ground, and their degrees of misery are predicated on the amount of fight they put up and the amount of hassle they are to kill.

"Thank you," he says to the bartender and then to the men collecting themselves from the floor. "You've helped me a great deal. I know my next course of action. As my mother used to say, if you don't succeed at first, try again."

"Get out of here before I call the cops," the bartender says.

"That would be foolish. But it would allow you to test your theory."

"What fucking theory, you nutcase?"

"Eternal life," Mr. Katz says. "You'd be dead before the cops arrived. How sure are you that living forever is the reward you've earned?"

"Get out of here, dammit!"

"Already leaving." Mr. Katz walks out of the bar and into the humid evening air. He gets into his car and calls Dice.

"What the hell is going on, Richie? Where are you?"

"Outside some Nazi bar."

"What the hell are you doing there?"

"Thinking."

"Richie, this isn't the time to be pulling this shit," Dice says. "Duchamp's people have been calling nonstop. They want to know if this thing is coming to a close."

"Tell them twenty-four hours . . ."

"Another day?"

"Yes."

"What about the delays? They're talking about cutting the last payment in half."

"I'll throw in a discount for any inconvenience my delays have caused."

"We don't discount, Richie. We're known for results."

"And there will be results," he says. "There's been a few hiccups, sure, but everything is on track."

"I don't know about this . . ."

"I don't pay you to know. I pay you to do. Offer the discount—10 percent for each day that the job goes unfinished. That should shut them up." He ends the call.

The bartender and bikers have congregated near the bar's entrance. He counts six, but there could be more. As the men converge on the vehicle, an empty beer bottle shatters against the hood. Another one strikes the passenger-side door. The men shout curses and slurs. Mr. Katz slams on the gas pedal, floors the car onto the road, and drives in the direction of the Bouchard farm, flipping the men the bird out the window.

• • •

When he arrives at the barn, he sees a familiar-looking Explorer. He gets out of the car and checks the license plate. It's state-issued, and the plate number matches the Explorer driven by Ranger Adams, but she's nowhere in sight. He looks through the windows and notes clean seats, and the vehicle is unlocked.

Back at his car, he loads a magazine into his Ruger, slips additional magazines into notches on his gun belt, then returns to the barn. He shines his flashlight around the barn. Mice scurry, along with roaches. He thinks Adams wouldn't have left her vehicle unattended unless her entry point was nearby, but he sees no other way in and out of the barn.

Ms. Bouchard's voice pierces the quiet; it's faint, almost a whisper. He exits the barn with his hand on the Ruger, shining the flashlight at the abandoned Explorer, then moves around the building. Still, no one is in sight, but he knows he heard talking. He's slightly tipsy from the beers but not drunk enough to conjure voices in his head.

After walking the barn's perimeter a third time, he goes inside, stomps hard, and listens closely. Detecting a hollowness in the ground, he kicks away dirt and debris and shines the light on the hatch. He reaches down and pries it open. Ms. Bouchard's voice is clearer now and is coming from inside the hole. He turns off the flashlight and waits until her voice fades. Certain she's gone, he turns the flashlight back on and climbs into the tunnel. He walks until the tunnel ends, and another hatch is visible above him, slightly open. He climbs the ladder, and pulls himself out of the darkness.

"Don't you move," Ms. Bouchard says, pointing the shotgun at Mr. Katz. "Who the hell are you?"

"I don't want to hurt you," Mr. Katz says.

"Hurt me? Then you've never seen what this thing can do at close range."

"I'm afraid you misunderstand," he says, aiming the Ruger and firing from the hip. The bullet slices into Ms. Bouchard's flank. She collapses on the ground, dropping the shotgun. Blood seeps from the wound; she struggles to breathe. "This is not a negotiation. Tell me where Al Bouchard is, or the next bullet goes through your skull."

"Last place I saw him was the grave." She presses her palm into her wound and grimaces. "I reckon he's still there."

He aims the barrel slightly above her nose. "Your attempt to protect him is futile."

"He's not the one I'm protecting."

A bullet strikes Mr. Katz's shoulder. He drops to his knees and looks toward the garage's entrance. Nia stands holding her pistol. "Can you get up, Ms. Bouchard?" she asks.

"I can try." Ms. Bouchard rolls over on her stomach, tucks her knees, and slowly rises. "Where's Amora?"

"Inside," Nia says. "Go to her. I'll deal with him."

"Deal with me?" Mr. Katz says. "You've got no idea what you've done, Adams."

"Says the man shot and bleeding."

"I should've killed you back in Ellis," he says, gripping his wound.

"You could have tried... Now, drop the gun and take four steps back."

He slowly places the Ruger on the floor and steps away. "Aren't you going to call it in?" he asks. "You caught me, the Devil of Waxahachie, the Ellis County Butcher. I'm sure it's a crowning achievement for a woman of your station."

"Shut up," Nia says, moving toward the abandoned Ruger. "You move, and I shoot you."

"I thought we already established that." Mr. Katz is limber on the balls of his feet and bides his time. "Although, I must commend you," he says, watching her every movement. "But even after all you've done, they still won't remember you. Not the way you want, anyway."

"Wasn't it enough to kill them? You had to rape the girl." She tries to pull the Ruger across the floor with her foot, but the unfinished cement inhibits the weapon from sliding easily. "Don't move," she says, keeping her gun aimed at his chest as she reaches for the Ruger. Mr. Katz steps to his left. "I said don't fucking move!"

Nia grips the Ruger. Mr. Katz leaps forward, slamming his shoulder into her body and sending her to the ground. Both guns drop from her hands. She scrambles for the weapons.

He mounts her, pulls his bowie knife from his pocket, and drives it toward her chest. "Perhaps I was wrong before," he says, drooling like a hungry wolf. "They will remember you, but not for stopping me . . . as another victim," he says. "Another name in my collection."

The sharp edge grazes Nia's skin. He presses the blade further; it digs into her flesh. She screams in pain, then drives her knee upward into his chest, knocking the wind out of him. He gasps. Nia works her legs free, slips from underneath his body, and gets to her feet. He reaches for her leg but isn't fast enough to take hold.

"I'm going to kill you," he shouts. "You're all fucking dead!"

She runs toward the back porch and enters the house.

"Fucking hell," he says, sitting up. He removes his suit jacket to get a better look at his wound. A lump of flesh is missing from his shoulder, ripped away by hot lead, and the shoulder is bleeding profusely. He removes his belt and notches it around his arm as a tourniquet. Sitting back on his haunches, he sighs. Maybe this is it, he thinks. Time to call it on account of rain. He's never left a job unfinished; he's never had to deal with a goddamn Texas Ranger, though.

But abandoning a job, especially when he's been hired by a family like the Duchamps, is bad for business. He's under no illusions about the family's capabilities. They've survived this long because of their power and their willingness to do whatever it takes to keep it.

All that matters now is finishing the job and leaving no witnesses behind who could ID him. He slowly stands, picks up his pistol and knife, and begins walking toward the house, blood trailing behind him.

CHAPTER ELEVEN
DESMOND

War has never been a mystery to Desmond. Even before enlisting in the Marine Corps, he understood the nature of warfare. The battlefield existed outside of space and time, somewhere between the pillars of heaven and hell, where men embraced their true selves. It was where he learned who he was, what he was capable of, and the sins he was willing to bear.

War spread like pestilence, blanketing Vietnam and infecting everything it touched. He watched his fellow soldiers stand in line outside a brothel, awaiting sex with a girl no older than sixteen. This was common in the bush. After each soldier had his way with the girl, a mama-san would hand her a warm washcloth and towel, and she'd wash away the stains the men left behind. There were days he thought about helping the girl escape, but he was one man, and the war was a beastly thing. There was no place for her to go. Neither he nor the girl could escape the machine, which was fueled by men in Washington who never set foot on a battlefield.

Even in the still moments, he was haunted by the heinous acts perpetrated by men who called him brother. He dreamed of the mangled and severed limbs of Vietcong. Napalm and cluster bombs that eradicated villages. Field rats larger than most lap dogs nibbling on corpses.

Then there was Mai, who made the days in the death den bearable. And when the time came for him to return to the States, he couldn't imagine leaving her behind. So, on a humid night, they walked hand in hand in the sticky air to a small gathering, miles from the base, where they swore their love for each other in front of Fletch, Mai's siblings, her parents, and her family's priest. It was the happiest day of his life, alongside the birth of Amora, and he knew in that moment that there was no limit to what he'd do to protect his family.

He ties the last of the steel twine around the banister and spray paints a red *X* on the wall. It isn't a sophisticated tactic, but the letter might be enough to distract the men from the trip wires he's secured along the stairs.

He had managed to find the spray paint and twine, along with nails, screws, and ball bearings, in Linh's garage. He filled an empty coffee can with the nails and screws and added broken glass, flour, starch, and gasoline. He drilled a hole in the top of the can, and ran a rope soaked with gas from the can's top to its bottom, where the flammable concoction had settled. Afterward, he cut the power to the building before going back inside, where he shut the blinds, darkening the boardinghouse.

Back in his room, he loads the assault rifle, puts on the night vision goggles affixed to head gear, and peeks out of the window.

A white van with "24/7 RESCUE PLUMBERS" written on its side pulls into the driveway. Four men, dressed in black fatigues and tactical vests and carrying rifles, exit the vehicle.

Seconds later, there's heavy pounding on the front door. He moves into the hallway, positions himself at the corner railing and readies his rifle. The door splinters, then rips from its hinges. Two men enter, brandishing AR-15s, and fan out along the walls. The other two men move across the center of the room, headed for the stairs.

Desmond holds his position. Stays hidden in shadows, studying the men's movements. The shortest man takes point and begins climbing the stairs. He looks at the X painted on the wall and stops with his fist in the air, signaling halt. The other men form a line behind him and together they continue up the stairs. Desmond counts the men's steps, and tightens his grip on his rifle. As the leader nears the booby-trapped step, Desmond aims and prepares to shoot.

The leader's foot catches the wire. As he falls, Desmond shoots twice, striking the man in the torso. The other men open fire, forcing Desmond to retreat further into the hallway. He sets the coffee can turned bomb next to the wall, pulls his Zippo from his pocket, and lights the improvised wick. Two men round the corner and open fire. Desmond quickly ducks into his room and shuts the door. Moments later, there's an ear-piercing cacophony, followed by screams. Desmond opens the door carrying the briefcase of stolen goods. Two men are covered in flames. Nails, screws, and glass are embedded in the walls. He runs across the hallway into Linh's room. He kicks out the window screen, and climbs onto the second-floor balcony. With the rifle strapped to his back, he tosses the briefcase to the ground and lowers himself down the drainage gutter.

He opens the back of the van and gets inside.

The last man emerges from the house, his face blackened from the explosion. He can't walk straight and looks disoriented holding his rifle. Desmond recognizes the signs of shock. The man opens the van's door and gets into the driver's seat. He struggles to put the key into the ignition, barely able to steady his hand. Desmond can see him closely. His face is badly burned, and portions of flesh are missing from his cheeks and jaw. Nails and glass protrude from his shoulder and arm. He gives up, unable to start the van, and slowly pulls a phone from the glove box and dials.

"They're dead," he says, struggling to get the words out. "The target neutralized everyone but me... How should I proceed?"

Desmond's cell phone vibrates in his pocket. The man drops the phone and turns around, looking down the barrel of Desmond's rifle.

"Hang it up," Desmond says. Their eyes meet. "Do it."

The man complies. "Please." His left eye twitches. Desmond is certain the other would be twitching, too, if it weren't burned shut. "I'll tell them we killed you," the man says. "You can walk away. I'll call them off. We won't follow. I promise."

"No," Desmond says. "You won't."

"Please? I have a family."

Desmond shoots the man in the head. Blood sprays onto the dash and windshield, along with brain tissue. "So do I," he says, lowering his gun.

He reads the text on his phone. It's a message from his mother: *Come now.*

He calls his mother. "Ma? What's going on?"

"Al," she says, desperately. "There's a man here. Says he killed Fletch and his family. He says he's going to kill us, too, unless you give back whatever you took."

"Are you and Baby Girl safe?"

"We are right now, but he ain't gonna stop, Al."

"Hold tight. I'm coming."

"And, Al," Ms. Bouchard says, working to calm her nerves, "we aren't alone. There's a cop here, a Ranger Adams."

"Ah, dammit."

"No, she's good people, Al. She saved my life."

"All right, Ma. Can you get to the escape tunnel?"

"Tunnel is no good. We're barricaded in my bedroom. Thought it was the safest place. But I can hear that man downstairs tearing up a storm."

"How are you on bullets?"

"Between the two of us, we're all right. But we're both bleeding badly."

"I'm coming now."

Desmond ends the call, opens the van's door, and shoves the dead man out. He gets behind the wheel, adjusts the seat, and places the briefcase on the floor. The van has half a tank of gas, enough to get him to his family's farm in Austin.

CHAPTER TWELVE
NIA

"We've got to stop the bleeding," Nia says, wrapping Ms. Bouchard's torso with a ripped pillowcase.

"Lord, that hurts." She squeezes her granddaughter's hand. "You have to be so rough?"

"I'm trying to stop the bleeding," Nia says.

"Hell, this is payback, ain't it? I think I'm starting to regret freeing your ass."

"Grammy," Amora snaps. "She saved your life, remember?"

"I know, dear. It's just the pain talking."

Nia ties the pillowcase tighter around the woman's waist, making a knot at her hip. "That should control the bleeding until we can get you help."

"What about you?" Amora asks Nia. "Look at your arm."

Nia had almost forgotten about her knife wound. It's a shallow laceration, and much of the bleeding has stopped. Still, when air finds the exposed tissue, pain registers throughout her arm. "Got any tape?"

"Might be some in the nightstand," Ms. Bouchard says. "Go on and look, Amora."

The girl rushes to the nightstand, opens the drawer, and searches. "Got some," she says, holding up a small roll of silver electrical tape. "Will this work?"

"That'll do." Nia holds her arm up for the girl to wrap.

"We've been fine here for years, and not once did I ever think it might come to this," Ms. Bouchard says, bracing her hand to her wound. "I guess that was naive on my part. Whatever Al's cooked up this time must be bad."

"That's an understatement."

There's a racket downstairs. Nia can feel shaking under her feet. "What's below us?" she asks.

"My office," Ms. Bouchard says.

"How many rooms are downstairs?"

"Three, not including the two bathrooms."

With Amora's help, Nia barricaded the door with a bookcase and TV stand.

"We just have to hold him off until Dad gets here," Amora says, crouching on the floor at the foot of her grandmother's queen-size bed. "Once he comes, that asshole is fucked."

Ms. Bouchard wags her finger in admonishment. "Watch the language, Miss Thang. I didn't raise no heathen."

The girl is grown by all standards, but she's been coddled. Nia thinks chastising her seems trivial, given what they're facing. But even in the midst of death, the girl is expected to exercise proper etiquette, and nothing may be more southern than that.

The noise downstairs grows louder. "Oh, Lord," Amora says, her voice strained by fear. "Sounds like he's tearing a hole in the wall."

"Stay calm," Nia says. "The door will hold."

"And if it doesn't?"

"Don't speak that way," Ms. Bouchard says. "We can't get discouraged. Understand?"

"Yes, ma'am."

Nia looks out of the bedroom's only window and down into the side yard, where grass has failed to grow. "We'll need a contingency plan," she says, steely-eyed. "Just in case . . ."

"What's that supposed to mean?" Ms. Bouchard says.

"It means we must be ready for anything. Can't get caught off guard."

Ms. Bouchard's mouth is dry. In the corners, sticky white has gathered. "But you said the door will hold? You think there's a chance he can get in here?"

"Nothing is absolute," Nia says, returning to the floor. "But I won't be cornered."

"So we're shooting our way out?"

"I didn't say that."

"But you didn't say we weren't, either."

Heavy footsteps boom outside the door. Nia clutches her pistol. She's breathing differently—softer, smoother—not as hard as when she and Powers breached Colonial Trust Bank. Maybe she's gotten used to the cortisol dump, the prickly bumps at the base of her neck, and the tingle in her chest—it all makes her sharper and more attuned, and it slows time so she can think.

The doorknob rattles.

"Oh my God, it's him," Amora says, pressing her stomach to the floor. "Why can't you just shoot him through the door?"

There's more doorknob rattling, followed by pounding.

"What if I miss or don't kill him?" Nia asks in a whisper. "It's too big a risk. The only thing keeping him from us is that door. I blast it to hell, and we're done for."

"Amora's right," Ms. Bouchard says. "Shooting first ain't a bad idea.

Here . . ." She offers Nia her shotgun. "This'll blast a hole right through him."

"No," Nia says, keeping her pistol low. "We need to stay quiet, so we don't give away our position."

The pounding on the door grows heavier and shakes the walls. "You're only delaying the inevitable," Katz says. "Come out, and I promise it will be painless." There's the sound of running, then bashing against the door.

Nia aims her pistol, prepared to fire if he breaches the door.

"You're a fool, Ranger . . . ," Katz says.

"He's got to have the devil in him," Ms. Bouchard says. ". . . crazier than an alley cat."

"I will rip this fucking door from its hinges," Katz screams till he goes hoarse.

Ms. Bouchard offers Nia the shotgun again. "Take it. Shoot him before it's too late."

"Just keep quiet," she says. "Trust me."

"All right," Katz says, clearing his throat. "So be it . . ."

He backs away from the door.

Silence.

"Did he leave?" Amora asks. "He wouldn't just give up like that, right?"

"No, he wouldn't," Nia says. "We need to get out of this room."

"How do you propose we do that?" Ms. Bouchard slowly gets to her feet. "Only way out is the window."

Nia removes the comforter and blanket from Ms. Bouchard's bed, strips off the sheets, and begins tying the bedding together.

"You're not serious . . ."

"If he wanted us out, he would've kept up with the door," Nia says, tying the tip of the blanket to a sheet. "He's got other plans."

Amora blinks as if dust is in her eye. "What do you mean, 'if he wanted us out'?"

"He knows we're trapped in here."

"And your idea is for us to climb out of the window? My grandmother can't do that. Look at her."

"We may not have a choice," Nia says, tying the last of the bedsheets into a knotted rope. It might hold her and Amora, but she isn't sure about Ms. Bouchard.

Katz returns to the door and begins pouring liquid through the threshold.

"What is that? What's he doing?" Amora asks.

The women move to the furthest corner of the room, near the window.

"Last chance," Katz says. "Come out, or I torch this entire fucking house."

Nia steps closer to the door and crouches down. "It's liquor."

Ms. Bouchard struggles to open the window. "We can't die in here."

"But Grammy," Amora says, the lilt in her voice suggesting a greater level of fear. "How are you going to get down?"

"I'll find a way. Now, come help with this window." Amora helps Ms. Bouchard open the window. "My F-150 is parked in front of the house," she says, already out of breath. "We'll have to cut through the side fence."

"Keys?" Nia asks.

"Under the floor mat . . ."

Nia can't imagine leaving her keys inside her vehicle, but Austin has a reputation for having little crime—it's nearly nonexistent. But that reputation might change after tonight.

"That's a good hundred feet, Grammy . . ."

"I can make it."

Nia smells burning. Katz struck a match. She quickly ties the sheet to the bed frame and tosses the improvised rope out of the window. "Amora, you go first. Your grandmother will follow, and I'll climb down last."

"You stupid bitch," Katz says. "You brought this on yourself. So much for quick and painless."

"Let's move," Nia says, giving Amora the rope.

Flames spread under the door, across the carpet, and inch up the walls to the ceiling.

Amora throws her leg over the windowsill and starts her descent. Nia keeps the rope steady while monitoring the flames. The smoke grows thicker by the second. It's becoming difficult to see.

Ms. Bouchard coughs; her eyes water. "What about the shotgun?" she asks.

"I've got it," Nia says. She's relieved when Amora's feet safely touch the ground. "It's your turn, Ms. Bouchard." She ties the rope around the injured woman's waist, hoping it'll give her more support.

Ms. Bouchard coughs more. This time, wheezing sets in. "Never been one for heights," she says, firmly gripping the rope with a tremble.

"Once you're down, I'll give you the shotgun." Nia helps her over the windowsill and begins to lower Ms. Bouchard down. "The second you're on the ground, you and Amora get to the truck. Don't wait on me." The strain sets in as Nia tries to control the speed of Ms. Bouchard's drop. Her arms tighten, muscles flare, and her grip slightly loosens.

"Ranger?" Ms. Bouchard sounds rattled. "You got it?"

"Everything's fine. Keep going," Nia says, leaning backward with a slight bend in her legs. The flames spread to the dresser, travel along the baseboards, and begin to overtake the nightstand. She can feel the heat at her back moving nearer.

"You dead yet?" Katz says.

Nia's surprised to hear him outside the door. She thought he would've fled to watch the burning from outside. The fire must be localized to the room. If she can keep him inside, it'll give Ms. Bouchard and Amora more time to get to the truck; it's best to keep him talking. "Still here, mutherfucker! Damn shame that you are too."

"Defiant to the bitter fucking end—that's the spirit, Adams."

Nia coughs and tries to steady the rope. "My heart just needs to beat long enough to kill you," she says. "Which I promise I'll enjoy."

"I respect your unwillingness to lay down and die for these people, but fuck, if you're not delusional. Two or three minutes is all you've got before that smoke suffocates you. That's if you don't burn to death first."

Ms. Bouchard is inches from the ground when Nia sucks in smoke, coughs hard, and unwittingly loosens her grip, sending the woman to the ground with a *thud*.

"My leg!" Ms. Bouchard shouts.

Nia looks out of the window and sees Ms. Bouchard rolling in pain. "Shit," she says, dreading the extent of her injury.

"It's her ankle," Amora says, untying the sheet from around her grandmother's waist. "I think it might be broken."

"Dammit . . . All right, I'm coming down." Nia pulls the rope up into the room, wraps it around her right wrist, then steps off the windowsill with the shotgun. She quickly rappels down the side of the house, the way she did in Ranger School, and settles on the ground.

"It looks bad," Amora says.

Nia examines Ms. Bouchard's swollen ankle. There's heavy fluid from the ankle to the knee. "Can you try to walk?"

They help Ms. Bouchard to her feet, but she can hardly stand.

"Come on, Grammy."

Flames explode through the window. Scorched debris sails into the night sky, landing dangerously close to the women. "We have to hurry."

Nia and Amora support Ms. Bouchard's arms on their shoulders as she takes a step. "Oh, Lord . . ." She winces. "I can't do it."

"We can make it," Amora says. "It's like you told me, Grammy. We can't get discouraged . . . we can't give up."

"Baby Girl," she says. "I'm sorry for all this."

"You've got nothing to be sorry about, Grammy."

"I tried to do right by you . . . I promised your father that I would. But I got old, sweetheart. I should've known this day would come."

"This isn't the time," Nia says. "Keep moving."

"It's all right, Grammy. We're going to be just fine," Amora says, supporting her grandmother up with her hip. "One foot after the other . . . Just like that . . ."

Nia sees the late-model truck parked in front of the house through the chain-link fence. It's close enough, but at the speed they're moving, they'll be exposed for too long trying to reach it.

"Stay here," Nia says. "I'm going to get the truck."

"If it doesn't start up right away, just keep at it," Ms. Bouchard says.

"Hurry." Amora struggles to keep her grandmother supported.

Nia opens the fence's gate and sprints across the front lawn to the truck. She gets into the driver's seat. Placing the shotgun on the floor, she reaches under the floor mat and finds the key. She depresses the foot brake and turns the key in the ignition. The truck struggles to start. "Come on, baby," Nia says. Black smoke seeps from the tailpipe. She turns the key again, harder. It backfires and starts with a roar.

She shifts into drive, gases the truck, and floors it across the lawn toward the gate. She gets out and opens the passenger-side door. "Let's get her inside," Nia says, helping Ms. Bouchard take the final few steps to the truck.

The house is engulfed in flames.

"Come on, Grammy. You've got this," Amora says, lifting her grandmother's leg onto the floor of the truck.

"God bless you both," Ms. Bouchard says, sliding onto the seat.

Nia looks at the binding around her body. It's blood-soaked near the knot. Ms. Bouchard has lost a significant amount of blood. She may die if she doesn't get to a hospital soon.

Once Ms. Bouchard is settled in the truck, Amora climbs into the middle seat, followed by Nia behind the wheel. She shuts the door and speeds toward the road.

"The house," she says, looking back as the fire consumes the remaining wood and brick.

"It's okay, Grammy," Amora says. "See, you were right. We did it—we're out!"

"We need to get your grandmother to a hospital," Nia says. "You know the closest?"

"Saint Martin's off Farmington Road."

"You know how to get there?"

"I think so," she says. "I'm not the best with directions."

"You all right, Ms. Bouchard?"

"I can make it." Ms. Bouchard sighs like a weight has been lifted. "Thank the Lord," she says. "We're going to be all—"

A bullet shatters the passenger-side window, enters Ms. Bouchard's skull, and exits from her left eye socket. Her body slumps over into Amora's lap, and she screams in horror.

"Grammy! No! No!" She cradles her dead grandmother in her arms. "God, no. Please, God!"

Another bullet shatters the rear window.

"Get down," Nia says, taking a sharp turn to evade the gunfire.

The rear tire blows out. The truck crashes into the front porch. Nia's head smacks against the window. She's veering in and out of consciousness.

The passenger door opens. Katz pushes Ms. Bouchard's body to the floor and takes hold of Amora, yanking her from the seat.

Blood collects in Nia's right eye. She reaches for the shotgun on the floor. Ms. Bouchard's body is pinned against the weapon. She can't reach the handle and instead, pulls her pistol from the holster, aims the gun at Katz's back but doesn't take a shot, fearing she might hit Amora.

She watches helplessly as Katz carries a screaming Amora over his shoulder toward the road.

"Amora!" Nia shouts. "Fight! You have to fight!"

Flames spread around the truck. Nia smells gasoline. She gathers the strength to open the door and get out. Fire surrounds her feet. She moves away from the truck and starts walking in the direction of Katz and Amora.

Moments later, the farmhouse's roof collapses. The facade breaks free, folds onto the truck, and erupts into flames.

Nia reaches the edge of the road and loses sight of Katz and Amora. The girl's screams resonate in the distance. Nia's body is failing. A sharp pain burns in her hip and pinches her thigh. The pain intensifies, and she's unable to move. Her eyes are growing heavy. She drops to her knees; she can't take another step.

The fire rages as her world fades to black.

• • •

Sirens wail in the distance.

Nia awakens to Desmond standing over her, holding an assault rifle. "It's you . . ."

"Where's my family?" he asks.

Desmond takes hold of her arm and tries to pull her up. "Shit. I can't move," she says. A wooden shard protrudes from her leg. She grips the splintered wood. "I need it out." She sucks in the air and her cheeks balloon.

"Don't," he says. "It's too deep. You'll bleed to death in minutes."

She exhales, falling back to the ground. "Leave me for the medics."

"I can't do that."

"I said leave me!"

He bends down, slips his arms around her waist, and begins dragging her across the lawn.

"Get the hell off me!" Nia swings, desperate to land a blow. Each time her heels bumps along the rocky field, blood spurts from the wound. "Let me go, dammit!"

"We don't have time for this."

He opens the van's sliding door and forces her onto the first bench.

"Do you know what you're doing?" she asks. "You're abducting a Texas Ranger." More blood pours from the wound; she moans.

"I can't be here when the police arrive." Desmond gets into the driver's seat. "And you have information I need."

"Where are you taking me?"

"Tell me where my family is."

She swallows hard and looks back at the burning house. "It was Katz . . . ," she begins. "He killed your mother and took Amora."

"Took her where?"

"I tried to stop him, but my leg . . ."

"Tell me where they went!"

"I don't know," she says. "He carried her off, and I lost sight of them."

Desmond pounds his knee with his fist. Emits a guttural noise, more beast than human. When the pummeling stops, he appears numb. "Where's my mother's body?"

Nia points to the F-150. Flames curl and twist throughout the cabin. "I'm sorry."

His jaw rattles, and right cheek twitches uncontrollably. He's on the verge of imploding, she thinks.

"He couldn't have carried her very far."

"He might've had his car waiting," Nia says.

"You know what he drives? Can you point it out if we see it?"

"Yes."

"Good—you're not completely useless."

The van eases off the property and onto the road, headed away from the lights and sirens.

"You should turn yourself in," Nia says. "Let the law do what we're trained to do."

"The police can't help me. Tonight is proof of that."

Nia tries not to lose her cool. Reminds herself that he's just lost his mother and daughter. "I'm sorry about your family, but it has nothing to do with me. I risked my life for them. Tried like hell to get them to safety. And we would've made it had it not been for—"

"Katz."

"Yes," she says. "Katz."

"He's the one who killed Fletch's family?"

"We believe so." The gruesome details are still fresh in Nia's mind. Fletch and his wife bloody and left to be found in their bedroom. Fontaine lying dead on her bed, face down on a pillow. Images that will haunt her until her last day.

Desmond asks, "What else do you have on him besides a name?"

"Nothing," she says. "But he's a pro. Resourceful. Determined. Well-funded . . . Whoever hired him has deep pockets. But you need to be straight with me. Tell me what you stole and whom you stole it from."

"That doesn't matter anymore."

"What the hell are you saying, 'it doesn't matter.' Can't you see what's happening?"

Desmond pulls over on the side of the highway and parks. He stares at Nia in the rearview. A single tear punctuates his stark reality: dead mother, kidnapped daughter. She wonders how a man like Desmond was shaped—the shades of violence, the unknowns—what has he lived through? And what's keeping him from breaking down?

"You think I don't see what I've brought on my family? I'm living through an ungodly clusterfuck. It hurts so much that I don't even know what to do with it. It's eating me from the inside out." He taps his fist against his chest. "What I've got in here is atomic, but it's all I've got. You understand? I can't grieve—I can't let go. All I want . . . all I can think about is killing the people responsible."

"Katz?"

"And the mutherfuckers who hired him."

"Then tell me who they are," she says. "And what is it you took from them? We can work together."

Desmond turns on the interior light, picks up the briefcase from the floor, and hands it to Nia. "See for yourself."

She opens the case, expecting to see rare gems or uncut diamonds that might warrant all the death, but the contents appear unremarkable. She investigates the satchel of tarnished coins. "Gold?"

"Keep looking."

She picks up the manifest, slides it out of the protective sleeve, turns the fragile pages, and reads. "Catchy Creek Plantation? It's a museum now."

"Wasn't back then."

She struggles to see in the dull light. "It's a slave ledger? This is real?" She focuses on a single name. "For the Estate of Sir Conrad Duchamp."

"The Duchamps have owned Colonial Trust for centuries but managed to keep it quiet, mostly with shell companies, part of larger conglomerates. It made it hard to track the bank back to them. Especially when most people don't think of a family owning a bank."

"You're saying the richest family in Texas is behind this?"

"Deep pockets, like you said. Whose pockets are deeper than those mutherfuckers?"

"Okay, so you're plan is to kill the Duchamps?"

"I'll take that." He reaches for the case. "Might be the only thing keeping that crazy bastard from hurting my daughter."

Nia puts the manifest and coins back in the case and closes it. "I'll help you get her back," she says, handing him the case. "But I can't let you go after the Duchamps."

"You on their payroll, too?"

"Hell no. Of course not. But they need to be arrested and brought to justice if they're guilty. You can't expect me to stand by while you assassinate—"

"Dr. King . . . Bobby Kennedy. They were assassinated. The Duchamps are crooks in fucking khakis. Goddamn killers hiding behind their money, but I've got bullets for each of them."

"Going after that family is suicide."

"It's like this, Adams... I kill whoever green-lit Katz or die trying. And I wouldn't recommend you getting in my way."

Nia has spent hours in interrogation rooms with men like Desmond, who speak with conviction, strike out when cornered, and embrace the carnage that follows. Men who refuse paths to contrition, never seeking to unburden themselves, even when facing death sentences. They maintain a constant discord between decency and their desire for brutality. Born in the wrong era, these men are better suited to be primitive warriors and hunters, defending and providing food for their villages.

"And Amora?" she asks. "What happens to her while you're in prison?"

"Who said anything about prison?" He turns around in his seat, shoulders hunched. "Enough talk. Let's go."

"I need this thing out of my leg. And since hospitals are out of the question..."

"I'll fix you up."

"What do you mean you'll fix it? Are you a doctor now?"

"I'm trained in field medicine."

"Right, you got that training in the military."

"You want your leg patched or not?"

"I do."

"On one condition."

"And what's that?"

"There is nothing I won't do to get my daughter back," he says. "I will remove any obstacle in my way."

"Does that mean killing a Ranger?"

"Like I said, there is nothing I won't do. Are we clear?"

"Fucking crystal... Just get this damn thing out of my leg."

CHAPTER THIRTEEN
MR. KATZ

For Mr. Katz, Houston's historic Sunnyside community is fucking Disneyland. He's never seen a place so ignored, so forgotten. It's home to Reed Dump, seventy-eight acres of land for waste disposal. Hundreds of bodies have been found in and near the dump, underscoring its convenience to the high-crime, poverty-stricken area.

He has conducted his last three jobs out of a two-bedroom rental home on one of Sunnyside's most undesirable streets. Having constructed a "kill room" in the home's basement with plastic sheeting, he's murdered two victims without worry about discovery. Removed their teeth and hands, then disposed of their bodies near the dump. Given the neighborhood's reputation, the murders received little news coverage, and the police investigation was overshadowed by a gangland killing the following week.

The predominantly Black and Latino neighborhood is volatile, and despite being the only white person for blocks, Mr. Katz is at ease. He drives down the poorly lit street, where people loiter on corners, smoking, drinking, and moving dope from hand to hand. His car's darkly tinted windows help ensure his anonymity, and when a local does catch a glimpse of him, he's certain they think he's a cop. Undercover, maybe. Working on some special operation. They've suspended dealing drugs in front of his rental home, and foot traffic has dwindled. While police roust corner boys, raid trap houses, and arrest prostitutes for solicitation, Mr. Katz hides in plain sight, free to operate as he pleases.

He pulls into the driveway of the rundown house, opens the garage door remotely, and drives in. Like most of the homes in the neighborhood, the house has been neglected and needs repairs. But its large basement offers generous square footage and took him four hours to soundproof.

He opens the trunk and lifts the girl out. Her mouth is sealed with electrical tape; her wrists bound with it too.

Dice enters from the basement. He's a tall, slender man with arms covered in tattoos: pentagrams, skulls, and a devil with its tongue out. His pointed nose and chin make him a dead ringer for Mr. Punch, the comedically brutal puppet from the Punch-and-Judy show. Growing up, Mr. Katz watched the puppet show in a small loft near Royal Air Force Croughton in Britain, where his father was stationed.

"This wasn't what we agreed," Dice says.

"I improvised."

"Do you know the fucking heat this is going to bring? It's kidnapping."

"Keep your voice down," he says, carrying Amora into the partially furnished basement—a TV is balanced on cases of beer in front of a stained yellow sofa. Mr. Katz drops the squirming Amora onto the cushions.

"You're bleeding," Dice says.

"No shit . . . Get me the handcuffs."

"Handcuffs?"

"You want her running off?"

"Get them yourself. I don't want any part of this."

Mr. Katz walks to a large box, digs inside, and removes cuffs, a bike chain, and a lock.

"What are you going to do with her?" Dice asks.

"This little peach is going to tell me how to reach our friend, Al Bouchard, aren't you?" He pokes Amora's ribs. She screams through the gag. "And if she doesn't . . . her stay here will be a short one."

"Man, we need to talk." Dice takes him by the arm and pulls him a few feet from the girl. "What the hell are you thinking bringing her here? You've got no business involving civilians."

Mr. Katz snatches his arm away. "You calling the shots now? I told you I'd finish the job, and that's what I'm doing."

"How exactly does snatching a girl help us get the goods back?"

"He'll come for her."

"How can you be so sure?"

"Because she's his daughter. And unless she's been resurrected, he faked her death the same as his own. She was living a few acres up the road with her grandmother near the Bouchards' old farm."

"So the address checked out?"

Mr. Katz nods. "There was a barn there. Somebody had dug a tunnel inside it."

"What kind of a tunnel?"

"Figure it was for escaping. Didn't do them much good, though."

"This is a fucking mess," Dice says. "I don't know what's gotten into you, but you're off, man. I mean, that business in Ellis and now this."

"What the hell do you know about Ellis?"

"They're saying the girl was," he lowers his voice, "raped."

"The job got done. What's it matter?"

"Fuck, man." He looks at Amora, still squirming on the sofa. "That's what you're into now?"

"You're judging me? After all the people you've slaughtered."

"None of them children," Dice says. "And I for damn sure didn't rape anyone."

"Congratulations. You're a real credit to humanity. The contract killer wants a prize for his modest decency." Mr. Katz walks back to Amora. He cuffs her leg to the bike chain, then locks the chain around a metal support beam. He looks back at Dice. "Tell yourself whatever you want if it'll make you sleep better at night, but we both know you're no better than me. The only difference is I know what I am—a goddamn predator—and they're the prey. Fucking sheep. How they die doesn't matter. And when you stop treating them as anything more than numbers, you'll be better off."

"You're fucked-up," he says. "What was I thinking getting into business with a freakshow like you?"

Mr. Katz can feel it. The fever starts in his gut, then rises around his neck and beats inside his head. He thinks about hurting Dice—taking a knife to him, cutting him enough so that he remembers he's cattle, too. "I'm going upstairs," he says. "Keep an eye on her."

"She's chained up. Where the hell can she go?"

"Well, then, Mr. Bleeding Heart. I'm sure she's hungry. Feed her. Give her some water. Make her comfortable. Otherwise, shut the fuck up."

Mr. Katz goes upstairs, leaving Dice to tend to the girl. He goes into the kitchen, takes a bottle of cheap bourbon from the cabinet, and carries it into the bathroom. He removes his jacket and shirt. The wound hasn't stopped bleeding. He looks it over in the vanity mirror. Adams's bullet did a little more than graze his shoulder, but he'll live. He washes away the blood with a washcloth and takes a sip of bourbon. He douses the wound with liquor once he's worked up the nerve. The surge of pain nearly sends him to the floor.

"Fuck!" His body shakes; he grabs the sink's edge and waits for the pain to pass.

After drinking more of the liquor, he applies greasy ointment to the wound and covers it with a bandage. He sits on the edge of the tub and keeps drinking.

The room is at full tilt when he slips into the scum-lined tub. It might be the liquor or the shock, reality is slipping and he's fading into nothingness.

• • •

The front door slams. Mr. Katz nearly jolts out of his skin. There's no telling how long he's been out. He climbs out of the tub and spills onto the floor. He struggles to get up from the slippery tile, his legs heavy. Reaching for the door, he takes hold of the knob and turns. The door opens, and he crawls into the hallway.

At the end of the hallway stands Dice, at the front door. "What are you doing?" Mr. Katz asks. "Where's the girl?"

"I let her go."

"You did what?"

"She's gone."

Mr. Katz works to stand, stumbles into the wall, then steadies himself. "Get out of my way." He tries to step past Dice in pursuit of Amora. Dice pushes him back to the floor.

"It's too late," Dice says. "You won't get to her."

"You idiot. Do you know what you've done? She's all we had to bargain with."

"Find another way."

"Another way?" He stands, bracing against the wall to steady himself. "You goddamn fool. There is no other way."

"Then it ends. Tell the Duchamps it's over, and they can fuck off."

"A fine time to get a backbone." Mr. Katz reaches into his pocket and pulls out his knife. "A little late, though." He lunges at Dice and sticks the knife into his neck. Blood pumps from his neck like a geyser; he collapses to the floor and convulses.

Mr. Katz steps over his body on his way out the front door. From the doorway, he sees Amora running down the street. She's too far ahead for him to catch on foot. He goes back into the house and downstairs to the garage. He gets into the car, impatiently waits for the garage door to open, then reverses down the driveway into the street. He flicks on his high beams and scans the night. He sees her cut across a home's dead lawn and into a backyard. He circles the block, eyes peeled for the girl in a flowered T-shirt and denim.

As he rounds a corner, she appears again, moving slowly. She looks out of breath.

He pulls alongside her and rolls the window down. "Get in the fucking car!"

"Go to hell," she says, keeping to a moderate jog. "My father is going to kill you."

"About that . . ." He hangs his arm casually out the window. "What do you say we go back to the house and call him before things get further out of hand."

"I'm not going anywhere with you."

"You won't make it out here alive," he says smugly. "These crackheads and pimps will sniff you out in an instant."

"I'll take my chances."

"This might be hard to believe, but you're safer with me."

"Leave me alone, asshole!"

"I've got no intention of hurting you, Amora. You're worthless to me if you're dead."

Red and blue lights flash up ahead. A police car idles in the distance. Amora notices and picks up speed.

"Don't do it," Mr. Katz warns.

She begins waving her arms, trying to get the officers' attention. "Hey! Help!"

"Stupid, girl. You're digging your own grave."

"Thought you weren't going to kill me."

"You force my hand, and I'll do worse than kill you—"

"Fuck you." Amora breaks into a sprint, headed for the police car at the end of the street.

Mr. Katz accelerates and keeps on her heels.

"Help! Please, help!" Amora's arms pump furiously. "Please, officers!"

The police stand over a man dressed in a frayed winter coat despite the warm evening. He's lying under an overpass and doesn't appear to be moving. Maybe he's dead or drunk. A female officer, a petite redhead, nudges the man's foot, and he stirs.

Katz speeds up, gaining on Amora. She looks back, petrified. The terror in her eyes thrills him. His stomach tingles, and he grins, convinced his excitement is what big game hunters feel when they're closing in on their prey. He contemplates clipping her leg with the bumper. Not to kill her, but enough that she loses her footing and falls to the concrete.

No . . . it's too risky with the cops nearby, he thinks. He slows down, keeping under the speed limit, allowing Amora to reach the police.

He parks a block away and watches her interact with the officers, both of whom have their hands at their waists as Amora talks. She looks to be growing more agitated and points to his car. It's time he made an introduction, but his shirtless and disheveled appearance won't lend credibility. He reaches into the back seat for his duffel bag, unzips it, removes a black collared shirt, and puts it on, careful of his wounded arm. He spits on his thumb and rubs away the blood that's dried on his neck.

He drives closer and lowers the window. "Evening, officers," he says.

The other officer, a broad-shouldered Black man, stands bowlegged with a hand on his hip. "It's almost midnight," the officer says. His redheaded partner watches intently.

Mr. Katz looks at his watch. Dice's blood is splattered on its face. "Would you look at that," he says. "You're right. It's been a long day. Don't know if I'm coming or going."

"It's him," Amora says. "That's the man who took me."

The officer assumes a strong stance—gun leg back and his hand on his weapon. "How about you step out of the car and show us some ID."

"Certainly." Mr. Katz opens the door and gets out of the car. "This is just a big misunderstanding. That young lady is my responsibility."

"That doesn't seem to be going well for you. Care to explain?"

"Sure," he says, taking his wallet from his back pocket. "I'm her social worker, and the state has charged me to return her to a facility in Dallas so she can get the care she needs."

"He's lying," she says. "There's nothing wrong with me! Please, go to the house. You'll see. There's a basement with plastic. He's killed people there, I know it."

"Such a vivid imagination," Katz says. "It really is a gift most of the time. Just not at midnight, know what I mean?"

"Tell them the truth, asshole."

"Hold on a second, Miss," the officer says.

Mr. Katz hands the officer his driver's license.

"You say you're a social worker with the state?"

"Left my badge in my sports coat. I'm happy to go retrieve it if you don't mind waiting with her. Fair warning, she can be a handful when she's off her meds."

"I'm not on any damn meds," Amora says. "Please, take me in, and I can prove everything at the station."

"No one's going anywhere yet." The officer examines Mr. Katz's license and then hands it to his partner. "Go ahead and run it."

The redhead sits in the passenger seat and pecks keys on what looks like a word processor mounted to the dashboard. Mr. Katz knows his alias is clean, but he never appreciates having his information run in any law enforcement database.

"Sir, what exactly are you doing in this neighborhood?" the officer asks.

"I thought Amora here might visit Sunnyside. A lot of our runners seek out family members and friends."

The officer looks at Amora. "That true?" he asks. "You have people around here?"

"I've never been here in my life. I mean, this is my first time..." She stutters. "I don't understand. Why don't you arrest him? I told you he's dangerous. He kills people."

"The only thing I kill is time," Mr. Katz jokes. "Usually with a crossword or Sudoku."

"People don't come to this neighborhood unless they know someone," the officer says. "How'd you say you got here?"

"He brought me in the trunk of his car—that car," she says, pointing at the Buick.

His partner returns with Mr. Katz's license. "He's clean."

"You can give the gentleman back his license."

The redhead hands Mr. Katz his license. "Thank you," he says. "I really am sorry about all this."

"I can show you where he kept me in the basement," Amora says. "It's a house a few blocks over."

"You got an address?" the officer asks.

"What?"

"An address for the house... Do you have one?"

"No."

"Do you at least know the street the house is on?"

"I... I don't know. But I know what it looks like."

"No offense, Officer," Mr. Katz says. "But I wouldn't be in this neighborhood unless I had to be. I got lucky when I saw her running along the road."

"How long have you been looking for her?" the officer asks.

"A few hours... maybe longer. As I said, it's been a long day. Now, if it's all the same to you, I'd like to get Amora back to her facility and under the care of her physicians."

Amora pleads: "You have to listen to me. He's lying. My grandmother is dead because of him."

"You're saying this man killed your grandmother?"

"Yes," she says emphatically. "He's the Ellis County Butcher."

"This again?" Mr. Katz chuckles. "The other day, she accused me of being a Terminator sent from the future."

The officer rolls his eyes. "Look, Miss, I can have a unit come get you and carry you to the station, but it'll be a wait. We're a skeleton crew tonight."

"That isn't necessary," Mr. Katz says. "I'm happy to get my badge and prove to you that I am who I say I am."

"Where's the badge?"

"Back in my motel room about fifteen minutes away."

"Afraid we can't hang around for that long."

"Please, Officer," Amora says. "Just take me to the station. I'll be safe at the station."

"Officers, this isn't the first time she's run. I found her in Las Vegas a year ago. She's a good kid. Misguided but good. I wish she understood that we're trying to help her."

"This can't be happening . . ." Amora buries her face in her hands. "Why aren't you believing me?"

A static-laden call comes over the patrol car's radio. The officer turns to his partner: "Patsy, check that out, will you?"

The redhead sits in the passenger seat of the patrol car and listens. "Code 3." She bangs on the car's hood. "We gotta roll, partner."

"Look, Miss, seems like Mr. Katz is trying to work with you. How about you two figure this out?"

"No," Amora grabs onto the officer's arm. "I'm begging you. You have to help me."

He shoves Amora to the ground and snatches his Mace canister from his Sam Browne. "Have you lost your goddamn mind? Don't ever grab an officer like that. I have the mind to hook you up for assault on a peace officer."

Amora is drained. "Please, just take me in," she says, pulling bits of glass and gravel from her palms. "Otherwise, I'm dead. Get it? Fucking dead."

"Partner," the redhead says, "we need to get moving."

"Un-fucking believable . . . Best of luck with this one, Mr. Katz." He looks at Amora as though he wants to upchuck. "Let us know if she runs again. It'd be my pleasure to put an APB out on her ass."

Amora stands, and brushes debris from her knees. "I'm not crazy! You have to help me."

"I suggest you both be on your way." The officer gets into the patrol car. The lights spin red and blue. Sirens blare. The patrol car peels out in a cloud of smoke. Amora and Katz stare at each other in the dark.

Amora backs away from him. "Don't you come near me."

"Pull something like that again . . ." He steps toward her. "And I'll—"

"I said stay back!" She raises her fists.

"You've got a strong will. It's commendable." He smiles; her antics amuse him—turn him on, too. "But you fail to see. I'm not the bad guy—not some villain in a fairytale. I'm a sanctified horror show. Pain is all I've ever known and all I will know. And when I get inspired, I dream up ways to explore that pain with people like you. The thing is, once I get started, I can't stop. So, I'm giving you one more chance, that way we don't have to journey down that road. Return to the house so we can contact your father, and when he brings me what I need, you'll be free."

"And if I don't?"

Mr. Katz opens the passenger door. "Think about your old man," he says. "Losing both mother and daughter? That's enough to break anyone."

Amora's face sours. "You're a monster."

"No argument there."

She walks toward the car. "And Dice? You kill him too?"

"He made his choice. Hopefully, you'll choose more wisely."

CHAPTER FOURTEEN

DESMOND

Desmond pulls the piece of wood from Nia's leg; she lets out a deafening scream. The air smells of blood. He thinks of Nam. Fallen men. Mowed down by gunfire, bodies blown apart. The air carried the scent of death, the same way it does now—metallic like copper or nickel, accompanied by a chemical sweetness reminiscent of antifreeze.

"Take this," he says, handing her two white tablets.

She looks skeptical. "What is it?"

"Ibuprofen. It's all I could find."

She takes the pills from his hand, puts them in her mouth, and swallows them down with water from a Styrofoam cup. "So, whose house is this, anyway?" she asks, her leg stretched across the couch.

"It's just a house," Desmond says, applying pressure to Nia's leg.

"It's never *just* anything with you."

The one-story, three-bedroom house is sparse and outdated and appears never to have been lived in. A couch, a table, three folding chairs, and cots in each bedroom for sleeping.

The objective of a safe house isn't to offer comfort, it's to provide safety, but the inhabitants must remain vigilant. Desmond has never spent more than a day in a safe house, and that time was spent strategizing. He doubts he and Nia will stay long. Too much time in the house would be dangerous. The Rangers could be searching for Nia, and members of the Fraternal Order of Thieves are likely scouring all of Texas for him.

"My handler maintains this place." Desmond lays another adhesive bandage on Nia's leg and lightly presses it against the wound. "Try not to put weight on it."

"Not planning on it," she says. "Thanks."

Desmond stands up from kneeling and works a tension knot in his shoulder. His body is sore; he's tired but can't afford to rest.

"Is your handler your boss? The guy you answer to?"

"Something like that," he says.

"Any ideas where Katz might've taken Amora?"

"He wouldn't have gone too far. He'll want to keep near so he can exchange Amora for the goods."

"I don't know how you do it," she says. "How can you be so calm knowing she's out there with him?"

He wishes he wasn't calm, that his capacity to compartmentalize failed, and he could scream until his lungs collapsed. But losing his shit won't get Amora back. In Nam, staying alive meant keeping his mind sharp and focused on the mission. Everything else was inconsequential. The same philosophy holds now. If Ranger Adams stops being useful, he'll have no choice but to leave her behind.

"I need to make a phone call," he says, then goes into the kitchen and dials Linh. Despite their shared intimacy, calling her feels strange, as though they haven't spoken in years.

The phone rings longer than he anticipates. Given the early morning hour, she's likely asleep, and he considers hanging up.

She answers. "Hello?" Her voice is strained.

"Linh?"

"Desmond . . . I mean, Al? Is that you?"

"Yes."

"What's going on? Are you all right?"

"Yes," he says. "But you can't go home. Not for a while."

"What are you talking about?"

"It's not safe for you at the house."

"What about the other tenants?"

"They're staying in hotels. The police will probably contact you soon. It's best to tell them the truth."

"But I don't know anything."

"Exactly. Tell them you're out of town visiting family. As far as you're concerned, the house is fine."

"Please tell me it's still standing." Worry weighs in her voice. "You know what it means to me."

"It's still standing, Linh."

"Thank goodness."

"Listen, I meant what I said before. The last thing I wanted was to hurt you, and I'm going to make this right."

"How?"

"I don't know yet. All I ask is that you consider space for me."

"You're a thief—a fugitive. You expect me to live a life built on secrets and lies? I can't do that—I won't."

"Things are going to change. I'm not going back to that life, and I won't lie to you again."

Her tongue clicks. "What am I supposed to say to that? Am I just supposed to trust you now?"

"Don't say anything. Not yet. We can have a proper discussion when I see you."

"That means you have to stay alive," she says. "Is that going to be a problem?"

"It's never been my problem. But I'm going to have to do things. Terrible things, but there's no other way."

"But if there was," she says, "you'd find it. Right?"

"Yes."

She sighs warily. "Then do what you have to do."

"All right."

"My aunt might wake up. I should go back to bed."

"See you later, Linh."

"Goodbye, Al."

"It's Desmond," he says. "Like I told you, Al is gone."

"Okay . . . Desmond."

He ends the call, takes two bags of corn nuts from the cabinet, and returns to the living room. Nia is worn out, eyes heavy. He hands her the snack. "In case you're hungry . . . You should sleep, too."

Nia rips into the bag, fills her palm with corn nuts, and loads them into her mouth. "What about you?"

"Might have a protein bar. Found some, only a month old."

"I'm talking about sleeping."

"I'll manage."

"I don't get all this," she says. "It's just that you seem like such a smart guy—"

"Don't patronize me."

"I don't mean to. All I'm saying is . . ."

"You want to understand me? Is that it?" Desmond begins to pace, circling Nia on the couch. "Let me guess, you were a criminal psych major?"

"I want to know why you did it. If it's worth the fallout. Tell me, was it about the money?"

"It's never been about the money. I did it for my family, to keep them safe."

"Safe from whom?"

"You wouldn't believe me."

"Try me."

"All right," he says. "Imagine for a moment that a world exists apart from everything you know. It's a shadow world, and the organization I work for built it. They don't fear cops, politicians, governments, or anyone."

"Organized crime?"

"No—nothing like that. They aren't about lining their pockets and ripping off laundromats. Money is a tool for them. Their currency is power. It always has been. And they wield that power to influence everything around them. I stole for them and made many enemies. Until today, I thought it was all for the greater good."

"What happened today?"

"They tried to kill me."

"Damn. Who *isn't* trying to kill you?"

"I'm the flavor of the month."

"Let me get this straight. Some ominous organization wants to control me?" She scratches her temple while munching on a corn nut. "And what? Force me to buy name-brand toothpaste?"

"Nothing so petty."

"Okay, then what?"

"I've already said enough. Believe it or not. The only thing I care about is getting my daughter back."

Desmond's cell phone vibrates. He flips it open. "It's a text from Amora. She wants me to call."

"How do you know it's her?"

"She signed it *7:21*."

"What's that mean?"

"It's the time she was born."

He dials. It rings once, then he hears his daughter's voice. "Dad," Amora says softly. "It's me."

He listens closely, focusing on anything that suggests her location. "Are you hurt?"

"I'm all right."

There's no echo. No background noise whatsoever. It's like she's being kept in a soundproof chamber. "What about the man who took you? Where is he?"

"He said if you give him what you stole, he'll let me go. Dad, he killed Grammy." She begins to sob. "I just want to go home."

"I know, Baby Girl. I know. Everything is going to be all right. Just hang in there, okay?" The line becomes quiet. "Amora, are you there?"

Katz grunts. The line isn't dead. "The address is 157 Maple Street in Sunnyside," he says. "If I hear a siren or see red and blues in front of this house, she's dead. Understood?"

"Let me speak to her again."

"Come alone. You've got an hour."

"Hey!" he shouts into the phone. "Hey, dammit!" There's a dial tone. "Shit."

"How is she? What'd she say?"

Desmond takes a beat before answering. "She didn't sound hurt." He walks toward the couch and circles it. Anger doesn't touch what he's feeling. "Katz said I have to come alone. No cops."

"No cops? He's the prime suspect in multiple homicides. Do you know the shit I'll be in if I don't notify my superiors?"

"You do that, and he'll kill her." Amora's words thump in his head—'I just want to go home.' "After I get her back, you can call anyone you want—the Army and National Guard for all I care."

"I'm violating procedure just being here. Now you want me to ignore that I've got an armed and dangerous suspect sitting at a location with a hostage?"

"She will die. Get it?"

"We train for this. The Rangers can get Amora out."

"I'm not going to risk my daughter's life so you can prove some point."

"I don't need to prove a damn thing to you or anyone else. I'm only suggesting what's best for Amora. You're one man. Even if he lets her go, do you think he's going to let you walk out of there?"

"What other choice do I have?"

"You go into that house alone, and he could kill you on the spot. What if he has accomplices? Let me help you."

"Look at your leg," he says. "What good are you?"

"I've been in worse shape before." She sits up and drops her foot onto the shag carpet. She winces, having aggravated the wound.

"It's a bad idea. I'm in enough shit without a Ranger dying on me."

"If only you knew what I went through to keep Amora safe, you wouldn't be questioning my capability."

"I know. I know," he says, circling, then pacing. "You risked your life for them, but you're still breathing. My mother is dead, and my daughter might be, too."

Nia's eyes track him around the room. "Look, I'm not fishing for gratitude. I did it because it's my job, and despite the hell you've clearly put your family through, I actually believe you."

"You believe what, exactly?"

"That the Duchamps hired Katz and that you work for some creepy-ass secret society. The thing is, I don't care about all that. I care about Amora, and right now, she needs all the help she can get."

He pauses. "Fine, but just remember, I gave you an out."

"An out? Well, aren't you a darling. But don't worry about me. I won't break a nail."

She's sarcastic and brash—same as his mother, who, in every conversation, would remind him of his frailty. "We all get to the finish line, Baby," she'd say. "The goal is to get there still knowing your name and walking upright." His mother had lived with the prospect of his death during his multiple tours in Vietnam, and she'd become accustomed to his absence. But she worried about Amora, believing her granddaughter languished, not knowing her father as more than a voice on the phone.

"We do it my way," he says. "You'll hold position outside. I go in, get Amora, and send her out to you."

"What good am I if I'm outside?"

"No cops, remember? Stay out of sight."

"Fine."

"But if everything goes to hell, you'll have to get her out."

"You mean if Katz—"

"Yes," he says abruptly. "If I don't make it out."

Death has never troubled him, not in the way it should have. He faced death more than a dozen times since leaving Nam, and never once did he shudder at the threat of its rapture. But things are different this time. It isn't his impermanence that he fears. It's Amora's.

Nia pushes herself up from the couch, almost loses her balance, then steadies herself on the couch's arm. "I'm okay," she says before Desmond can balk or change his mind about her coming along.

"Wherever he's keeping her, he's dampened the sound," he says.

"Houses in that neighborhood tend to have basements. Maybe he outfitted it so no one can hear her?"

"He'll want to keep her isolated while we make the exchange."

"Bad move," she says. "You need proof of life before going in."

"Agreed."

"And if he does have other suspects inside, what then?"

"I'll have to be ready for anything." He walks back into the kitchen. Nia hobbles behind him. He opens the oven door and removes three handguns, suppressors, a sawed-off shotgun, and three boxes of ammunition from the racks.

"Damn," she says, leaning in the doorway. "Are all the safe houses like this?"

"Most of them."

"How many are there?"

"Hundreds across the country." He opens the pantry and removes a tactical vest and flashlight. "Some states have more. Others less."

"It's like a fast-food franchise for criminals."

"It's the Fraternal Order of Thieves—not some purse snatchers."

"What's your deal with them? One minute, you make them sound like devils, and the next, you're revering them as if they're Robin Hood's merry men."

"It's complicated."

"About as complicated as a cartel?"

"The Order doesn't push drugs."

"Right. Right," she says. "But they do kill people?"

Desmond sighs.

"So, what happens when members of this thieves club stop hiding and decide to flex their power?" Nia asks.

"Won't happen."

"And why's that?"

"Because they aren't some street gang needing to prove anything." He lays the shotgun on the counter and begins to load it. "They don't need you to believe in them to exist."

"So, how is it you got mixed up with them in the first place? Soldier to thief seems like an odd career path."

"What's any of this matter?"

"Because, tonight, we're partners."

"We're not partners."

"Okay, then, teammates—who, mind you, are facing a highly trained killer, which I prefer not to do with a stranger."

She isn't backing down. He needs to give her something, meet her halfway; he needs her. "All right," he says, loading the last slug into the shotgun. "Anything else you want to know, I'll tell you in the van."

"Anything I want to know?"

"Yes . . . anything."

• • •

Desmond observes the speed limit, keeping the van between white lines. Police habitually pull over motorists headed into Sunnyside, usually looking for felonies such as drug and illegal firearm possession or outstanding warrants. Nia sits in the back seat, still probing, which is what he expects from a cop.

"What else do you want to know?" Desmond asks with his hands on the wheel at ten and two o'clock.

"Why did you hide Amora for so long?"

"It's what Mai and I decided, if anything happened to us. My mother would keep her secluded until she was old enough to take care of herself."

"Mai? She was your wife?"

"We met and married in Nam. I needed to get her out of the country when she got pregnant. But it was hard. Damn near impossible."

"So what'd you do?"

"Got drunk," he says. "There was a little bar where the war and what was left of society came together. It was neutral ground. A man struck up a conversation . . . the business type. Linen suit. Flashy shoes. Plenty of cash in his pocket. Said he worked in antiques. Scoring items across the globe for resale."

"Asia's black market?"

"Back then, we just called it business. The war had destabilized the entire country. Priceless artifacts, gold, art, even exotic animals—everything had been looted, and there were plenty of unscrupulous people trying to get their hands on goods. So, I didn't question him. He told me he could get us out of Vietnam and safely to the US, any state of our choosing. In exchange, I'd work for him, helping to secure and transport goods out of the country. The thing was, I wasn't working a job. I was paying a debt. And as time went on, there were more jobs and bigger risks."

"Like bank robberies?"

"Some," Desmond says. "Mostly, I'd target private residences. Say a person with a large watch collection. Rare timepieces they didn't want anyone to know about with complicated histories. Like a Rolex that once belonged to a Jewish banker, confiscated by the Nazis before he was executed in a gas chamber. Those are things most people aren't supposed to have. Years later, I learned about the Fraternal Order of Thieves—their mission and my true purpose in it. By then, Amora wasn't a little girl anymore, and I'd missed every achievement, every significant moment of her life. Except for the death of her mother."

"I'm sorry you lost your family."

"I didn't just lose them. I failed them," he says, walling in his emotions. "Changed my name but couldn't change what I'd done."

"So you stayed away. I get it."

"I was the problem. Staying out of their lives was the only solution."

"Sounds like something my father would say."

"Your father?"

"Joseph Turner. He's incarcerated."

"Name rings a bell."

"It should," she says. "You two were like contemporaries."

"He was in the life?"

"Since the day I was born."

"How long has he been locked up?"

"Almost twenty years. Probably will be for the rest of his life. And I'm the one to thank for that."

"You? How so?"

"I made the call. Told the Rangers he was planning something big. I wasn't sure what, but I was convinced he was signing his death warrant, and I didn't want him to die. I thought calling the law would stop that from happening—and it did. Now, he sits in a prison cell for fourteen hours a day, and the most he has to look forward to are visits from me and strawberry milk."

"Was it worth it?"

"Sometimes, I'm not so sure."

Desmond makes a right turn into the neighborhood, then brakes lightly at a stop sign on Maple Street. "We're close," he says, looking at Nia in the rearview. "Should be a couple of houses down."

Nia grabs the passenger seat's headrest and pulls herself closer to Desmond. He can hear her better over the police sirens in the distance. "Will you kill him?"

"What do you think?"

"I'm not saying he doesn't deserve it. He deserves it a hundred times over, but—"

"But you're the law."

"So you understand?"

"He nearly killed you."

"And he should face prosecution. That's true justice."

"Sorry, but that's not my definition of justice."

Desmond points toward an unlit house. "This might be it," he says, pulling into the driveway.

"I don't see his car. The place looks empty."

"Probably in the garage. Keeping it out of sight."

"I don't know," she says. "You sure this is it?"

The porch light turns on. "That's the green light." He attaches the suppressor, pulls the Glock's slide, and chambers a round. His tactical vest holds the flashlight and additional magazines. "I'm leaving the shotgun with you," he says. "If Amora isn't out in ten minutes, you know what to do."

Nia cocks the shotgun. "What about you?"

"Don't worry about me. Just stick to the plan."

He gets out of the van with the briefcase, walks the driveway, and then up the concrete steps to the front door. He looks back at the empty street. It's eerie. Feels like death. He knocks hard and waits.

"It's open," Katz yells. His voice bounces off the walls of the empty house.

Desmond opens the screen door and tries the front door's handle. It turns. "I'm coming in," he says, clutching the Glock as he steps inside. He sets the briefcase down, pulls out his flashlight, and attaches it to his Glock. It sits heavy on the barrel, and it takes a moment for him to get acclimated to the firearm's added weight. He turns the flashlight on and walks.

The house smells the way it looks. Decrepit ceilings show long-term water damage. Mold and fungus grow on rotted patches of Sheetrock. The floor creaks with each step. Wooden planks are warped, broken, and missing. Some are spotted with blood—the walls, too.

He picks up the case, tucks it under his arm, shines the flashlight around the corner, and glimpses inside the bathroom. There's a body in the tub. He approaches slowly and sees a blood-soaked man with a hole in his neck. He blinks fast, then turns and continues searching. Two bedrooms are on the east wall. The doors are shut. He checks them out, opening them quickly and scanning the rooms.

Both rooms are clear.

He walks into the kitchen. The leaking faucet drips into the rusted porcelain sink. Roaches scatter from the light.

Katz shouts from the basement: "We're down here!"

His voice burns Desmond's ears. He leaves the kitchen and moves toward the stairwell. Coming around the corner, he points the pistol and shines the light into the dark. "Amora?" he calls. "You down there?"

"I'm here, Dad."

"We're just waiting on you," Katz says. "Our guest of honor."

He takes slow, deliberate steps until he reaches the last stair and sees Katz sitting at a table in the dark. Amora is next to him with her wrists bound. His gun is pressed to her head. "Lower your weapon to the floor and kick it over there," Katz says, pointing to the far end of the basement.

Desmond kicks the gun with enough force to send it a few feet. The flashlight dies.

"Satisfied?"

"There's a light switch to your right? Flick it on," Katz says. "Then take your vest off and put it on the floor."

Desmond feels for the light switch and flicks it on. He removes the tactical vest and drops it at his feet. Fluorescence fills the space. The walls are dutifully padded. Everything has been covered in plastic, prepped for a bloodbath.

"Put the case on the table," Katz says. "And back away."

Desmond walks toward the table, makes eye contact with his daughter, and gives a knowing nod. He puts the case down and takes six steps back. He watches as Katz opens it, pulls out its contents, and looks them over. "It's all there," Desmond says. "Coins and the manifest."

Katz laughs. "The hell we went through for this. It's ironic, isn't it?"

"How's that?"

"The lengths some will go to bury the truth, but you know all about that, don't you, Mr. Bouchard?" Katz puts the items back in the case and closes it. "It's no easy feat staying dead as long as you have."

"You got what you wanted. Let her go."

"No—not what I wanted." He toys with Amora's hair, twisting his finger in her coiled locks. "What I want is far more complex. It's primal—an ache that never soothes. Fighting it is a losing battle. See, we're not so different, you and I." His hand moves down Amora's neck. "We go after what we want and don't mind a little collateral damage. The Fletchers, your mother . . . How many have died over the years so that Al Bouchard could live again . . . have his second chance?"

"I'm not asking. Let my daughter go."

"Well, she is exquisite. Beautiful. Smart. I admire her spirit. I can see where she gets it from." He cups her breast and squeezes. "But everyone's spirit can be broken."

Desmond sees the light fade in Amora's eyes, the aura around her face stripped of what it once held—a dazzling vibrance. "I'm going to kill you," he says.

"I don't question that you want to. Nor that you'll try." Katz stands and wraps his fingers around the base of Amora's neck. "Get up." Amora slowly rises, eyes welled with tears. "Go to him."

Amora walks around the table. She takes wide steps until she reaches Desmond. He embraces her, tight against his chest, and keeping an eye on Katz. He hasn't hugged his daughter in sixteen years, hasn't smelled her or felt her heartbeat. This was not the reunion he dreamed of. The ordeal's grimness is beyond comprehension. In all his years as a soldier and later a thief, he's never witnessed anyone as violent and debased as Katz.

Desmond speaks into Amora's ear, "Adams is outside. Run."

Amora pivots and sprints up the stairs. Desmond faces Katz, whose gun is aimed and slightly askew. Katz seems to favor his right shoulder, subtle but noticeable.

"You shouldn't have involved my family," Desmond says.

"You left me with few options."

"Do the Duchamps know what you've done?"

"Why?" Katz smirks. "Do you think they would disapprove?"

"No . . . I don't."

"So what do you intend to do, Bouchard?"

Desmond looks at his pistol at the end of the room. He estimates it'll take twenty steps to reach it—approximately three to five seconds. Enough time for Katz to fire multiple times, and even nursing an injury, his aim wouldn't falter.

Desmond will have to level the odds.

"The way I see it," Katz says, gripping the pistol firmly, "you can turn your back and try to walk out of here. In which case, I decide to pull this trigger and drop you where you stand or let you reunite with your daughter. Say I choose the more merciful option. Maybe months go by . . . years, even. Then, one day, when I'm feeling exceptionally chippy, I track you down and let you watch as I break your little girl's spirit, and afterward, when I've gotten my fill, I'll bleed you both. Slowly."

"Neither works for me." Desmond springs for the light switch, slaps it down with his fingers, and dives to the floor. Darkness covers them. Muzzle flashes overhead. Katz hollers, firing wildly. "You're a dead man!" he cries. "I swear you're fucking dead!"

Bullet casings ricochet off the metal and concrete walls. *Keep digging. You've got to fight for it*, Desmond tells himself. He feels for the pistol, takes hold of it, and aims low. He fires in Katz's direction. Two shots, then three more, until he hears a thud, and the shooting stops.

He crawls toward the light switch, hops up, and turns it on. Katz lies, holding his knee—a shattered kneecap and shin. There are tissue and bone fragments. Plenty of blood.

"Do it," Katz says. "Finish it."

Desmond kicks Katz's gun away. "No."

"Don't leave me like this." Katz is slobbering over himself, trembling. Shock is setting in.

"You're going to take me to the Duchamps," Desmond says. "Then, if you're still alive—what was it you said about bleeding us slowly?"

"The Duchamps are untouchable. You'll be dead before you reach the front door."

Desmond picks up the tactical vest and slips it on. "No one's untouchable," he says.

"You'll never get past the gates—"

"You'll get me in." Desmond presses his foot against Katz's bullet-torn leg. Blood oozes in thick clumps. "Right?"

Katz screams.

Desmond continues to apply pressure, listening as the broken bones grind on the cement floor. "There are worse things than death," he says, looking at the mangled leg bend and flatten in unnatural ways. "Adams is outside with Amora. If you don't help me, I will leave you for the Rangers."

"Fuck!" Katz takes short, panicked breaths. "All right," he says, trying to calm his breathing. "I'll do it."

"Like you had a choice. Get your ass up," he says, grabbing hold of Katz the way he would a soldier injured on the battlefield. "This door leads to the garage?"

"Yes."

Desmond takes the briefcase from the table and continues toward the door. He opens it and sees Katz's sedan parked. He hits a dimly lit button near a light switch. The garage door opens. Nia stands in the driveway with the shotgun, shielding Amora.

"That you, Desmond?" Nia asks, hoisting the shotgun.

"It's me," he says.

"Dad!" Amora moves to greet her father when she sees Katz clinging to his shoulder. She freezes, then runs toward Katz and spits in his face. The saliva glides down his cheek.

"He's alive," Nia says, surprised.

"For now," Desmond says.

"Should I call it in?"

"No."

"I can't let you kill him."

"Dad, as much as I want to see him dead, let Nia take him," Amora says. "We can go—this all can be over."

"Afraid not, Baby Girl. Me and Katz here are going to have a conversation with his employer."

Nia adjusts her grip on the shotgun. "You're going after the Duchamps? I told you that was the wrong move."

"It's the only move."

"If what you say is true about the Fraternal Order, killing the Duchamps will only bring more heat on you and them. It's time to walk away. Take Amora and go. Leave Katz to me."

"What are you saying?"

"I'm giving you a chance, Desmond. You both have been through enough. Leave, and everything that happened here won't concern you. But if you go after the Duchamps, I can't ignore that."

Katz is fading fast: "Maybe you should listen to the Ranger, Bouchard." He moans from the effort to speak. "She's smarter than she looks."

"Dad, we should just go. We've already lost so much . . ."

"You both don't understand," Desmond says. "It's the only way it'll end."

"You always said when the time was right, we could be together again. Disappear to someplace nobody would find us. The time is now, Dad. No one else has to die."

"But they will," he says. "I understand that more than I ever have before. People like the Duchamps don't suffer like the rest of us . They don't feel fear because they don't face consequences. They go their entire lives never having to face the ramifications of their actions. They're at the top of the food chain, sharks feasting on everything they desire. Convinced they can't be touched. But all that's going to change. People will see that sooner or later, we all have to answer for our crimes. Especially those who have fattened their wallets off the backs of the meek."

"You're right—we do have to answer for the things we've done. That means you, too," Nia says. "Doesn't it, Desmond?"

"I accept what's coming my way. I'm already paying, and I'll be paying still."

Nia shifts her weight to her good leg and fights to stay upright. "So you're a crusader now?"

"No," he says shamefully. "I'm just a man with more than a fair amount of killing under my belt. And I've spent most of my life killing the wrong people. I finally got a chance to remedy that."

Katz's laugh turns into a coughing fit. He spits blood. "A noble murderer . . . a little contradictory, don't you think?"

"Shut the hell up," Desmond says.

"I can't let you leave," Nia says. "You know that."

"Move, Adams." Desmond heads for the van. Nia doesn't budge.

"You kill them, and you'll be hunted for the rest of your life. There will be no place you or Amora can go."

"I know," he says, looking at his daughter. "But it's time for you to find your own way Amora."

"Dad, what are you saying . . . ?"

"It's going to be all right, Baby Girl. Your grammy raised you strong. Trained you swell."

"Dad? No. Please don't do this."

Desmond snatches the shotgun from Nia's grasp. She lacks the strength to oppose him. He continues dragging Katz to the van. He sets the briefcase down, opens the van's sliding door, and shoves Katz inside. Given the amount of blood Katz has lost, he might live for another thirty minutes, an hour if he's lucky. Unless Desmond can slow the bleeding. He removes his belt and ties it around Katz's leg. The pain should be unbearable, but Katz barely makes a sound. His eyes are empty, and his face is drained of color. Skin washed in a cold sweat. The nerves must be dead, Desmond thinks.

"Dad . . . Just be careful."

"I'll see you soon, Baby Girl," he says before climbing into the van. He starts the engine and flicks on the headlights.

"I'm not going to make it," Katz says. "You're going to get pinched transporting a corpse."

"Here," Desmond says, taking the car phone from its base and handing it to Katz. "Make the call."

"And say what?"

"Tell them you've got the goods, and you're ready to deliver."

"That's not how it's supposed to work."

"Call an audible."

He spits more blood. "They'll know something's up."

"Convince them."

Katz dials. "It's me," he says. "Change of plans. I'm coming to you."

Desmond holds the Glock to Katz's head and listens for anything odd: a tip-off, maybe.

"You want the goods or not?" Katz asks. "Then I'm coming to you." He ends the call and gives Desmond the phone. "Happy now?"

"I will be. Where are we headed?"

"Hunters Creek Village. 3211 Timberwolf Drive."

Katz looks as though he's going to nod off.

"Try to stay alive, mutherfucker," Desmond says, backing out of the driveway. He looks out of the windshield to see Amora wiping her tears. She mouths *I love you*.

He mouths the words back.

CHAPTER FIFTEEN
NIA

Morning breaks over the horizon. Ocher sunlight blankets the distressed neighborhood, illuminating the squalor.

"I need to call this in," Nia says. "My cell is dead. I'm hoping there's a working phone inside."

"You're going in there?" Amora asks.

"I don't have a choice," she says. "Stay in the garage. I'll only be a minute."

"There's a body in there. A man . . . I think he was working with Katz."

"Katz had a partner?"

"I think so," Amora says. "He tried helping me escape and Katz killed him."

"I'm sorry." Nia puts her hand on Amora's shoulder. "I wish you didn't get sucked into all this."

"It isn't your fault. You did what you could, and I'm grateful for your help. Even if my father won't say so, he appreciates what you did to save us."

"Still," Nia says. "I couldn't save your grandmother..."

"Grammy," Amora says, remembering the beloved matriarch with downcast eyes. "You don't know how many nights I prayed for a normal life, a normal father. And still, after all of this, I can't hate him."

"I know."

"I love him too much. He's all I've got left," she says. "Despite everything, I know he was just trying to do the best he could for us."

"I know what that's like..."

"Do you think he's going to make it?"

"I haven't known your father long, but he may be the most driven man I've ever met—certainly the angriest."

Amora forces a smile. "I suppose that's good, right?"

"Means he won't give up, and maybe that's the trouble... knowing when to quit. I still haven't learned."

"You're going after him, aren't you?" she asks. "Stop him from hurting those rich people."

"I'll do what I can to ensure he doesn't get hurt." Nia lets her hand fall from Amora's shoulder. "But it'll be up to your father how it all ends." Together, they walk into the garage. "You sure you'll be okay out here?"

"I can't go back in that house—I can't stomach it."

"Okay."

Amora stares at Katz's sedan. As if triggered by the sight of it, she begins to cry. Nia reaches out to comfort her. Amora directs her hand away. "I'm okay," she says. "Just do what you have to in there."

"You sure?"

"Yes. Go make your call."

Nia limps into the house, makes her way across the basement to the phone, and dials McCann.

"Adams?" He's alarmed, either by her voice or that he's been woken up at 6 a.m. "Where the hell have you been? We've been calling you and trying to get you over the rover all night."

"Never made it back to the Explorer. Phone died."

"Where are you?"

"A crime scene. I'll explain everything, but right now, we need units out here to Sunnyside."

"What the hell are you doing in Sunnyside?"

"Tracked the Ellis County Butcher suspect here. I've got a live victim, and there's a body in a bathroom." She looks around the basement and notices the plastic sheeting and power tools. "And you'll want to get forensics. I've got a feeling he brought his work home."

"Where's the suspect now?"

"Gone when I arrived. We'll need at least a dozen Rangers. Probably should loop in the feds."

"A dozen Rangers at this hour?"

"Whatever you can spare."

"And the feds? It must be bad."

"It's big, sir. Far bigger than I realized."

"And the survivor?"

"She's a little skittish, but she'll talk."

"How'd you get to Sunnyside without the Explorer?"

"Commandeered a vehicle, sir. Defense of necessity."

"Not looking forward to that paperwork," he says. "Stand by. I'll get a team together."

"Copy."

"And Adams?"

"Yes, sir?"

"Good work," he says. "We'll be there soon."

"Thank you, sir . . . There's something else."

"Go ahead."

"I have reason to believe the Duchamp family is involved."

"The Duchamps? What the hell do they have to do with this?"

"I'm still piecing it together, but they may be in danger. I'd suggest notifying the local authorities that there is a credible threat to their lives."

A car engine revs. Nia startles and looks to the open door where Amora was standing moments ago. She drops the phone and totters toward the garage. Amora is behind the wheel of Katz's Buick. Nia approaches the driver's side window and bangs on the glass. "What are you doing? Get out of that car!" she shouts. "It's evidence."

Amora doesn't lower the window. The car starts to back out slowly, inching to the edge of the driveway. Nia is slow to move. She gathers her strength and drags her injured leg. She can't keep up with the car, even with its incremental speed and Amora's novice driving ability.

Amora continues to back out and into the street.

"Shit . . ." Nia is beyond fatigued, and her leg is swollen with fluid around the puncture wound. Each step is excruciating. She crosses the lawn, then drops to her knees beside the mailbox, and watches Amora drive away.

• • •

It takes thirty-four minutes for McCann to arrive with three Rangers in a Chevy Suburban. Two FBI agents in a Crown Vic follow behind. No forensic team. Given the gravity of the crime scene, Nia expected a more considerable response. She watches the men exit the vehicles, all dressed in civvies, and meets them in the garage. McCann looks her up and down. It's hard to gauge what he's thinking, but Nia knows she looks like hell.

"Morning, sir." She acknowledges the other men. "Gentlemen."

"Good Lord, Adams," McCann says, concentrating on her leg. "You need a medic." He turns to Ranger O'Donnell, a dopey blond with a shit-eating grin Nia has never cared for. "Call a medic for Adams and check on that forensic team."

"Yes, sir," O'Donnell says, rushing back to the Suburban.

"So, this is it?" McCann says, surveying the shabby home. "His base of operations."

"Seems like it. No telling if he owns it."

"You said there's a body inside?"

"Older male. Caucasian. Looks like he lost a lot of blood."

An FBI agent wearing an Allman Brothers T-shirt and acid-washed denim walks into the garage. "There's fresh oil here," he says. "What happened to the vehicle?"

"Must be what he fled in," McCann says. "Is that right, Adams?"

"Correct, sir."

"Mind if we go in?" the agent asks. "Just to get a feel for things before forensics shows up."

"Go on ahead," McCann says.

The agents enter the house through the garage while the other Rangers secure the perimeter. A few neighborhood gawkers congregate across the street—mostly dopers, homeless, and people on their way to the bus stop.

"What's this business about the Duchamps being in some kind of danger?"

"Did you call the locals?"

"Apparently, they get plenty of threats on account of their oil drilling. You know, those Greenpeace types—environmental warrior freaks."

"It's a credible threat, sir."

"I conveyed that to the locals," he says. "But they won't set foot on the land."

"Why not?"

"Apparently, it's sovereign."

"The Duchamps live on tribal land?"

"Appears so."

"How the hell did they pull that off?"

"Who knows, but they've got their own jurisdiction and security team to go with it. Commando types. Supposed to be some real badasses."

Nia sighs. "What a shit show . . ."

"Maybe you should take a seat and keep still until the medics can have a look at you?"

"I'm fine."

"You don't look fine."

"Sir, I'm fine!"

"Easy now, Adams. Keep a cool head."

"You don't understand, the Duchamps are involved in this and trouble is headed their way."

"What kind of trouble?" McCann strikes his thinking pose. "Is it the Butcher?"

"I can't explain it to you right now. Too many moving parts."

"You have to give me something, Adams."

"The Duchamps may have hired the Butcher suspect."

"What?"

"The Butcher isn't some fringe killer, he's a hit man."

"You're saying the Duchamps hired a contract killer?"

"I know how this sounds, but the Fletchers weren't random victims."

"You have any substantial proof?"

"No."

"Did this Butcher escape before you could get him into custody, or was he in custody and escaped?"

Nia is silent. She's never lied to a colleague, let alone a superior. She knows anything she says could be considered an obstruction of justice and a violation of her oath. Her actions would be prosecutable and grounds for termination, but she doesn't see another way. "Acting on a tip, I tracked him to a residence that I thought was abandoned. I was ambushed. There was a gunfight."

"Why didn't you call for backup?"

"No radio access."

"What else?" he asks, looking eager to challenge her story's credibility.

"The suspect fled, and I managed to follow him here to Sunnyside."

"In the vehicle you commandeered?"

"Yes—a work van. I presume the suspect got wind I was on his tail and doubled back. I lost him but came upon the open garage at this residence. On a hunch, I parked, surveyed the home, and observed suspicious activity."

"What was so suspicious that you needed to gain entry without a warrant?"

"The garage door was up," she says. "That's unusual in this neighborhood. No one leaves anything open around here, especially not a garage."

"That's thin, Adams."

"Nevertheless, sir. It's what happened. I entered and found the surviving victim and the dead man in the tub."

"And this survivor—where is she?"

"Gone," Nia says. "Something spooked her. She bolted and took the van. I was in no shape to stop her."

"If the news stations get wind of this, we might be getting a call from the governor."

"We can turn it around, sir. The Duchamps are the key."

"I expect all of this to be thoroughly detailed in a report."

"Yes, of course, sir."

"We need to concentrate our efforts on locating the suspect and the victim. Did you get the license plate number of the suspect's vehicle?"

"Unfortunately, I didn't. Visibility was low, and distance was a factor."

The ambulance arrives. Two medics exit the vehicle and approach O'Donnell, who directs them to Adams and McCann, standing a few feet away. "Go ahead and get checked out," he says, stepping aside so the medics can evaluate her.

The medics help Nia to the ambulance. She shouts to McCann, "Sir, we need to get to the Duchamps!"

"Just tend to that leg."

"You got this one?" the younger medic with shaggy hair asks. Nia didn't think medics were allowed to grow their hair long—the man looks like he's come from a grunge concert.

"Sure," the tall, mahogany-skinned medic says. He has a pretty smile. Perfect teeth—white and straight. "She's in good hands."

The grungy medic nods. "I'll monitor the radio," he says, then climbs into the front seat of the ambulance.

"Must've been some night," the pretty boy says. "Take a seat, and we'll get that leg fixed up."

"You don't know the half."

"So, you're a Ranger," he says. "Impressive."

Nia never knows whether people suggest it's impressive because she's Black, a woman, or both.

"Decent patch job on the leg," he says, removing the dressing. "I'll have to give you something to keep the infection at bay. Might hurt a little." He unlocks a drawer, reaches in, and removes a vial and syringe. He dips the needle into the vial, pulls the plunger, and fills the syringe with a clear liquid. "You're going to feel a little pinch in your arm."

Nia is too exhausted to care. He wipes her skin with an alcohol pad. The needle pierces her arm, feels cool at first, then burns in the muscle. The medic slowly pulls the needle out of her arm, applies a cotton ball, and puts a Band-Aid over the injection site. He cuts away the bandages Desmond had administered and cleans the wound with an antibacterial foam.

"You need stitches," he says.

"No time for all that."

"It's a serious puncture."

"Feels real serious," she says, flustering him. "I just need to move better. You got anything to numb it?"

"An analgesic can help, but you really need to get to a hospital. The wound isn't even closed."

"So, let's close it. How long will it take for you to stitch it up?"

"I'm not really supposed to do that."

"But you know how, don't you?"

He gives a lukewarm nod.

"Okay, then. Let's go," Nia says.

He sighs and begins to cut the rest of the shredded pant leg. Then he douses the wound in sterile water. "This will hurt," he says, pulling a surgical stapler from a sealed bag. "I've only done this once . . . it's against protocol."

"You have the green light. I won't sue."

"Good to know," he says, with a circumspect expression. "Here goes." He presses the stapler's head into her skin and bears down with force. Nia wants to cry out but shoves her thumb between her molars. He continues stapling along the track of the wound.

"Just a few more," he says, his forehead wet. Nia worries the sweat will get into her wound, but he's quick to wipe it from his face. "All done. It'll hold until you get to a hospital."

"Thank you."

"You got it, Ranger . . . ?"

"It's Adams . . . Ranger Adams."

"I hope you don't mind me asking, but are you the first?"

"I am," she says, no further explanation needed.

He extends his hand. "It means a lot," he says. "You having that badge. I appreciate you."

"For what?"

"Not giving up. I bet they'll write about you in the history books," he says. "I can't wait to tell my little girl about you."

Nia feels compelled to smile but feels unworthy of the admiration. It isn't enough to be a Ranger; she needs to be good—one of the best. And so far, she's failing at the biggest case of her career.

She steps out of the ambulance. The leg pain is more manageable. She knows it's only temporary.

McCann walks over to her with the FBI agents in tow. All three men look indignant. "It's a goddamn horror show in there," McCann says. "We'll need to issue an APB while we arrange for a statewide manhunt.

These agents are going to need the suspect's physical description, along with what you can tell them about the vehicle."

"All right," Nia says. "And afterward are we good to go?"

"We'll look into what's going on at the Duchamps' ranch."

Nia can only hope they'll get there in time.

"Let's have it," O'Donnell says, holding ready to take her statement in his notebook.

Nia gives an accurate description of Katz and his car, knowing both are dead ends. Desmond needs Katz alive long enough to get access to the Duchamps. The moment he's no longer useful, he's dead. Amora is smart. Nia didn't anticipate her giving the slip. She probably ditched the car and vanished.

O'Donnell stops writing. "Anything else you recall? You might think it's minor." He speaks with condescension, pressing the end of the pen into the cleft of his chin. "Something you may have overlooked."

Under other circumstances, she'd tell him to fuck off for implying that she doesn't know her craft, including how to gather evidence with a sharp eye, but there's no time to lecture or belittle him.

Nia feigns deep thought. "No," she says. "That's all I've got."

"All right, then," McCann says. "Let's go see about the Duchamps."

CHAPTER SIXTEEN
DESMOND

The Duchamps' security gate looks to be crafted from steel or iron. It's elegant with an aristocratic flair. An obnoxious *D* is centered among winding lattices like a crest.

Getting to the property wasn't easy. It required traveling down a long, dirt road. Desmond worried security cameras were monitoring their approach, and he half expected an ambush when he arrived at the gate. But there was no ambush—only an intercom.

"Get out and push the button," Desmond orders Katz.

"I can barely move." Darkness has settled around Katz's eyes, and his blanched skin is the result of significant blood loss. "You expect me to walk like this?"

Desmond puts the shotgun to Katz's head. "It's five fucking steps."

"I can't." His leg steadily bleeds despite the tourniquet.

"Fine," Desmond says, moving out of the front seat. "Get up here and talk through the window."

Katz crawls between the front seats, finally sitting in the driver's seat, almost collapsing over the wheel. He rolls the window down and presses a white button on the intercom.

"Yes?" a man's voice says through the metal box. "Can I help you?"

"I'm here about a job," Katz says. "I need to see Big Ed."

"What job?"

"A recovery . . . It really is best if I talk to Big Ed."

"Name?"

"Katz."

"Mr. Duchamp doesn't like to be disturbed during breakfast. You should have called first."

"This isn't a subject he'd want to discuss over the phone."

"Hold on." The man's voice cuts out. It comes back after a few minutes, sounding slightly less annoyed. "All right. Drive on through."

The gate opens. Desmond pulls Katz from the driver's seat and pushes him to the floor. "Stay down." Katz flops on the floorboard like a fish out of water. His body is shutting down. Death is imminent.

Desmond drives toward the Duchamps' sprawling palatial estate, which dots the flat land. There are four buildings adjacent to the mansion. ATVs and construction equipment are parked near an airport hangar that houses two commercial jets.

Further in the distance, oil wells fail to blend into the landscape. He steadies the van, keeping it to a moderate pace so as not to cause alarm. Two men appear near the front of the mansion holding rifles, standing near large white columns reminiscent of the antebellum South. The guards are suspicious, as Desmond suspected they would be. He stops the van and shifts into park.

"What's happening?" Katz asks.

"It's the end of the road." Desmond climbs out of the driver's seat, takes hold of Katz, and props him behind the wheel.

Katz's mouth is dry. Lips chapped and peeling. "What are you doing?"

"Sending you home," he says, shifting into drive. The van rolls toward a large fountain in the center of the roundabout driveway.

The guards aim their weapons and shout commands.

"Home?" Katz is barely coherent, his body limp.

"You're hell-made," Desmond says. "Your mama might've popped you out, but the devil gave you breath." He presses the gas pedal. The van gathers speed. He opens the side door as it barrels forward, set to collide with the fountain. He jumps out with the shotgun and briefcase. Tucks and rolls, stopping in the manicured shrubs bordering the cobblestone driveway.

The guards open fire in steady, controlled bursts. Then, a bombardment of bullets tears into the van. Holes riddle the metal and glass. Gasoline hangs in the air. Desmond sees fuel pouring from the undercarriage and gets to his feet.

A golden spark ignites the fuel. The fiery explosion propels the guards onto their backs and demolishes the fountain, scorching the cement and flowers around it.

Flames swell. Plastic and metal truck debris falls from the sky. Desmond races into the woods to take cover. He stays low, keeping his shotgun trained at the guards.

The guards recuperate, picking themselves up from the ground. They hold their positions near the porch and take cover behind the columns. After a few minutes, they carefully approach the burning van. Desmond watches as they probe the vehicle. Looking at the burning man in the driver's seat, they shout into their radios and fan out. There's no way to be sure how many guards are patrolling the premises, but if the men are separated, Desmond has a better chance at dispatching them.

He sprints through the woods, clearing downed branches and thick foliage. He's back in the bush, survival mode. Twelve hours, no sleep. It's a test of will—discipline and endurance. He hides the briefcase near an oak stump, hollowed and infested with termites, then rounds to the back of the house, concealed behind a pack of trees. A guard stands on an expansive deck with his rifle ready, overlooking the empty field.

A sawed-off shotgun is no good at Desmond's range; he needs to get closer. He tears out of the woods, running at full speed.

"Stop!" the guard says. "I said stop, dammit!"

Desmond pushes forward, ready to pull the trigger. He's nearly close enough to make it count. The guard fires. Bullets veer wide. Desmond cuts sharply, rolls, and fires from the ground. The buckshot sprays the guard's face. Eviscerates his nose and leaves tiny craters.

The guard falls dead over the railing.

Another guard appears from the French doors leading to the deck. He's massive, a corn-fed white boy who looks as if he deadlifts concrete. Desmond gives up his shotgun, opting for the dead guard's assault rifle. As the guard comes down the steps, Desmond steps out with the gun poised for a kill shot. "How many others are there?" he asks.

"Me and one inside with the boss." He's the calmest man at gunpoint Desmond has ever seen, and he's threatened many men with guns.

"Who's the boss?"

"Big Ed."

"Any other Duchamps in there?"

"You itching for Corbin, ain't ya? Fat chance, fucker. If you were smart, you'd put the gun down and turn yourself over to the boss, and he might have mercy on you."

Desmond shoves the rifle's butt into the guard's chest, knocking him to the ground. The guard struggles to gather his wind. "This Corbin kid—the one running for office. Where is he?" Desmond asks.

The guard wheezes and coughs, holding his hand to his stomach. "Corbin is campaigning in San Antonio. Big Ed calls the shots."

"Take me to Big Ed," Desmond says. "Fuck around again, and I'll shoot you."

"All right, Action Jackson," the guard says, getting up slowly. "So, what's your big plan?"

"Shut up and walk." Desmond nudges the guard up the deck stairs.

They enter a sunroom, enclosed with tinted glass. There's wicker furniture: a couch, chairs, and end tables. A cigar box sits on a coffee table, along with a cocktail setup: a bottle of bourbon and two tumblers.

"Where's he eating?" Desmond asks.

"Like I'm going to tell you . . ."

Desmond slaps the guard across the face. "Keep testing me."

"Gotta be shitting me." The guard notices the tattoo on Desmond's arm. "You're a Marine, aren't you? Then you should know how important the Duchamps are to the movement."

"What the hell are you talking about?"

"All the things the Duchamps have done for us . . ."

"Speak for yourself. They've never done shit for me."

"Can't you see they're heroes, brother? I did my time. Operations in Iran and the Persian Gulf. Then Iraq after 9/11. Came home with PTSD. Couldn't even piss straight. No fucking job. No prospects. Then Big Ed stepped in. Kept me from living on the streets. Gave me a way to make a living when the government left me high and dry. But if Corbin becomes president, all that changes and our voices will be heard."

"If you believe that, you're a damn fool. The Duchamps only care about themselves—nobody else."

"Of course you'd say that. You're not a real patriot, just some spook."

"Newsflash, mutherfucker. All the patriots are dead."

Desmond shields himself behind the guard as they move in tandem down the hallway, passing watercolor landscapes that look old and expensive. Aged portraits of silver-haired white men in debonair suits and hats. Shifty-eyed swillers standing next to oil rigs with their arms around indigenous women—maybe Tonkawas or Comanches—sitting on the hoods and fenders of big-bodied Cadillacs. Generations of Duchamps loony from riches, sometimes on horseback, drenched in black gold as if it were their indisputable birthright.

Near the end of the hallway, a man's gruff voice rises and peaks. There's the clanking of a fork and a coffee cup banging on a saucer.

Desmond pushes the guard forward, keeping the rifle's barrel close to the man's head. "Go on in," he says.

The guard mumbles and enters the dining room. Desmond follows.

A long table spans the room. It's archaic, like something from the Dark Ages. Pieces of dead animals are preserved, still lifelike, and mounted high on the walls: a lion's head with a flowing mane, a stag with a royal crown of antlers, and an elephant's baronial tusks.

Trophies for the weak.

Big Ed Duchamp is older than Desmond imagined, maybe mid-seventies, with strawberry blond hair sprayed stiff. He's a hefty man in a white polo shirt, with a pasty complexion and jowls like Jabba the Hutt, which explains the moniker. He's a real Boss Hogg type, feasting on a jelly-filled pastry, with bacon and eggs that rest greasy on a plate to the right of his coffee.

A radio hisses and pops on the table.

Desmond doesn't see a gun, but it doesn't mean the fucker isn't armed.

"Come on in, Dove. Don't loiter," Big Ed says, motioning to the guard.

"Sir, I'm not alone."

"I see that. This the fella who destroyed my fountain?"

"Yes, sir."

"Well, don't be shy," Big Ed says, cocking his neck to get a better look at Desmond. "Come in so we can talk."

Desmond nudges Dove aside and steps further into the room. "Where's the rest of your security team?" he asks.

"Sent them away to tend to the mess you made. I thought we could discuss things man-to-man. I've got plenty of food if you're hungry."

"Fuck your food."

"All right. How about you let Dove help put out the burning van you've gifted us this fine morning?"

Desmond doesn't budge, keeping his gun aimed at Dove's head. "Why didn't you call the fire department?"

"I prefer to handle matters such as this in-house. As a sovereign nation, we operate self-sufficiently," Big Ed says, taking another bite of the pastry.

"Sovereign?"

"The land you're standing on is tribal. Been in my family for centuries."

"That explains the pictures. How'd your great-great-grandpappy do it? Force an Indian woman to marry his ugly ass?"

"You have a very poor impression of me and my kin, don't you? I'd have you know it was a business arrangement. One that paid off for both parties."

"Yeah, I bet . . ."

"I take it that's Mr. Katz burning in the front seat?"

"Yes."

"He didn't strike me as a likable man. I don't reckon anyone will come looking for him."

"Probably not."

"We'll dispose of the remains accordingly."

"He's not the only one."

"My guards?"

"One is dead out back."

"Dead men present challenges to our sovereignty. I do wish you would have done without the bloodshed."

"You gave me plenty of cause."

"No matter. I think we can manage one." He sips from his coffee cup and dabs his mouth with a cloth napkin. "I've made it a point to avoid dealing with law enforcement. Government agencies can be pesky. I find them to be far too overreaching."

"Yet, your son is running for the highest office in the land. Seems like a contradiction."

"Before we get into all that. Is Dove free to go?"

Desmond takes his finger off the trigger and relaxes his shoulders.

"I prefer to speak privately," Big Ed says. "So, either shoot him or set him free."

"You'd advocate for him to die?"

"Never. He's one of my best men. But I've come to accept death as a cost of doing business. If killing him means we can discuss our matters, so be it."

"You should find a new job," Desmond says, shoving the rifle barrel into Dove's back. "Hurry up. Get the hell out of here before I change my mind."

Dove hurries out of the room, not looking back.

"You are a fascinating man," Big Ed says, wiping jelly from his fingers with a napkin. "I can see why the Fraternal Order sent you."

"What do you know about the Order?"

"Oh, my family and the Order have been doing this dance longer than I'd care to admit."

"I don't understand."

"Did you think this was the first time you people have tried to sabotage a Duchamp's success? Every generation going back to 1903 has had to deal with your meddling. Blackmail, threats, espionage. The Fraternal Order's attempts to destroy what my family has built is a timeless tale told around our dinner table. But you, my friend, are a new chapter."

"I just work for them."

"Oh, no, my dear, boy. If they sent you, you've got to be the best. And seeing all the trouble you went through to get here, you're not just some lowly thief. I can tell you possess skills far beyond what they recognize."

"I'm here because of Katz. He murdered people I care about."

"Yes, he did."

"I hold you responsible."

"I see," he says, digging food out of his teeth. "While some may kowtow, I prefer to meet force with force. Did you honestly believe stealing from me wouldn't come with consequences?"

"He killed my mother."

"An unfortunate outcome, but never the intention."

"Doesn't matter." Desmond raises the rifle and lines his sight with the center of Duchamp's forehead. "You let him off the leash."

"So, you kill me?" Big Ed asks. "Then what?"

"I don't care what happens, as long as you're dead."

"I respect your resolve, but you aren't thinking it through. Is there someone out there you love? Someone you're protecting? Because we won't stop. We never stop. That's why I can look you in the eyes and tell you that if you pull that trigger, anyone and everyone you care about is dead. Family members. Friends. They'll be plucked like fruit on a withered vine."

"That goes both ways, mutherfucker."

"Killing me accomplishes nothing. Corbin will ascend to the presidency, and he will dedicate his life to eliminating the Fraternal Order, starting with you. And the best part is, the country will love him for it." Big Ed shoves the rest of the pastry into his mouth and licks the sugary icing from his fingers. "These people—the ones out there chanting his name on the campaign trail—they're hungry for him. They're lonely, angry, looking for someone to blame. There's the offshoring of American jobs. The wars. Record-high interest rates. Illegals jumping our borders. Rising gas prices. And no one cares about the people anymore—the down-home, blue-collar, salt-of-the-earth people. Nobody's listening to them. They go off to fight wars. Work shit jobs, pulling double shifts. And every day they wake up to a country they barely recognize."

"What the hell do you know? You're a goddamn billionaire with gold shitters."

"I know their frustrations. I know their rage."

"People won't just swallow that."

"They already have," he says. "Because they'll believe anything that makes them feel like they matter." He slowly rises from his chair. "And that's all people want—to know that someone out there sees them and understands them, fights for them."

"Don't fucking move!"

Big Ed raises his hands. "You kill me, and the country—the entire world—will learn what you and the Fraternal Order truly are. Terrorists. Enemies of the free market looking to make slaves of the American people. There's money to be made here, but you cowards would rather hide in the shadows believing you can shift the tide with your little robberies. But it's in vain. My son is going to become president whether the Order likes it or not. He will usher in a new era of truth. No longer will people wonder whether secret societies and shadow governments are out to get them. They'll know. All their fears realized, but Corbin will be the cure. Your coming here all but guarantees his election." He points to a small camera mounted in the corner of the ceiling. A tiny red light blinks incessantly. "Smile. You're going to be a part of history."

It's a punch to Desmond's gut. All the oxygen is sucked out of the room. He wants to collapse—ball up and disappear into nothing. How could he have slipped up so badly? He broke the cardinal rule and let his emotions cloud his judgment. Coming to Duchamp's compound was an unmitigated error. Adams was right. He didn't have a plan. He didn't perform recon; he had no tactical analysis, no strategy. He was just a man riding his rage.

"Is it sinking in yet?" Big Ed asks. "After this footage circulates, no one will believe those items you stole are remotely authentic."

Incoming sirens draw near. Desmond looks outside the eighteen-pane window, where unmarked vans are beginning to flood the driveway. The radio buzzes. A guard's voice cuts in. "Mr. Duchamp. Come in, Mr. Duchamp."

Big Ed snatches the radio from the table. "What is it?"

"Trespassers."

"Get rid of them."

"But, sir—"

"I said handle it!"

The sirens grow louder. Gunshots ring like thunder, only slightly louder than the sirens.

"So much for sovereignty," Desmond says, his ears ringing. "Sounds like you've got yourself a welcome party."

"Who's out there?"

"My guess: feds and Rangers."

"Cops? You drew cops here?"

A frantic voice blares through the radio: "We've been breached! I repeat, we've been breached!"

"You've got dead men on your property, and one of them is the Ellis County Butcher," Desmond says. "Add that to the video recording of you confessing, and you're fucked. I go down and you go down."

"You think this means our fates are aligned?"

"It's in your best interest to tell me where that tape is."

Big Ed clams up. His eyes dart every which way—first to the door, then to the camera. "Katz should've put a bullet in you."

"For that to happen, he'd need to be far better than he was. Unless you want that tape to end your world, you've got less than five minutes to tell me where the surveillance room is before they come in here and arrest us both."

More desperate yelling emits from the radio. It sounds as though Big Ed's guards are being rounded up, and the ones dumb enough to resist are taking fire.

"What's it going to be, Duchamp?"

"By God, if you're trying to fuck me . . ."

"The clock is ticking. Any second, this hallway is going to flood with Rangers and agents."

Big Ed mumbles something under his breath about Desmond,

something derogatory, then says, "Down the hall. Last door on the left."

Desmond pivots and rushes out of the room and into the hallway. He makes sure it's clear, then works his way to the end, coming upon a narrow door. It looks as though it belongs to a storage closet. He crouches down and suspends his fingers near the threshold. There's warm air and the hum of electricity. Desmond aims the rifle, prepared to shoot through the door.

"Wait, goddammit!" Big Ed says, waddling down the hallway. "There's no need for that. I've got the key right here."

Desmond stands back, his rifle still poised to fire. Big Ed unlocks and opens the door. Inside is a small workstation with a video bay—monitors displaying the entire grounds. On the screens are a half dozen guards on their knees in cuffs. Two guards look to be shot, and an agent is giving one man CPR.

Desmond counts three feds and two Rangers moving through the airport hangar. Additional agents have breached the mess hall. The estate is more than a showcase of wealth; it's a paramilitary training camp where Duchamp has been building his army.

"These assholes are everywhere," Big Ed says.

"Just get the tape."

Big Ed presses the eject button on the DVD deck and removes the disk. "Don't pussyfoot," he says. "Destroy the damn thing."

Desmond snatches the disk from his hand and strikes him in the stomach with the rifle butt. The fat man doubles over and drops to the floor. Desmond fires on the equipment. Sparks fly. Monitors shatter. Smoke fills the space.

"You bastard," Big Ed whimpers, unable to get up. "I will come for you. Best believe I will—"

Desmond knocks him out with another blow to his forehead. The front door rattles as if someone's kicking it in. He runs down the hallway just as agents and Rangers burst through the front door.

He turns a left corner, then another left. The house is winding—long hallways, fancy wallpaper. He passes a Baccarat crystal vase setting on a console table. He's sure it's worth at least a quarter million, maybe more. Expensive antique mirrors and more paintings line the walls. Desmond keeps moving to what he thinks is the rear of the massive home. The agents' and Rangers' footsteps bang behind him, heavy combat boots against the hardwood. He comes upon a large bedroom—likely Big Ed's master suite. The room is easily five times larger than his studio in Linh's boardinghouse. French doors lead out the back. He opens the doors and steps onto a patio where an abundance of potted plants are flowering.

Big Ed has a green thumb—won't do him much good in prison, he thinks.

Desmond steps off the patio, makes sure the law isn't in sight, and runs toward the woods. The trees provide cover; if he's lucky and quick enough, he can make it off the property and down the road without being spotted by the cops. After that, he'll need to get to Houston. He'll contact Marco, if the Fraternal Order hasn't already killed him.

Desmond runs deeper into the woods and then drops into a prone position. He fixes his aim at the house. An oak slightly obscures his view; his knees and elbows sink into the soil. Two agents appear on the patio, having exited from Big Ed's suite. They stand a moment, scanning the empty field.

Desmond has managed to evade law enforcement for decades. No matter what he stole or which people he stole it from, the cops never pieced together his crimes. It's been a source of pride; he's lauded himself for never having killed a law enforcement officer, but he fears what he may do if ever a cop backs him into a corner.

The agents observe the open space a few moments longer, then go inside the house. Desmond begins crawling back to the hidden briefcase. He uses his rifle to push through moss and ivy, careful not to allow the plants to touch his skin.

After eight minutes of arduous crawling and staying out of sight, Desmond reaches the briefcase. When he looks back at the house, the small band of agents and feds are gathering near the demolished fountain. The van is smoldering, and the roof and hood are still burning.

The men converse and speak into their radios.

A fire engine speeds down the road. Ambulances follow behind. Soon, EMTs enter the house, carry Big Ed Duchamp out on a stretcher, and load him into the ambulance. The wounded guard is placed into another ambulance. The dead guards are laid in front of the house, covered with sheets.

Firefighters hose down the van, snuffing out the small remaining fires. Katz's charred corpse won't be removed until the coroner arrives. His body fat likely melted into the seat. The van will need to be dismantled and the seat unbolted to get him out. It was a horrible way to die, and Katz earned every excruciating minute.

Desmond anticipates that more law enforcement officers will arrive soon with a coroner and forensic team. It'll take the entire day to process the scene, and he can't remain in the woods much longer. He continues his journey, fending off stinging insects and crawling over anthills. When he reaches the end of the woodlands, he estimates he's traveled half a mile. He can still see the police lights flickering in Duchamp's driveway.

More vehicles arrive: an SUV and another unmarked sedan. If he moves now, he might be seen. It's best to wait it out before crossing the road.

A housing subdivision looks serene in the distance. Modest homes compared to Duchamp's sprawling estate. Desmond could find a car there, boost it, and drive back to Houston. Maybe something that's late-model, easy to hot-wire. It's worth a try, he thinks.

The minutes ebb away. He notes the vehicles traveling on the road. Two FBI vans turn onto Duchamp's private access road and park in the long row of vehicles stretching away from the mansion.

A minivan packed with children, a motorcycle, and two sedans pass by along the two-lane road separating Desmond from an open field.

After a five-minute lull in traffic, he determines it's time to move. He stands, tucks the briefcase under his arm, and breaks free of the trees. He crosses the concrete divide and climbs over the guardrail. He looks at the field. In the far distance are grazing cattle, an indicator that the land is private. Armed individuals usually patrol private lands, which could lead to a violent encounter. He's relieved when he's able to see a short wire fence. The cattle land looks to be secluded from the overgrown and dry field, which is probably state-owned and earmarked for development in the future or a road expansion.

The direct path to the neighborhood is across the center of the field. There'll be no cover, making him easily seen, so he'll need to be quick.

Desmond's drained, almost depleted. He isn't sure how he's made it this far. Deep breaths do little to ease the tension in his body. His legs are sore from crouching in the dirt. He shakes them out and starts running. He taps into a reserve of energy and darts across the road.

"Not another step!" Nia stands on the other side of the road with her gun drawn and a radio clipped to her belt. It's a miracle she's standing at all. "I told you not to come here," she says.

Desmond turns to face her. "You look like hell, Adams."

"You're not one to talk."

"How'd you find me, anyway?"

"Spotted you from the van," she says, pointing at one of the white passenger vans lined along the private road. "It's a fucking mess, Desmond."

"It could've been worse . . ."

"Can't imagine that."

"You have Duchamp. What else matters?"

"It all matters."

"I could've killed him. Now, you've got a case. Someone to answer for all this."

"So, you did me a favor?"

"He's alive, isn't he? Be satisfied."

"So, why'd you change your mind about killing him?"

"Killing him would've put others in danger. If he's locked up, it'll show people that even the fat-cats must answer for the shit they do."

A semi approaches with two trailers attached. A string of cars follow it.

"And Amora?" Nia asks. "What happens to her?"

Desmond stays quiet, watching behind her for the FBI or Rangers, hoping he won't have to kill one of them if they converge on him.

"She stole Katz's car back at the house," she says. "Seemed like a page out of your playbook."

"This isn't Amora's world. She deserves better. Leave her out of it."

"She's a victim and a witness to Katz's crimes. We need her to make the case."

"Find another way."

"There is no other way," she says. "You want Duchamp to pay, don't you?"

The truck is closing in. Desmond struggles to hear Nia above the road noise. "She's been through enough," he says. "Don't pursue her, or we'll have a problem."

"An easy fix is if you turn yourself in."

"Go back to the van, Adams—"

"You know I can't do that."

"Then, what are you waiting for? Call it in."

Nia unclips the radio from her belt. "It'd be a lot easier if you surrendered. Save us both the trouble."

"They'll have to kill me."

"You don't mean that."

He shrugs. "I won't rot in a cage like your father."

"And Amora? Does that mean she'll be running, too? That's no life for her."

"She's nimble," he says. "It probably wasn't hard giving you the slip."

The truck's gears grind as it picks up speed. Desmond prepares to flee, shifting on to the balls of his feet.

"You'll be a fugitive forever," she says. "Is that what you want?"

"Nothing's forever, Adams. You ought to know that."

The truck crosses between them. Desmond jumps the metal guardrail and enters the field. He runs hard, nearly dropping the briefcase twice. When he looks back, Nia is plodding across the road at a zombie's pace. She reaches the guardrail and hurls herself over with all her strength. She's winded and in pain and takes a moment to rest. She can't catch him, but he marvels at her will—she's got the heart of a Marine. He watches as she tries to remain upright but falls back onto the guardrail when the pain is too much. Then, as if summoning her last bit of strength, she gets up and continues across the field. He doesn't understand why she doesn't shoot him. She stops posing a threat when she teeters as if she's under a spell, then collapses in the high grass. The injury to her leg has taken its toll.

Desmond keeps moving. He's already wasted enough time with Adams.

But Nia isn't moving. If she calls in her location, the feds and Rangers should be along to tend to her. He waits a moment, thinking she'll mobilize. Every second in the field undermines his chances of escaping. It's better to leave her, he thinks. But she isn't calling for help, which means she can't . . . maybe she isn't breathing.

"Get moving, Adams!"

Nia remains still. A breeze moves across the plain, stirring up dust that collects on her back.

"Come on, now. Get up."

There's no response. Not even a twitch.

"Ah, shit." He runs to her, crouches down, and places two fingers in the cranny of her neck. Her pulse is weak, fading. "Damn you for this, Ranger," he says, picking up the radio. He opens the channel. There's no point in trying to mimic Nia's voice. "Ranger down," he says. "She needs medical attention in the field across the road from Duchamp's estate. Hurry your asses up." He wipes the radio with his shirt, to eliminate his fingerprints, and hustles across the field toward a house with a green Mustang that's begging to be boosted parked in the driveway.

He's almost home free . . .

CHAPTER SEVENTEEN

NIA

It's sometime after midnight. The hospital is frigid. Nia can't remember being in a hospital room that's been remotely comfortable. An IV drips saline into her arm. Every six hours a nurse administers a painkiller, which numbs the biting pain in her leg. Had she not gotten to the hospital when she did, the doctors say the sepsis would have killed her; they say she's lucky to be alive. *Lucky* is a funny word, she thinks. It makes it sound as though living requires no effort on the survivor's part—no drive or commitment to keep going. Hearing that she was close to death does little for her. In some ways, she feels as if part of her already has died—that she has one foot in the netherworld, and the other still anchored to living.

The TV drones. The local news is reporting on the story they've labeled "Destruction at the Duchamp Estate." The screen displays sensational aerial footage of the burned-out van, demolished fountain, and bodies of the dead guards. Even with the sound off, Nia knows what the reporter is saying: "No updates at this time, but we'll keep a close eye on this developing story."

She turns off the TV, and her thoughts get louder. She'd give anything to erase the past twenty-four hours and not have to think about Desmond and Amora, or Katz and Duchamp. But that's not how it works. She'll mull over what went wrong and how every misstep brought her to this point. Her greatest fears realized—this botched case will be her legacy.

If only she could get the pieces to fit, then it all wouldn't be in vain, from the murder of the Fletchers to Katz and the gunfight at Duchamp's—deaths spread across multiple crime scenes. Without Desmond or Amora, there's no hope for the case. Any evidence potentially linking Duchamp to Katz will be circumstantial. She knows this, and so does McCann . . .

There's a knock at the door.

"Come in," Nia says, adjusting the bed so she's upright.

McCann enters holding a bag of mixed nuts and a cola. "The vending machine was the pits," he says. "This is the best I could do." He sets the snacks on the tray next to Nia.

"Thank you," she says, opening the bag of nuts. "Is Duchamp talking?"

"Not a word. He's got a lawyer coming in from San Antonio. Supposed to be the real deal."

"What are the charges?"

"Nothing that'll stick." McCann takes a seat in a vinyl chair and tries to get comfortable. "We found two bodies on the premises. One victim seems to have worked for Duchamp as a guard. The other likely perished when the van caught fire. The best we can do is charge Duchamp with evidence tampering and failure to report a crime. Of course, he can argue his sovereignty and the immediacy of the attack were factors."

"We can't go after Duchamp with this. His lawyer will argue it down. Portray him as the victim of a witch hunt."

"I know," he says. "Which is why the DA has the mind to throw it out unless we bring something substantial to the table."

"We need to look at his books. See how money moved."

"And even if we were to get a warrant to go fishing, what do you think we'd find, huh? Duchamp is worth billions. I'm pretty sure he didn't pay an assassin with a check. Whatever evidence exists is buried, and it would take a forensic accounting team an entire year or more to uncover it."

"He had the Fletchers killed, sir."

"Again, where's the proof?"

"I don't have any," she says, softly.

"Say that again, but louder."

"I don't have any."

"Well, there you go. Finally, the truth." He gets up from the chair and stands at the foot of her bed. "Look, Adams. I'm telling you this because I'm a friend and you need to hear it. I think it's time to bow out."

"You want me to quit?"

"Spare yourself the embarrassment and keep your pension."

"I did my job. Everything was by the book."

"Everything? Are you willing to testify to that? Because that's where this is headed. Let's look at what we know. Someone used your radio to notify us that you were passed out in a field. Yet, you can't tell me who that person was."

"Like you said, sir, I was passed out."

"A bystander just happened to find you?"

"That's correct," she says. "Maybe a motorist who didn't want to be identified."

"Well, how fortunate," he says, sarcastically. "What are the odds?"

"I don't know . . ."

"I wasn't being literal, Adams."

"Yes." She sighs. The pain in her leg is beginning to return. "I'm sorry, sir."

"And how did you know to go to Big Ed Duchamp's home? You claim he was in danger, but you can't explain how or what the nature of that danger was. Then, a man you claim to be the Ellis County Butcher appears to have died in a vehicle fire, but you offer nothing to support why the man was there. Given the extent of the man's injuries, it could take weeks to identify him."

"I think Katz went to collect what was owed to him for the killings. Maybe something went wrong, and Duchamp didn't want to pay him?"

"You're a shit liar, you know that?"

"Sir, please . . ."

"All that business about the disappearing witness and commandeering a van . . . You must think I'm an idiot?"

"I'll explain everything in the report. I just need more time."

"Listen, Adams, I'm only going to say this once, but it's time for you to think about a career change."

"And if I don't?"

"Then there won't be much I can do. The feds are going to lay this at our feet. You have an open disciplinary investigation already pending for the Central Bank heist. You don't need any more attention; frankly, neither do the Texas Rangers." McCann turns toward the door, ready to walk out.

"Sir, please . . . Work with me here."

"I've *been* working with you, Adams," he says, unmoved by her plea. "I'm giving you two weeks to think it over."

"You're suspending me?"

"Medical leave. The paperwork is already being processed."

"I see," she says. "Tell me, did you urge Powers to resign, too?"

"Powers isn't your concern." McCann refuses to look at her. "Rest up." He leaves, and every thread holding Nia's world together threatens to snap.

She's abandoned . . . again.

Sharon hasn't come to the hospital or returned Nia's calls. Not that Nia blames her. They haven't spoken in the days leading up to her nearly dying, and that's no way for a relationship to function—not a healthy one, anyway.

The nurse comes in with fresh dressings for Nia's leg. After changing the bandages, the nurse delivers the final dose of painkiller into her IV port and leaves. Drowsiness sets in immediately. Nia puts the nuts aside and closes her eyes. The painkiller is the only way she's been able to sleep, and she can't imagine sleeping without it—an admission that would trouble her if she had the capability to give it more thought.

• • •

In the morning, Nia is discharged and given a prescription for morphine. She fills it at the hospital pharmacy before taking a taxi home. The driver drops her off in the driveway, rather than in front of the house. It's a shorter distance she'll have to limp. She enters the house. After all she's been through, her home is her constant. She stands at the door, inhaling the sweet-smelling potpourri Sharon keeps in a brass dish on the coffee table.

"Sharon?" Nia walks into their bedroom. The closet door is open, and Sharon's clothes are gone. Nia goes into the bathroom and opens the mirror cabinet over the vanity. Sharon's toothpaste, deodorant, perfumes, creams, and moisturizers have been cleared out, too. The same goes for the drawers that held her flat iron and hairbrushes.

Sharon's never left before. She's threatened to plenty of times but never carried through. It's the end of them, Nia's certain of it. She returns to the bedroom and sits on the mattress. Her heart pounds, and there's a tingle in her right arm. It's probably a panic attack, but maybe it's a heart attack? Her breathing is rapid. Tears flow. The pain in her leg pales in comparison to what she's feeling. If it is a heart attack, she hopes it's massive. Not the kind that results in a stent or pacemaker.

It needs to be catastrophic. If she dies, her survivors receive a decent payout from life insurance. Sharon deserves that after all Nia's put her through.

"Jesus, you look like you're about to pass out." Sharon steps into the room. She's holding an envelope and dressed in jeans, a Janet Jackson T-shirt that reads "Rhythm Nation," and a pair of Converse All Stars. It's the same outfit she wore the day they moved in.

Nia tries to compose herself. "I thought you left."

"I did," Sharon says. "I wasn't sure when you'd be back, so I was going to leave this for you."

"A goodbye letter?"

"It wasn't an easy decision for me. I need you to know that."

"Well, that's nice."

"There's a check in here," Sharon says, holding up the envelope. "It's enough to help you with the mortgage for the next couple of months. I thought maybe you could get a roommate. It could help shoulder the burden."

Nia rolls her eyes. "A fucking roommate?"

"It's just a suggestion."

"And where will you be?"

"Consulting for a law firm."

"You're not going to be a judge anymore?"

"No, Nia, I'm not. I've stepped down and leaving Texas."

"Leaving to go where?"

"It's a firm in Albuquerque. One-year contract. If it works out, they'll keep me on."

"New Mexico . . . you're just up and moving to another state?"

"It's been a long time coming. You know that. This place will never change."

"Is this about what someone wrote on your car? I told you to report it. But you can't let some isolated incident run you out of a state."

"That's the thing, Nia. It isn't isolated. It's everywhere. Do you think I like deceiving people? Telling them that we're best friends from college because God forbid that us sleeping in the same bed should make them uncomfortable."

"It's none of their damn business."

"That's exactly my point. So why are we the ones hiding, in 2004?"

"Because it's my career, Sharon. I don't have it the way you do. You're a federal judge. No one can take that away from you, but everything I've worked for can be taken away, and then it's over. Maybe it already is."

"What are you talking about? Did something happen?"

"It's not your problem anymore. I guess it was never your problem."

"I still care about you, Nia."

"And yet, you're walking out of my life."

"No," Sharon says, getting up abruptly. "You don't get to make me into the villain. I tried with you. God knows how I tried, but you are who you are. I will never matter to you as much as your job."

"Not this shit again..."

"Yes, this again! I've got no fucking clue where you've been for the past two days. Do you know how messed up that is? I didn't know if you were alive or dead. Here I am, this basket case, watching the news and wondering whether there will be some mention of you. Do you know what that's like?"

"No," Nia says, looking to the floor. "I don't."

"Of course not. How many times a day do you wonder about me and ask yourself, 'Is Sharon safe? What might be happening to her on account of being Black or gay or a woman simply existing?'"

"C'mon..."

"Give me a number. Once, twice, three times... five times? Or is it never? You are so consumed with what you've got going on that you never stop to think about me or anything that doesn't revolve around you being a Ranger. If I'm wrong, then tell me. Tell me I'm way off base."

Seconds lapse. "No, you're right," Nia says. "I don't think about you the way I should. I feel burdened by you. Having to call and check in. Needing to be sure the fucking steaks are thawed. My mind is on work—it's always on work. It's why I'm good at what I do. I felt safe with you, and if I were to die, you were there to remember me . . . to tell people that I mattered outside of this fucking job."

Sharon's eyes well. She tucks in her lower lip and tries to fight back the tears.

Nia continues. "But it isn't fair to you. It's not what you signed up for, because you're right, this place isn't going to change, and neither am I."

"Thank you for the honesty," Sharon says, before dropping the envelope on the dresser. "I hope everything works out for you."

Sharon leaves. Nia doesn't try to stop her. The front door slams, and the house is quiet again.

She opens the envelope on the dresser. Inside are house keys, the check Sharon mentioned for the mortgage, and a letter, which only solidifies her heartbreak. Nia reads two paragraphs and sets it aside. Somehow reading the words hurts more than hearing them come out of Sharon's mouth for the past two years. But the letter offers permanence—a way for her to always remember what she's lost, to know that once upon a time, she had somebody who loved her despite her flaws. And to remember that if she ever finds love again, she'll be wise to protect it.

Her cell rings and she answers. "Hello?"

"Adams, we need you down at headquarters," McCann says.

"What's going on?"

"The disciplinary board has scheduled a meeting. I did my best to get them to postpone it on account of your leg and all, but—"

"It's fine, Lieutenant. I'll call my union rep."

Nia goes into the kitchen, pours a glass of water, and swallows a morphine pill. She knows she needs to appear strong and capable if she has any hope of projecting confidence.

• • •

Nia's union rep is Guillermo Gutierrez, a stodgy man in his sixties with a thick gray mustache that he's steadfastly maintained even after retiring as a Ranger almost fifteen years ago after being shot by coyotes crossing the Rio Grande. Like most people in law enforcement, Nia calls him by his last name. Aside from today, Nia's met him once at a state benefit for fallen officers. She's always seen their minimal interaction as a positive sign, a testament that she's a good Ranger and has managed to stay out of the fray.

Gutierrez wears a gray suit over a white collared shirt and a bright floral tie that would never be acceptable if he were still wearing the badge. He carries a black leather attaché case and walks hard, coming down the hallway. Nia waits on a bench outside the conference room, and as Gutierrez approaches, nerves set in.

"Mr. Gutierrez," she says, hopping up and extending her hand. "How was the drive?"

"Decent," he says, sitting on the wooden bench. "I managed to get a copy of Powers's deposition." He opens the case, removes a clasped folder, and hands it to Nia. "Take a look."

Nia removes the documents from the folder and begins to read. "Wait . . . this is accurate," she says. "He's admitting the suspect wasn't armed?"

"He came clean about the shooting. Evidently, he attributes his capitulation to a meeting with his priest."

"Priest or not, this means I'm off the hook."

"Correct."

"Then why am I here?"

"The board is willing to close the Central Bank investigation without imposing any disciplinary action on you. However, this situation with Edward Duchamp has caused serious concern. They are alleging that you falsified information to justify an unsanctioned raid on his home."

"A raid? We were attempting to prevent his murder."

"Yes, by some unknown assailants?"

"Well, someone gave him a concussion. Who do they think it was, Casper the friendly fucking ghost? And did they even bother asking him who shot up his surveillance system?"

"He's claiming memory loss from the trauma."

"A lot of that going around lately."

"Due to the sovereignty of his land, he is arguing his civil rights were violated. He's threatening a federal lawsuit."

"It's an active investigation. No one's going to entertain that."

"I've been told the FBI are not going to pursue charges at this time, and the Rangers have agreed to issue a formal apology to Mr. Duchamp."

"This is bullshit. He gets a pass because he's rich and his son is running for office?"

"Do you know how much money he's contributed to charities for fallen soldiers and officers in the past year alone?"

"No one is above the law, right?"

"That may be, but it doesn't change the politics of this."

"People died out there."

"If the FBI determines Mr. Duchamp or a member of his security team acted beyond the scope of self-defense, they will build the appropriate case against him."

"Dead men tell no tales," she says with a sideways glare. "They're sweeping it under the rug."

"You need to understand the optics here."

"Oh, I understand," she says. "I understand exactly what's happening. Duchamp hired that man, Katz, to kill the Fletchers and numerous others, and now, he's going to get away with it."

"I must advise you to refrain from making those types of accusations. It will only give Edward Duchamp cause to go after you civilly."

Nia sighs. "I've got nothing left to take."

"You still have your badge."

"What about the Fletchers?"

"The FBI has taken over their homicide investigation, and they are adamant that they will seek justice for the family. As for the altercation that occurred at the Bouchard residence, the local sheriff's department will continue to investigate, and I encourage your cooperation."

"This whole thing is a wash."

"It's no longer your concern, Adams. The fact they haven't brought you up on charges is astounding. Not only did your pursuit of the man you claimed to be the Butcher end in people's deaths, but he has yet to be identified. No dental records, and his condition makes facial identification impossible."

"He went by Bartholomew Katz. That's all I know."

"Likely a fictitious moniker, if it is him. Unless a family member comes to claim him, your supposed Butcher is a John Doe. It's a dead end, Adams, and if you keep down this path, you won't have much of a career to salvage."

"What are you recommending?"

"Admit you operated under bad intel and that the investigation suffered due to your failure to adhere to standard policies and procedures. And after all that, if they decide not to terminate you, gratefully accept whatever assignment you're given. Keep your pension, live your life, and don't ever go near the Duchamps again."

The door to the conference room opens. A brown-skinned woman with honey-colored eyes smiles generously and says, "They're ready to see you, Ranger Adams."

Nia straightens the arms of her sports coat, rolls her shoulders back, and brings her chin high. She reminds herself that it's about confidence. Whatever choices she made in the field, she did to preserve life and property, and that's what she was trained to do. Anything outside of that was a condition of survival.

"Right this way," the woman says.

Nia enters the room, with Gutierrez a few paces behind. They sit at a rectangular table across from three white men in suits—stone-faced and glaring. A stack of plastic cups and a pitcher of water are positioned between them, along with notepads, pens, and a cassette recorder.

Nia removes her hat. "Afternoon, gentlemen," she says, eager to break the ice.

"This interview will be audio and video recorded," one man says before putting on a pair of oval-framed glasses. "We keep the audio recording as backup." He proceeds to angle the video camera so that Nia is in the frame and presses the record button.

Another man, wearing a bolo tie crafted of turquoise and silver, slides a Bible in front of her. "For the swearing-in," he says. "You have any questions before we start?"

"No, sir," she says.

"All right then." He presses the record button on the cassette deck. "Start with your full name."

"Nia Lissette Adams."

CHAPTER EIGHTEEN
DESMOND

Desmond looks out the window of the Greyhound bus. A dusty sign reads, "Welcome to El Paso." The bus pulls into an old station. Rows of charters are parked and ready to be boarded. Passengers wait under a metal awning, fanning themselves in the sweltering heat.

When most of the passengers have deboarded, Desmond grabs the briefcase and follows the last few people off the bus.

Outside, taxicabs are parked along the curb. A couple of men he takes to be drivers stand laughing, drinking colas, and smoking cigarettes. He quickly finds a cab with the driver behind the wheel and gets into the back seat. The vinyl is hot. He feels it through his pants, and the cab smells of the tropical breeze air freshener that dangles from the rearview.

"Ah, hola, señor," the driver says. "Destination?"

Desmond hands him a small piece of paper with an address written on it. "Can you take me here?"

The driver reads the address, then wipes the sweat from his face with a handkerchief. "I can. But this place . . . are you sure?"

"I'm sure."

The cabbie starts the meter. "Okay, señor." He pulls away from the curb and onto San Antonio Avenue.

"How long will it take?" Desmond asks, holding the briefcase on his lap.

"Fifteen minutes. Maybe less. Don't worry, I'll get you there."

The cab merges onto Interstate 10, eastbound, and then onto US-54, before exiting onto Gateway and making a right on Dyer. The area has seen better days. Most people are barely surviving by doing what they can. Narcotics trafficking and prostitution have become synonymous with the poverty-stricken neighborhood known as Angel's Triangle, though there's nothing holy about the place. Gangs and Mexican cartels brought about the crime, adding to the already dire conditions. It was renamed Angel's Triangle after being known for decades as Devil's Triangle, to reflect the hope its residents held for the neighborhood.

The cabbie parks outside the brick building. "Here we are," the cabbie says.

Desmond glances at the meter and pays the cabbie ten dollars, including two bucks for tip.

"Maybe I should wait a minute, yes?" the cabbie asks. "Just to be sure you make it inside okay."

"I'll be fine." Desmond gets out and shuts the cab door. He begins walking toward the white building, taking a second to look up at a metal sign from the art deco era that reads "Shangri-la Motel" in large red letters alongside two palm-tree cutouts. Another sign reads "Closed for renovations."

The lobby's glass door is tinted black, far from welcoming. A surveillance camera is fixed above the door, angled at Desmond. He makes eye contact with the lens, and seconds later, the door opens. Desmond enters to find a young man, Mexican, no older than eighteen, in a filthy tank top and jeans. His rough appearance complements the patched drywall and water-damaged ceiling tiles. Even the wooden counter is chipped and warped. A table fan and a wall AC unit keep the tiny room from reaching the boiling point. It's a shit gig, Desmond thinks, but when it comes to moving up in the Fraternal Order, everyone has to start somewhere.

"Reservation?" the man asks.

"Desmond Bell. Room 7."

He hands Desmond a key. "Will you be needing anything else?"

"No." Desmond hands the man fifty dollars, which he graciously slips into his pocket.

He leaves the lobby and walks to room 7, unlocks the door, and enters. Immediately, he's assaulted by the sharpness of ammonia. The room has been doused with it. The cabinetry in the kitchenette has missing doors, and a small bistro table has been paired with one dining-room chair and another chair, made of white plastic, belonging to a patio set.

The oven has also been removed. In its place is a small refrigerator, topped by a microwave.

It's a shithole, but places like this are how the Fraternal Order stays hidden from those curious about its dealings. Who would think an organization funded with millions in stolen goods would consider a roach-infested motel to be a fitting meeting place?

Desmond dials and puts his cell phone to his ear.

"That you, Desmond?" Marco asks loudly over the phone. "Are you at the location?"

"El Paso, like you said." The connection is poor; there's static, and his voice echoes with delay. "Checked into room 7."

"Do you have the briefcase?"

"Right here with me," he says, placing the briefcase on the bed. "How long am I going to have to wait here?"

"As long as it takes. You want this to end, don't you?"

"It has to . . ."

"Then be patient."

"And you're sure this is going to work?"

"Did you follow my directions? Do everything I said?"

"Right down to the letter."

"Good. Relax," Marco says. "We'll be along shortly."

Desmond hangs up and goes into the bathroom, where the scent of cleaning products is stronger. Despite smelling sanitary, nothing appears to be cared for. The sink and shower are rusted; there's heavy limescale and broken tiles, and a bulb is out over the vanity.

He returns to the eating area, sits in the lawn chair, and faces the door. Sore from the eleven-hour bus ride from Dallas, he rests his head back and looks up. Speckles of dried blood are on the ceiling above the door and bed; some blood is smeared near the window. Bad things have happened in this room. People died—maybe even wished for death after what the Fraternal Order inflicted upon them. Desmond knows what the Order is capable of and how far they'll go to silence anyone they believe is untrustworthy, but he'll be damned if he meets the same fate. He opens the briefcase, removes his pistol, and sets it on the table.

• • •

An hour after sundown, there's a knock at the door. Desmond gets up from the chair and moves cautiously to answer, with the gun aimed and his finger on the trigger. He unlocks the deadbolt. "It's open," he says, backing away.

A tall and massively built Black man, bald with a gray goatee, and a dark-haired man with a military haircut and tanned skin enter, wearing well-tailored suits. Overtly posh. Marco enters behind them, his face bruised and wearing the same clothes Desmond last saw him in. His shirt is blood-stained and ripped, and his hand has been bandaged. He wonders what kind of damage the bandage is hiding. Broken fingers? Extracted fingernails? A missing thumb?

Noticing Desmond's gun, the Black man in the navy pinstripe suit quickly pulls his small-caliber pistol and aims it at Desmond. "Marco, I thought you said this would be a conversation?"

"Please, gentlemen," Marco says. "Let's keep things civil."

"Drop the gun," the bald man says. "Or I drop you."

The line sounds like dialogue from a Blaxploitation film, something Dolemite would utter before karate-kicking a man in the head. Under different circumstances, Desmond would laugh. But these men are here to kill him.

"I won't ask twice," the man adds, doubling down on the one-liners.

"All right," Desmond says. "You got it." He slowly places his gun on the table.

"Thank you for your cooperation," Marco says.

"As you can see," the man utters shrewdly, "we needed to be sure Marco was telling us the truth about your escape. We're here to restore the balance."

Marco begins: "According to the *praecepta*, as established by the Fraternal Order of Thieves, you have carried out an egregious act."

"Which one? There've been a few."

"You killed multiple members of the Order."

"To be fair, they tried to kill me first."

"So, you don't dispute this?"

"No," Desmond says. "I killed the men in your home and eliminated the team that came for me at the boardinghouse, and I'd do it again."

"Let's note the lack of remorse, shall we?" the bald man says. "I don't even know why we're bothering with all this. Let's just kill him and be done with it."

"Wait . . . please," Marco says. "Let's hear what he has to say."

"I've given you years of service. Does that mean nothing?" Desmond asks.

"The tenets dictate our actions here. Nothing else," the man says. "Trust and loyalty above everything."

"Then, I'd like to make the Order an offer," Desmond says.

The man smirks. "What can you possibly offer the Order?"

"I turn over the gold and slave manifest stolen from the Duchamps' bank, and you release me from the organization."

"Let you go? You mean like a resignation?"

"I give you the goods and walk out that door. The coins must be worth at least a couple million."

"And does that include a severance package?"

"I'm serious. There's no reason to draw a line in the sand. We can come to an agreement."

"What the hell do you think this is, McDonald's? There's no walking off the job, and we know exactly what the coins are worth. But trust is invaluable."

"Take the coins and the manifest. Do what the hell you want, but I'm out. Done."

"Seems like Marco did a poor job with orientation," the man says. "There are only two ways out: prison and death. And since you've admitted to killing members of the Order, I don't see the point in talking as if you hold any cards."

"What are you prepared to do?" Desmond asks.

"Not me," the man says. "Marco brought you into the Order, and now he's got to clean up his balance sheet." He hands Marco the pistol and takes hold of Desmond's arm. "Best not to fight this . . ."

Desmond tries to break free, but the dark-haired man slugs him in the stomach. They drag him into the bathroom.

"Put him in the tub," Marco says, checking the pistol's chamber in the doorway.

The men push Desmond into the tub and hold him down. "You better make it clean," the bald man says. He punches Desmond again, this time across his jaw.

Marco steps toward Desmond, who is trying his best to stay conscious. He aims the pistol as the brutes back away. "You don't want to get blood on your fancy threads," Marco says. "Might want to wait in the other room."

The men gather by the doorway. "Don't get sentimental. Do it already," the man says, dabbing sweat from his bald head with a handkerchief.

Marco fires twice, striking Desmond in the chest. Then he moves closer and fires an additional shot into his leg. He quickly reaches down, presses his hand against the wound, works the blood on his fingers, and smears it across Desmond's face.

The bald man angles for a better look at the kill, but can't see around Marco. "Is he dead?"

"Just checking for a pulse."

"Well?"

"Dead as disco."

The men walk to the tub and halt at the sight of the bloody Desmond. "That wasn't so hard, was it?"

"No," Marco says, sounding surprised at the facility with which he was able to shoot his friend.

"Let's get the fuck out of here. This place is stinking up my suit," the man says, leading his partner into the other room. Marco follows.

"I'll clean up," Marco says.

"Full disposal," the bald man says. "All the trouble this asshole caused us . . . I want to make sure he's wiped off the face of the earth."

"The works, then?"

"That's right, mutherfucker. The works."

"Got it."

"You came close to getting your ticket punched, Marco. But you fixed it. It would behoove you to be more mindful about whom you recruit in the future. Nonetheless, your privileges are curtailed. No recruiting. No jobs. Any move you make needs to go through us."

"For how long?"

"Until we say otherwise. Just be glad you aren't laid up in that tub, too. Now get this fucking place in order."

Once the men leave, Marco rushes to the bathroom to find a coherent Desmond still slouched in the tub. "Help me out of here," he says.

Marco takes hold of his arms and pulls him onto the tub's edge. "Did it go through clean?" he asks, looking down at the gunshot wound in Desmond's leg.

"Just clipped the thigh." He begins removing his shirt and the bulletproof vest that had prevented the slugs from entering his body. "Can't believe you'd really give me the works."

"You'd be dead. What would it matter?"

"Still, man—a fucking lye bath?"

"I'm pretty sure a thank-you is in order."

"You're right," Desmond says. "Thank you." He looks at Marco's bandaged hand. "They do that?"

"It's nothing I didn't deserve."

"I'm sorry, Marco."

"Do me a favor and stay dead this time."

"I'm going to need someplace to get patched up."

"I have a first aid kit in the car, but you'll need to get to Juarez for complete care."

"Who's in Juarez?"

"I have an associate there. Doesn't ask questions. He can help you."

"He's a doctor?"

"He's whatever you need him to be. He knows people who will get you set up with papers and get you back across the border, but after that, you're on your own."

Desmond gets to his feet. "Where'd you park?"

"Around back," Marco says, helping Desmond from the bathroom onto the bed. "I'll bring the car around."

Marco hurries out the door. Desmond watches from the window as he disappears around to the back. He notices the briefcase housing the gold and slave manifest is gone from the table, taken by the Fraternal Order, and he hopes it brings them as much grief as it brought him.

CHAPTER NINETEEN
NIA

"This is it," the chief says, directing Nia to a small desk along the back wall. "You can get set up here, and then I'll take you down to meet the trainees." He's a portly white man in brown suede boots and a matching sports coat. There look to be other open desks, some as dusty as hers. She counts six spaced out in the large room, some closer to the door and more visible to anyone who would walk in, yet she's been consigned to the rear.

"Sure, Chief," she says, setting her box of office supplies on the assigned desk.

"There's a coffee machine in the kitchen. All we ask is that you keep it clean between uses."

"Yes, sir."

"I know this isn't the same as field work, but we run a tight ship. Your job will be to get these trainees in order. If you need something, you come to me. We observe the chain of command. Understood?"

"I understand, Chief."

"All right," he says. "Get settled in, and I'll swing back by after chow time."

Nia takes a seat in the dusty leather chair. It squeaks under her weight. She opens the desk drawer and starts placing her belongings inside: framed awards and certificates, a stapler, pencils and pens, notepads, and field manuals. Her entire life as a Texas Ranger fits neatly in a drawer. She doesn't know why, but the thought makes her melancholy.

For years, she kept a photo of her and Sharon vacationing in the Bahamas hidden at the bottom of her drawer and was worried that someone might find it, but it never kept her from pulling it out when times on the job got tough. Sharon was her anchor—her North Star—until she wasn't. Nia, at least a part of her, is relieved their relationship is over. She'll be a better Ranger not having to worry about coming home to anyone, but it doesn't mean she doesn't miss her.

"Excuse me, Ranger Adams?" The thin man with coke-bottle glasses is barely visible behind a mail cart stacked high with packages. He hands Nia a small box. "This was rerouted from your previous office," he says. "Came in last week."

"Thank you," she says, setting the box on her desk.

"You're welcome, ma'am." He heads back toward the door, pushing the cart with one hand and keeping the tower of packages in place with the other.

Nia takes out a box cutter and proceeds to slice the packing tape. Inside the box is a DVD. She looks for a note, but there isn't one. She leaves the office with the DVD in hand and walks the long hallway to a small media room. Two carts with TVs and DVD players are in the corner of the room. She quickly plugs in the master power supply and turns on the TV and DVD player. She pops the disk in and hits play. Black-and-white footage of Desmond and Duchamp appears on-screen. She watches, trying to make out where the footage had been recorded. There's the faint murmur of voices. She turns up the volume and can clearly hear Duchamp. She watches long enough to ascertain that it's evidence, proof of Duchamp's involvement with Katz.

She goes back to her desk, dials McCann, and tells him to meet her at the training building.

• • •

"What exactly am I looking at here?" McCann asks, arms folded.

In ten minutes, the media room had become populated, with McCann and a state prosecutor.

"This was the surveillance footage taken from Duchamp's compound the morning of the alleged raid."

"Yeah, but how'd you get it?" McCann asks.

"Someone mailed it to me."

"Someone?"

"There wasn't a note or anything," she says. "My guess would be it came from someone familiar with Duchamp's dealings."

"Who's the other man?"

Nia had told herself she was done lying to her superiors. Covering for Desmond and Amora had gotten her nowhere. "His name is Desmond Bell . . . at least that's one of the names he uses."

"You know this man?"

"I learned of him during the course of my investigation."

"And what's his relationship with Duchamp?"

"From what I could gather, he was attempting to blackmail Duchamp to get his son to drop out of the presidential race."

"Who's he working for? Black militants? Environmentalists? Religious extremists?"

"I don't know."

"Why is it we're just now hearing about this guy?"

"I needed more evidence," Nia says. "I didn't want to come to you unless I knew for certain of his involvement." More lies: they may be inescapable now. The words come out with ease. "I just wanted to be sure."

"Any idea where we can find this man?"

"No."

"If he is targeting the Duchamps, what's stopping him from going after Corbin?" the elfin, big-haired prosecutor in a dark skirt suit asks. "He could be a major threat to the candidate."

"What about the footage, ma'am? Edward Duchamp's confession."

"A confession under duress. Not to mention, the disk is inadmissible in any legal proceeding. We don't even know where it came from. Nor can we speak to its authenticity."

"It still warrants further investigation, doesn't it? At least it gives us something on Duchamp. We should be able to lean on him, draw out a confession."

"You mean to force a confession," the prosecutor says, tauntingly.

"I didn't say that."

"My understanding is that you've been removed from the case. Isn't that right, Lieutenant McCann?"

"Yes," he says. "Ranger Adams will be serving in the training division from here on out."

"An instructor, not an investigator," the prosecutor says, "Which means this investigation is out of your purview, Ranger Adams. I suggest you focus on your current post and leave all probes into the Duchamps to the investigative division."

Nia stares at McCann with pleading eyes. "Sir, we can't just ignore this."

"You're dismissed, Adams. We'll discuss this later."

Nia leaves the room and ducks into the hallway, avoiding eye contact as she passes colleagues. She can't help but feel that every stare is rooted in judgment, and each person she passes somehow knows that she's been demoted. It's an open secret, something the good ole boys cackle about in the men's room or while filling their cups with scorched coffee, laughing about how the Black girl couldn't cut it.

Back at her desk, Nia surmises that Desmond sent her the DVD, but why? What good would it do him to be implicated along with Duchamp? Unless . . . She considers two possibilities: he's dead, or he wants her to think he is. Either way, the exposed footage means Desmond Bell won't be found, especially if law enforcement isn't looking. She wonders what will become of Amora. The girl was raised in the equivalent of a petri dish. No life skills. No understanding of the world. How does a girl like that survive?

More questions than answers . . .

But Nia has done enough prying, looking for the truth. What good has come from her pursuit of justice for the Fletchers and the countless others Katz murdered? It's time Nia put herself first, and that means forgetting about Desmond, Amora, and the Duchamps. She needs to fall in line. As her father says, "We all have to bow out sooner or later," and she won't lose her pension. It's the only thing she has left worth fighting for.

"Excuse me, Ranger Adams?" A young brunette cautiously stands at attention with an armful of documents. She's dressed in the traditional cadet uniform: a brown shirt and pants, a royal-blue tie, and a tan cattleman's hat.

"At ease," Nia says, allowing the woman to settle into a casual stance. "What can I do for you, Cadet?"

"Brianna Castro." She chews her inner cheek and flushes. "I mean, Cadet Castro."

"Okay, Cadet Castro." Nia senses the woman's nervousness. "What's on your mind?"

"I read about you in the *Tribune*," Castro says, barely taking a breath. "Even cut the article out and posted it on my wall."

"Glad to know someone besides my father read it."

"It changed my life."

"A half-page article changed your life?" Ordinarily, hearing such a confession would make Nia feel good, but instead, she's bordering on irritated. "I'm flattered, Cadet, but I'm not sure you should take everything you read to heart."

"You let me know it was possible. No one in my family thought I'd make a good cop, and when I told them I was applying to be a Ranger, they took bets to see how long I'd last . . . What I'm trying to say is, if I hadn't come across that feature written about you, I don't think I'd be here."

Nia is reluctant to say anything out of fear she might discourage the cadet. Castro is riding high on hope, and Nia's lost most of that. After a short silence, Nia says, "You'd be here. If this life was meant for you, you would've found a way. Tell me, what is it you want out of this job?"

"What do I want?" Brianna looks flustered. "A long career and to make an impact."

Nia nods. "Okay."

"I . . . um," Brianna stammers. "Did I say something wrong?"

"No. You said exactly what I would've said when I was in your shoes. But here's some advice: ask yourself that question every morning you put on that badge. Maybe the answer changes over the years. Maybe it doesn't. But the day you can't answer that question, do yourself a favor and walk away."

"Yes, ma'am."

"My days in the field are over. All I've got are cadets like you. So rather than try to break you, like what was done to me, I'm going to build you up so you're a better Ranger than I ever was. And one day, who knows? Maybe they'll be writing articles about you."

Brianna smiles. "Thank you, ma'am."

"All right . . . You should get to wherever you're supposed to be."

Brianna nods, spins on her heel, and heads back the way she came, leaving Nia to question how much of what she told the girl was sincere and how much was a delusion.

CHAPTER TWENTY
DESMOND

Desmond's ball cap shields his eyes from the midday sun as he walks the long dirt road leading to the yellow house perched in the meadow. Two dogs roam freely, trotting with their tongues out across the wraparound porch.

A knapsack is slung over his shoulder, containing a change of clothes and cash. A cigarette is tucked behind his ear. Linh sits on the porch in a rocking chair, reading a book. Her pale blue sundress sways in the breeze while the playful dogs dance at her feet. He's no poet. Never had time to figure out the difference between a metaphor and a simile. But she's as majestic as a lightning flash in the evening sky. He draws closer to the house. The dogs get wind of his scent and approach. The barking alerts Linh. She steps to the edge of the porch, stands a moment, then steps down onto the dry soil and begins walking toward him.

Desmond sets into a jog, running toward Linh. They meet on the road, and she throws her arms around him. "You're alive," she says, her body glued to his. "I prayed that I'd see you again."

"I told you I'd come."

"Are you okay?" She steps back and looks him over.

"I'm fine," he says. "But the boardinghouse—"

"The police told me it was a botched home invasion," she says. "They asked a lot of questions about my boarders, but I told them I rented on the honor system. Never kept records on people who stayed with me."

A dog nips at Desmond's feet.

"We can talk about it inside," she says, taking Desmond by the hand.

"Is your auntie home?"

"She went to play bingo with friends. Won't be back until late."

Desmond follows Linh inside the house. While the quaint exterior suggests a homely decor, the inside is furnished with burl wood furniture crafted by artisans and woodworkers in Vietnam. Glazed ceramic vases and oil paintings depict ancient times in Vietnam, before the occupations and wars tore the country apart.

"Have a seat," Linh says. "I'll put on some tea."

Desmond lays his knapsack on the floor and sits on the couch, admiring Linh's beauty as she goes into the kitchen. He could never forget her beauty, but amid so much ugliness and killing, he'd forgotten how being around her made him feel. She calls forth in him a joy he wonders whether he deserves.

"I'm sorry about the boardinghouse," he says. "I know how much it meant to you."

"It'll take some time, but I'll get it up and running again." She drops tea bags into two cups and fills a kettle with water. "That business you had to take care of, is it over with?"

"Yes."

"What will you do now?"

"I have to leave here."

"You mean Texas?"

"The States. It's no longer safe for me . . . or my daughter."

"Your daughter?" Linh stops filling the kettle. "Why wouldn't you have told me you had a daughter?"

"I was trying to keep her safe, but it's like you said—no more lies."

She takes a deep breath. "Okay," she says. "You're right. I want to know everything . . ."

"There's so much I wanted to tell you before, but I was afraid."

"Afraid of what?"

"That if you knew who I was—the real me—that you wouldn't want to be with me. You asked me before if I'm a good man. The easy answer is no. I'm not good. I haven't been good for a long time. But it isn't because I don't want to be. I want it more than anything, and it's all Amora wants for me . . ."

"That's your daughter's name?"

"Her mother named her. It means 'love' in Spanish and that's all I've ever wanted for her. A life filled with love."

The kettle whistles. Linh pours the hot water over the tea bags. She carries the cups to the living room, sets them on the coffee table, and sits next to Desmond. "Can you tell me what happened to your wife?"

Desmond gazes into the cup as the tea bag steeps and the water darkens. "Time slips away," he says. "We don't feel it when we're in the moment, believing it's infinite. But it's far from that. My wife's time was cut short because of me, and for a while, there wasn't a day that went by that I didn't wish I had died instead of her."

"What happened to her?"

"We were run off the road. No one was supposed to survive. But Amora and I lived, and from that moment on, everything I did was to protect her."

"Where is she now?"

"There's a place in Vietnam where her mother grew up. Years ago, I bought the land and the home that resides there. It's a safe place. It's where she knows to look for me."

"You should go there. Find her."

"I will, but I won't be coming back, Linh."

She's quiet, befuddled maybe... then, "What?"

"I want you to come with me," Desmond says.

"What are you saying, Desmond?" Linh nearly knocks over her tea. "Go with you... to live in Vietnam?"

"Yes."

She stands and begins to pace. "Do you know what you're asking?"

"I know I love you and I want us to be together."

"My life is here in Texas. My aunt. The boardinghouse."

"I understand what you'd be giving up, but we can get someone to manage the boardinghouse..."

"And my aunt? She's getting older."

"When the time comes, we can send for her."

Linh sighs. "She hasn't lived in Vietnam for decades."

"Then we can go somewhere else," he says, getting to his feet and resting his hands on Linh's shoulders. "But I need to be clear. We can go anywhere you'd like, but I... *we* can never come back to the United States."

"What will we do for money?"

"I have enough to last our lifetimes and those that follow."

She starts pacing again. Desmond watches anxiously, wondering whether seeking Linh out was foolish. He's spent six weeks in Mexico with Linh on his mind, as he healed from Marco's gunshot wound and obtained a new identity, a passport, and a Social Security card, hoping she would run away with him. And now, facing her with his proposition, he worries that he's been bullish to a fault. After all he's put her through, why would she entertain the idea of life with him?

"Maybe I shouldn't have come here." Desmond picks up his knapsack and throws it over his shoulder. "Thank you for the tea. I'm sorry... for everything."

He heads toward the door.

"Wait," Linh says.

"Yes?"

"All right . . . I'll go with you."

"You will?"

"But you need to promise me something."

"Anything."

"No more stealing," she says sternly. "I won't be with a criminal."

"You have my word."

"If you break it, I'm gone. Period. No conversation . . . no back-and-forth. You'll lose me forever, got it?"

"I understand, Linh, and I won't let that happen."

"Good." Her sincere warning gives way to a budding smile, and she falls into Desmond's arms. "Oh, and cool it with the cigs. After everything you've been through, do you really want this shit to kill you?" She snatches the cigarette from behind his ear and crushes it in her palm.

"I'll get the patch or something," he says, with an uncontrollable smile.

"So, we're really doing this?"

"We are."

"I need to find a way to break it to my aunt. She's going to have a lot of questions."

"That might be a problem."

"Why?"

"We have to be at the border by nightfall. I have people waiting who will help us across, and then they'll take us to Mexico City. From there, we can fly to Hanoi. But we need to leave now."

"But my aunt won't be back until the evening."

"I'm sorry, Linh, but our window may close if we don't go."

"She won't understand."

"You can call her once we're across the border. It'll be safer that way."

"And tell her what? That I fled the country with a man she's never met? She'll think I've been kidnapped."

"I don't know," he says, the joyous moment collapsing under reality. "But I was in your shoes once. The only thing that made sense was telling my mother how much I loved her and to trust me—trust that I was making the right decision."

"And that was enough?"

"Sometimes, it has to be."

Linh walks to a painted desk accented with gold embellishments and silhouettes of bamboo forests. She opens a drawer and removes a pen and notepad. She begins to write. Tears build and fall onto the paper.

Why do risks so often come with pain and heartbreak? It doesn't seem fair to have to give up something to gain something. Desmond knows all too well what Linh is giving up, and he can never forget this moment. No matter what comes between them—disagreements, misunderstandings—he can never forget Linh's sacrifice to be with him.

Linh finishes writing, folds the letter, and places it on the coffee table. She wipes her tears and says, "Let's go."

EPILOGUE
NIA

Palestine, Texas
2023

Nia lies in the ICU. A muted news broadcast airs on a TV mounted to the ceiling. Nia prefers the news with the sound off, always has.

The room is cold, but the two blankets the night nurse provided her with are keeping her legs warm. Poor circulation causes frequent chills throughout her body. She should have known another heart attack was on the horizon. Her doctor says it's from years of opioid abuse. When the painkillers took hold, it took three stints in rehab to get the monkey off her back.

She owes Castro for getting her clean and for saving her life not once, but twice. After Nia collapsed on her living room floor, Castro called an ambulance, and Nia was rushed to the Regional Medical Center. Two heart attacks in five years. Even though she's retired from law enforcement, she can't shirk the daily prospect of death. Sure, it's universal and will happen to every living thing, but why does it have to hound her so? Most people probably live their lives considering the notion of dying occasionally—thoughts maybe brought on by the death of a family member or the sight of roadkill on the highway. Death doesn't dog them the way it does her. With each pinch in her chest, she wonders whether it's the big one.

In all her years in and out of hospitals, no one has ever come to visit her. Not that she has anyone left. But, for a time, Sharon was checking on her. Then she got married and moved to Taos, where she opened a wellness retreat. *Essence* magazine named it one of the best Black-owned businesses in the nation, a favorite among celebrities and politicians.

Nia tries to recall the last correspondence she received from Sharon. Perhaps it was five years ago? She gives it more thought. No, it's been more like a decade.

The monitor beeps loudly. Diodes are attached to her chest, and an IV line runs into her arm. A pulsometer is clasped on her finger, so tight she's lost feeling around the knuckle. Another night of tests, sucking down watery cherry Jell-O, and she'll be back home.

There's a knock at the door.

"Yes?" Nia calls. Must be time for her pills, she thinks. "Come in."

A nurse she doesn't recognize enters without her chart. The woman has long, jet-black hair and a fair complexion. Tattoos cover both arms—glyphs and odd shapes. She's wearing oversize scrubs. The top fits loosely on her shoulders and cuts a deep V over her breasts.

The hospital has interns who make rounds, but they are rarely unaccompanied by an RN or a physician. "New to the rotation?" Nia asks.

The woman silently inspects Nia's IV monitor.

"I believe the night nurse already checked that," Nia says. "What's her name?" She tries to recall her usual nurse's name. "Ms. Clara . . . that's it."

"Clara is on break," the woman says.

"Break? I thought her husband was coming to get her."

"Oh, yes, that's right," the woman says. "Her husband picked her up a while ago."

Nia sits up in the bed and glares. "Clara doesn't have a husband. She's got cats. Calls them fur babies. Now, who the hell are you?"

The woman stops fiddling with the IV monitor and takes a seat at the edge of Nia's bed.

"You better start talking, girlie, or I push that button." Nia looks to the glowing orange call button. "Talk, dammit!"

The woman straightens her back, crosses her legs, and rests her hands on her knees as though she's posing for a grade-school photo. "It's been some time, but I'm sure I don't look that different."

Nia stares with uncertainty. "I know you?"

"You, on the other hand, Ranger Adams, have not been taking care of yourself. Know what they call you around the nurses' station? John McClane," she says. "Misogynistic, but I guess they couldn't think of an imaginary cop who routinely escapes death who doesn't have a penis."

"It can't be . . ." Nia rubs her eyes. "Amora?"

"Howdy, Ranger."

"What the hell are you doing here?"

"Checking on an old friend."

"After all these years?"

"I was in the neighborhood."

"You shouldn't be here," Nia says.

"Two Texas Rangers recently visited you—"

"You've been watching me?"

"No," she says. "I've been watching them. Monitoring their investigation."

"What do you know about their investigation?"

"Everything worth knowing."

"The thing they're looking into," Nia says. "You're a part of that, aren't you?"

"More than a part—I orchestrated it. But it's only the beginning, which is why I need you."

"What are you playing at, Amora?"

"I want you to help them."

"Help them do what? I didn't bother looking at the case file. I want no part of it."

"Unfortunately, Adams, you don't get a say."

"The hell I don't!"

Amora pulls a smartphone from her pocket and scrolls through photos. "Here we go," she says, holding the phone up for Nia to see. "I hear the facials are tremendous."

"How do you know about her?"

"Times have changed, Ranger. Information lives and breathes in cyberspace. There is no past. No future. Not even now. It's all binary code—ones and zeros—zipping through the ether. It wasn't hard to find Sharon. Property records were digitalized decades ago, and with her name, I traveled down the rabbit hole, and it took me less than five minutes to learn about an old roommate who wasn't a roommate, was she?"

"Leave her out of this."

"That's up to you. If you want to keep Sharon and the life she's built safe, all you have to do is cooperate with those Rangers."

"And feed you information? Be your accomplice?"

"No," Amora says, putting her phone back into her pocket. "Be Sharon's hero—her protector. You help me, and I promise no harm will come to her or her business."

"And if I don't?"

"Every dollar. Every red cent that Sharon has will disappear overnight." Amora snaps her fingers. "And just like that, she'll go from glam to sham. Destitution is an ugly thing, but it's even uglier for those who once had more than they could imagine."

"You can do that?"

"Black girl magic, baby. Besides, I already have." Amora looks at the TV, then grabs the remote bound by a coil to the end of the bed and turns up the volume. A stoic reporter rambles. The lower third of the screen reads "CORPORATE CYBER ATTACKS ON THE RISE."

"You're the one behind these attacks," Nia says. "Blackmailing companies."

"A revolution in the making..."

"Good lord, what the hell happened to you?"

Amora grins. "The same thing that happens to everyone if they're lucky—I grew the fuck up," she says, walking toward the door. "I'll be in touch, Ranger."

On her way out, Nia notes Amora's black leather boots with two-inch soles and wonders how she didn't notice them before. Must be the meds, she thinks.

The news broadcast continues to play. She doesn't know the first thing about how the internet works or cybercrime, but she knows every good thing that's come to Sharon has been despite the many cuts Nia inflicted on her when they were together.

She owes Sharon everything, and her love for her will ensure that Nia will do whatever it takes to keep her safe.

ACKNOWLEDGMENTS

I would like to thank my team who helped put this project together: my literary agent, Marc Gerald; my publicist, Amanda Ruisi; and my general counsel, Steve Savva. Working with Aaron Philip Clark was a perfect partnership to help bring this story to life. Additionally I would like to thank Patrik Henry Bass, senior editor at Amistad; Brian Murray, president and CEO of HarperCollins; and Judith Curr, president and publisher at HarperOne Group, for continually being great partners for me in the literary space.

ABOUT THE AUTHOR

Award-winning rapper, entrepreneur, actor, and producer 50 Cent, born Curtis James Jackson III, is from Queens, New York. Recognized as one of the most talented and prolific music artists of his time, the Grammy Award winner rose to fame with his record-shattering debut album *Get Rich or Die Tryin'* and has since sold more than 30 million albums worldwide and been awarded numerous prestigious accolades. Jackson has leveraged his star power to cross over with unparalleled success as an entrepreneur, actor, and producer. From *Get Rich or Die Tryin'* being one of the fastest-selling albums in history to creating one of the most influential deals in hip-hop with the sale of Vitaminwater, Jackson continues to break records. He currently has the biggest premiere of a series ever on Starz with *Power Book II: Ghost*.

Jackson has carved out a thriving television and film career as both a best-in-class producer and star. In 2003, he founded G-Unit Film & Television, Inc., which has produced a wide range of content across numerous platforms and sold myriad shows to various networks. Among these is the critically acclaimed #1 show on Starz, *Power*, in which he not only costarred but also served as an executive producer and a director. He has successfully focused on the expansion of the *Power* universe with spinoffs *Power Book II: Ghost*, *Power Book III: Raising Kanan*, and

ABOUT THE AUTHOR

Power Book IV: Force. G-Unit Film & Television also produced ABC's *For Life*, is currently in production on season three of the hit series *Black Mafia Family* for Starz, and recently released the *Black Mafia Family* docuseries. In 2023, Jackson announced a nonexclusive multiproject development deal with FOX. G-Unit Film & Television is also in development on the scripted series *Fightland* and *Queen Nzinga* for Starz as well as *Trill League* at BET+. "Untitled" is in development for Paramount+ with Chad Stahelski attached to direct. *Lady Danger* starring Nicki Minaj is set at Freevee. G-Unit Film & Television recently released *Hip Hop Homicides* on WeTV. Jackson is also expanding into the podcast space through his new G-Unit Audio banner with the return of *Surviving El Chapo: The Twins Who Brought Down a Drug Lord* in partnership with iHeart Media and Lionsgate Sound. The company is also building out its feature slate, starting with a three-picture horror deal as a collaboration with horror phenom Eli Roth and 3BlackDot, and *Expendables 4* upcoming with Millennium and Lionsgate.

The exceptional businessman has served as CEO of G-Unit Records since its inception in 2003 and has since signed a host of multiplatinum artists. In 2003 Jackson launched the G-Unity Foundation to support programs that foster social and leadership skills in young people living in cities nationwide. Jackson also continues to widen his brand, and in 2016, launched luxury wine and spirits company Sire Spirits, which owns Le Chemin du Roi Champagne and Branson Cognac. Jackson is the author of seven books, three of which—*From Pieces to Weight*, *The 50th Law with Robert Greene*, and *Hustle Harder, Hustle Smarter*—were *New York Times* bestsellers.

Additionally, in 2020, Jackson received a star on the Hollywood Walk of Fame and was awarded an NAACP award for Best Director in a Drama Series. In 2023 Jackson embarked on a global tour, The Final Lap Tour, with over 103 shows across 35 countries, which kicked off in North America and continued through Europe and Australia with over a million tickets sold.